Diana was loo
getting her co-worker's opinion on
several aspects of the murder case

But first she had to get things moving on Connie Pearce's defense, which meant this meeting with the private investigator couldn't be delayed. Still, the second she saw the man waiting for her at reception, she came to an immediate stop.

He was in his early thirties, over six feet and wearing a hand-tailored suit that emphasized his wide shoulders and long legs. His thick, dark hair had been sculpted, not cut. His Technicolor blue eyes and wide-screen smile could easily stop a female heart at fifty feet.

He was Jack Knight. No wonder the receptionist had been so breathless. White Knight Investigations had sent her an actor!

Diana cursed to herself. What in the hell was she going to do now?

Dear Reader,

Courtroom dramas—where talented legal adversaries match wits and reveal shocking new evidence with every witness they call to the stand—have always been favorites of mine.

But once I had a chance to work on real criminal defenses, I met the unseen and unsung heroes of the legal process—private investigators. Without the skillful and dedicated private investigator tracking down both evidence and crucial witnesses, most defense attorneys wouldn't have the proverbial leg to stand on in a courtroom.

This is a story about a defense attorney and a private investigator fighting to free an accused woman. But it isn't full of the dramatics played out in front of judge and jury. Rather, the story focuses on how the two work together to build their case before the trial starts. Because the truth is that's how a case gets won—or lost.

Now one expects defense attorney Diana Mason to win her case. Jack Knight of White Knight Investigations is her only hope. But what can Jack do when eyewitnesses verify the defendant committed the crime, and the defendant herself admits she did it? You might be surprised.

I hope you enjoy Jack and Diana's story. Drop a SASE in the mail to me (at P.O. Box 284, Seabeck, WA 98380) and I'll send you an autographed sticker for the front of your book.

Warmly,

M.J. Rodgers

For the Defense
M.J. Rodgers

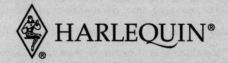

HARLEQUIN®

TORONTO • NEW YORK • LONDON
AMSTERDAM • PARIS • SYDNEY • HAMBURG
STOCKHOLM • ATHENS • TOKYO • MILAN • MADRID
PRAGUE • WARSAW • BUDAPEST • AUCKLAND

ISBN 0-373-71137-9

FOR THE DEFENSE

For **MARGUERITE DUCHARME,**
because her heart is filled with love.

CHAPTER ONE

JACK KNIGHT COULD THINK of at least a dozen other places he'd rather be about now.

He rested his shoulder against the cold stucco wall as he watched the entrance to the gambling casino. The wind swirled rain up his nose and whipped the soggy rope of long, black hair against his neck. His pinched toes ached inside the beat-up triangle-toed boots he'd dug out of the Goodwill rejection bin. The chilly night air seeped through his threadbare overcoat, sending shivers up his back.

Being a private investigator was such cushy, glamorous work.

It was almost midnight. A minute before, he'd stood at the casino's window, watching the man cash in his chips and the woman heading for the rest room. They should be along anytime. Jack made sure the video camera lens was peeking through the enlarged buttonhole in the front of his ragged overcoat, his fingers firmly on the controls inside the torn pocket.

Places! Camera! Action! The words echoed in his head bringing a wry smile of amusement to his lips. A rain-drenched Indian Reservation was about as far away from a dry and comfortable television studio as a guy could get.

When the doors to the casino burst open, he tensed in anticipation.

The couple staggered out. The man's face was flushed from too many drinks, the woman's from having to lug him around for the past hour. His heavy arm was draped over her sagging shoulders. As they hobbled by, the woman's eyes scanned Jack.

He knew what her look meant. She'd hold on to the man she was with only until a better offer came along.

When she was close enough to make out his filthy features in the shadows, Jack sent her a toothless grin. The woman grimaced and quickly turned back to her companion.

Jack's grin faded as the couple headed toward the Lexus at the curb. This man and woman were such a pathetic cliché. Not even a burned-out soap writer would sink into the banality of including their characterizations in a script.

After using a keyless remote control to open the car door, the woman dumped her drunken companion onto the passenger seat and circled around to get behind the wheel.

When she drove away, Jack turned off the video camera. He didn't need to follow them. He'd already filmed them in a body-crunching clinch that morning at the SEA-TAC airport. He'd shot more footage of them that afternoon mauling each other on the open patio of the condo where the woman was living and chronicled their subsequent evening out on the town. Considering how much bourbon the man had put away, Jack doubted he'd be capable of any more debauchery tonight.

Not that it mattered. Jack had the conclusive proof his client needed. Her husband's business trip to Washington State was an excuse to meet with his mistress. The guy hadn't even gone to see the employees at his new Seattle branch office.

Jack sprinted through the rain to the old blue pickup at the far corner of the casino parking lot. Once settled on the driver's seat, he pulled the wet black wig off his head and carefully hung it up to dry on the hook beside him. A private eye had to take good care of his props.

Sometimes on nights like this, he missed his life in show

business. Sure, he'd played some villainous parts, but at least at the end of those days, he didn't have to deal with a flesh-and-blood victim.

His client was a scared Idaho housewife who had recently seen the last of her five children leave home. She had a high-school education and no marketable skills. A vague feeling of unease had generated her call to Jack. All she really wanted him to do was relieve her mind.

He wasn't going to be able to do that. Her husband was not only cheating on her, he was also planning to divorce her to be with his twenty-five-year-old mistress.

Jack had found a bank account the guy had taken out in his name only the year before. A lot of cash had since been deposited into that account. The condo where he'd stashed his mistress was also in his name only, as was the Lexus she was driving.

No doubt in Jack's mind that the guy was hiding other assets as well so that when he sprang the divorce on his wife he could cheat her out of as much community property as possible. The best his wife could do was to get a good lawyer and get her husband before he got her.

And that's how their thirty-year marriage would end.

Jack grabbed some hand wipes and worked at removing the mud he'd earlier smeared on his hands and face to camouflage his features. The more he saw of marriage, the more convinced he became that it was a sucker's bet.

Hell, the majority of men and women he knew had trouble committing to the same cell phone carrier for six months, much less another person for a lifetime.

He flicked the black-tinted contact lenses out of his eyes and carefully placed them in their protective case. Next, he slipped the false, blackened teeth out of his mouth and stowed them away.

Since joining his family's private investigation firm the year before, he'd become an expert at surveillance. His theatrical background enabled him to blend into any crowd, much to the dismay of the errant husbands and wives he'd caught on videotape. Problem was, he'd gotten so good at tracking them, cheating-spouse cases had become his specialty.

Thank God this was his last one.

Yanking the too-tight boots off his feet, he threw them in the back seat and eased his aching toes into loafers. He slipped his watch back onto his wrist and combed his hair with his fingers.

His father had agreed that Jack had proved his mettle and was ready to take on the meaty stuff. Next Monday he'd tackle his first criminal case—a nice, clean murder.

Amazing how refreshingly wholesome murder could sound after the sordidness of marital deception.

Jack turned his cell phone back on and checked the messages.

His twin had called a couple of hours before. Doubtful he'd still be warming a barstool at their favorite watering hole. Still, some of the regular Friday-night crowd would definitely be milling around, including, in all likelihood, an unattached female eager to engage in some wrestling under the sheets.

All the more reason Jack wouldn't go there. He wasn't interested in women who frequented bars.

When Jack saw his second message was from Heather, he smiled. She was an actress he'd worked with, someone who wouldn't dream of letting herself be picked up in a bar. Being with a woman who valued herself made the exchange of physical pleasure so much more enjoyable.

Jack punched her number on his speed dial, a smile on his lips. She'd been shooting a movie in Canada for the past six months. Getting reacquainted was going to be fun.

Heather's voice greeted him with warm enthusiasm. "Jack, I'm so glad you called. I have great news!"

She'd gotten that new hot tub installed?

"I'm getting married!"

Damn. All Jack's hot tub fantasies swirled down the drain.

As Heather's excited voice related all the scintillating details of the whirlwind courtship with her new co-star, Jack diligently deleted her name and number from his cell phone list.

He'd give the marriage ten months, tops.

Jack had already selected another candidate for late-night company by the time Heather had finished her tale. Wishing her well, he released the connection and punched in the next number.

Thankfully, his address book still listed a dozen or so women who knew their demanding careers didn't give them time to think about marriage.

DIANA KNEW she didn't have time to think about marriage with everything else going on in her busy life, but she couldn't help herself. The whole idea was so mind-boggling.

When her mother had announced her upcoming nuptials the week before, her face had positively glowed. The groom-to-be had looked pretty happy, too. Ray Villareal was not as handsome as Diana's father had been. He was something better. He was in love with her mother.

Because of that, Diana was ready to forgive him for both his obnoxious stepson and for making her move.

But damn, she hated moving. She had neither the focus nor energy for the chore. Connie Pearce's life was in her hands. Guilt poured through her when she even thought about taking time to—

"Mason, are you listening?" Vincent Kozen, one of the two senior partners at the law firm, demanded from the other side of the conference table.

The insipid argument had been droning on for more than an hour. Diana's only hope of staying awake had been to tune out. Snapping back to attention, she stopped doodling on her pad and raised her eyes to Vincent.

"To every word," she lied, straight-faced.

Replaying her set-to-automatic mental tape, she retrieved the rapidly fading sentences. Yep, the topic was still Vincent's new, incredibly complicated time-allocation study, which would see if the law firm's staff was tracking case expenditures correctly.

Just another one of those useless projects that was so dear to Vincent's little number-crunching heart.

"If you've been listening, Mason," Vincent challenged in his typically high and condescending tone, "then by all means tell us how you would handle the matter."

He folded his hands in front of him and glared at her. She knew he was looking for a target. He always seethed when one of his "wonderful" time-tracking ideas met with dissension, as this latest had.

Diana plastered a look of concern on her face. "Although I recognize that the contributions from everyone at this table have been both thoughtful and insightful," she said, intent on not offending anyone who actually was naïve enough to express their real opinion, "I do believe that the wisest course would be to heed your considerable expertise in this area."

Bushy gray eyebrows rose in surprise as Vincent shifted his bony butt in the chair. "In the future, Mason, don't make me have to prod you," he said in a tone still annoying but far less combative. "I want to hear everyone's opinion."

Like hell he did. Vincent Kozen didn't care what she or anyone else at the law firm thought, unless that person was agreeing with him. He and his brother, Ronald, were very similar in that regard.

Still, Diana had learned when to fight, when to surrender and when to walk away. This morning's subject required a waving, white flag and nothing else.

Vincent pontificated for another ten excruciating minutes on his open-mindedness before the meeting finally came to a close. A sigh of collective relief wafted through the air as the staff members stood and gathered their belongings.

One of the midlevel associates at the firm, Leroy Ripp, sent Diana a look of open disdain as he shuffled toward the door.

"Nice going, Mason," he said, his whisper hot with ill humor. "Now we have to waste fifteen minutes out of every hour filling out one of his idiotic forms."

She didn't answer Leroy. No point. Whenever Leroy got angry at anything, he ended up angry at everything. Vincent had already made his decision to institute the new time-tracking procedure. Nothing she nor anyone else had said in this meeting would have affected the outcome.

As Diana headed toward the door of the conference room, Gail Loftin, another one of her colleagues, fell into step beside her.

"Was Leroy accusing you of crossing over to the Dark Side?" Gail asked, a big grin on her face.

Diana chuckled.

She'd known Leroy for three years, Gail for nine months. All the words in the world wouldn't get a point across to Leroy. Gail often understood without any.

"What's gotten Leroy in such a foul mood these days?" Diana asked.

"Our *favorite* prosecutor creamed him in court last week."

"Ah." Diana knew Gail meant Silver Valley's thoroughly detestable Chief Prosecutor, George Staker. Although she'd never classify Leroy as a friend, at this moment she felt for him.

"Hard not to take it personally sometimes," Diana said. "At least three of our other attorneys have lost cases to Staker recently. Getting to be a damn epidemic."

"Except Leroy keeps insisting that Staker knew things he shouldn't have when they went to trial. I overheard Leroy tell Ronald that there must be a mole in our office."

Diana shook her head. "Shoot me before I get that paranoid."

"You have my promise," Gail said, unlocking the door to her office. "Come in for a minute. I need to talk to you."

As soon as Diana had stepped inside, Gail firmly closed the door behind them.

"I heard you got the Pearce case."

"Ronald gave it to me a couple of weeks ago when you were tied up in that trial on the coast," Diana confirmed. "He told me Earl said the case conflicted with another one he had."

"What the case conflicts with is his drive to become a junior partner," Gail said, the irritation thick in her tone as she circled her desk and plopped onto the chair.

Yes, Diana had figured that as well.

With Gail's smarts, experience and expertise, she should be a shoo-in for the junior partner slot that the Kozen brothers had dangled before her eyes to get her to join the expanding private law firm of Kozen and Kozen.

But Earl Payman was vying for the position as well. Although Earl possessed not one tenth of Gail's talent or experience, he wore Armani suits, had finagled a membership in the private club the Kozen brothers belonged to and always said the politically correct thing. Gail wore a size fourteen bought off the rack, never played golf and often made the mistake of speaking her mind.

That latter failing was one Diana shared with her friend.

"You shouldn't have let Ronald dump the Pearce case on you," Gail said.

Diana snorted in amusement as she slipped onto Gail's guest chair. "You think I had some choice when our beloved senior partner charged into my office, dropped the file on my desk and said, 'You need to take over this court-appointed defense case that goes to trial in two months, so get up to speed'?"

Gail exhaled heavily. "I'm sorry. Of course, you didn't have an option. I'm only mad at the unfairness of seeing this happen to you."

"Don't be," Diana said as she stretched her arms above her head, trying to encourage some circulation back into her shoulders after sitting hunched over for so long in that pointless meeting. "I know Ronald only gave it to me because everyone else probably ran the other way when they saw him coming. But I'm glad I've got it."

Gail rested her elbows on the desk, regarding Diana gravely. "When I was in the prosecutor's office last year and the sheriff's reports landed in my in-basket, I was salivating in anticipation of taking the case to trial. A prosecution like that can make a career, which is why Staker grabbed the case right out from under me. Diana, the evidence is so overwhelming there's no way you can come out looking good."

"The case may not be as open and shut as everyone thinks."

Gail's eyebrows climbed her forehead as she inched forward in her chair. "You know something that no one else does?"

A knock came on the door. Gail looked decidedly put out at the interruption. "Come in," she called out.

The door popped open and Kelli, the firm's receptionist, poked her head inside.

"I'm sorry to interrupt," Kelli said, oddly out of breath, "but Mr. Knight is waiting at my desk. Do you want me to show him to your office?"

Diana's eyes went to her watch. Startled to see the time, she shot to her feet. "No, Kelli. I'll see him now." She headed for the door. "We'll talk later, Gail."

"Make that sooner," Gail said. "You can't keep me hanging like this."

Chuckling at Gail's frustrated look, Diana followed Kelli toward the reception area. She was looking forward to getting Gail's opinion on several sticky aspects of the case. Having worked both sides of the legal fence, Gail was a wealth of insight.

But first Diana had to get things moving on Connie Pearce's defense, which meant this meeting with the private investigator couldn't be delayed. Still, the second she saw the man waiting for her, she came to an immediate and startled stop.

He was in his early thirties, over six feet, wearing a deep-blue, hand-tailored suit that emphasized his wide shoulders and long legs. His thick, dark hair had been sculpted, not cut. His Technicolor blue eyes, wide-screen smile and leading-man features could easily stop a female heart at fifty feet.

Dear heavens, it was Jack Knight. No wonder Kelli was

so breathless. White Knight Investigations had sent her an actor!

Diana cursed to herself. What in the hell was she going to do now?

JACK FOLLOWED DIANA as she led the way to her office, his smile broadening. Well, well. The lawyer he'd be working for was a knockout—despite a formless gray business suit and no makeup—and she wasn't wearing a wedding ring. This had to be fate.

No, not fate, he corrected. Opportunity. He didn't believe in fate, but he sure as hell believed in opportunity.

He caught a whiff of her scent, something cool and sweet he couldn't quite place. She was maybe thirty and at least five-eight. Her gleaming black hair was gathered with a silver clip at the nape of her neck and fell to the middle of her back.

The way the light caught the curves of her face, highlighted her hair and settled in the soft centers of her eyes was absolutely arresting. She had what in the business was called "screen presence." He knew stunningly beautiful actresses who worked for years, and for naught, to try to attain what came naturally to Diana Mason, Attorney at Law.

Jack took a quick look around her small office as they stepped inside. Well-used law books lined the shelves that covered every available inch of wall space. Dozens of pieces of scrap paper stuck out of them marking passages. Several rather high but neat stacks of paper covered the beige metal desk.

Her functional office confirmed what Jack had already surmised. She was about substance, not show. The only personal touch was the half-dozen pots of geraniums, full of pink blossoms, that adorned the south-facing windowsill.

He sat in the offered guest chair as she slipped onto the

chair behind the desk. Scooting forward to the desk's edge, she rested her elbows on the small space of available surface and regarded him silently.

He smiled.

The expression on her face changed slightly, but not in a way he anticipated. He wasn't used to this kind of reaction to one of his smiles. The lady was something less than overjoyed to see him.

Ah, a challenge. Jack loved challenges.

"Frowns like the one you're wearing can leave permanent marks on a guy's delicate ego," he said projecting the faint hint of pain designed to amuse and maybe even elicit a defensive apology.

"I was counting on working with your brother, Richard," she said with such absolute candor and no hint of defensiveness that he almost laughed.

"Not to worry," Jack said. "I come with a sixty-day warranty and a money-back guarantee."

Her frown did not abate. "Your brother cleared up a very sticky case for me that another investigator had badly bungled. He came through on two other difficult cases as well. I trust Richard."

"Really?" Jack said, feigning surprise. "When we were kids, he used to put his spinach on my plate and tell Mom he'd eaten it."

"This case demands the best," she said pointedly.

He was disappointed that all his efforts to lighten her up weren't working. A good sense of humor in a woman always added to her sex appeal. Still, he could be serious with her if absolutely necessary.

"Fortunately for you, the best is here," he said, straight-faced.

An eyebrow raised on her forehead. "Are you always this modest?"

"Modesty is a false cloak when it covers competence, wouldn't you agree?"

"*If* it covers competence," she said, brutally.

He leaned forward, the better to emphasize his sincerity. "I understand that relying on a known quantity is always more comfortable. But Richard will not be available for a month. I was given to understand that you need help immediately. At least that's what my father said when he persuaded me to take this assignment."

Actually, he'd talked his dad into giving him this case, but he saw no reason to reveal that part. He'd been warned that Diana would be expecting Richard. Jack had told his dad not to worry. Charming women into accepting him had never been a problem.

But considering the continuing displeasure on this woman's face, he was beginning to wonder if he'd spoken too soon.

"Your brother, David, found a missing witness for me once. I was also quite pleased with his work. Is he available?"

Jack almost laughed. Next she'd be asking for his father or mother to take her case. What did this woman have against him?

"I'm the only one who is both available and right for this job," he said.

"How long have you worked at your family's private investigation firm?"

He pitied anyone who got drilled by this lawyer while in a courtroom. Thankful he wasn't sitting in the witness box, he avoided answering her sticky question by asking one in return.

"Do you think that my father would risk our firm's forty-year reputation for excellence by sending you someone who couldn't handle the job?"

Jack was well aware Diana had hired White Knight Investigations half a dozen times during the past two years. She'd come back because she'd been satisfied. Yes, she trusted Richard and David. But Jack also felt certain that she trusted their firm.

"You used to be an actor," she said. Her tone was almost an accusation.

Ah, so that was the problem. She'd seen him on TV and was mixing up the character he'd played with the man he was. A common failing. Still, he would have thought someone with her obvious smarts would have hesitated before making such an assumption.

"I used to be a very *good* actor," he corrected. "I'm very good at whatever I put my mind to, Diana. I have a strong sense that you are as well."

He knew no one was immune to a compliment, as long as it was delivered with sincerity. Knowing when to mix a compliment with a first name had become second nature to him. The timing on these two had been right. Now he waited to see how well the combination had worked.

And waited.

She finally extracted a form from her middle desk drawer and slid it toward him. "This is our standard contract and confidentiality statement. Please initial beneath each clause, sign your full name at the bottom and we'll get started."

Jack told himself he hadn't really doubted the outcome of this conversation. Nonetheless, he was relieved to hear her confirming words.

Scanning the contents of the two-part form she'd handed him, he noted that the confidentiality statement demanded absolute secrecy from him. It also warned that if he were to repeat anything about this case to an unauthorized party, he would be subjected to all the legal racks and thumbscrews at Diana Mason's disposal. He had not a doubt that she'd be happy to apply them, too.

Jack took a pen out of his shirt pocket, initialed where she'd indicated, signed his name and passed the document back to her.

"I understand your client is charged with murder," he said.

"First degree," she said slipping the confidentiality statement into the fairly thin folder in front of her. "This is a court assigned defense."

She pulled a stack of blank forms from her desk. "I'll need your time and expenses recorded daily and turned in weekly on these."

Damn, he hated paperwork. Dutifully taking the stack of forms she handed him, he decided to let Harry, the clerk at the firm, do this part for him.

"Does court assigned mean that you're acting like a public defender?" he asked.

A new frown appeared on her forehead. "Don't tell me this is your first criminal defense case?"

"If you don't want me to tell you that then I definitely won't," he said and sent her one of his most engaging smiles.

She shook her head, clearly not engaged. "When there are more cases than there are public defenders to handle them, a judge drafts the services of lawyers from legal firms in the area to represent a defendant. We're paid by the state, not by the client."

"When were you drafted into service?"

"I got the case two weeks ago in a workload shuffle. But the court assigned Connie Pearce's defense to another lawyer at this firm ten months ago."

"Connie Pearce?" Jack repeated. "Isn't she the kinder-garten teacher who killed her lover?"

"That's what all the banner headlines proclaimed last year."

"I remember hearing about that case."

"You and nearly everyone else in this county. Getting a panel of jurors that hasn't heard wasn't easy."

"She was supposed to have hit him with her car," Jack said as the details began to come back to him. "There were a couple of eyewitnesses."

"Are you having second thoughts about accepting this assignment?"

He smiled into the serious look on her face. "On the contrary. I love being on the side of the underdog."

The tenseness in her shoulders seemed to increase with his assurance.

"Well, then you're going to be ecstatic working this case," she said. "The victim's father suffered a fatal heart attack after witnessing his son's death. The victim's mother is one of our most prominent and politically connected superior court judges."

"And this prominent, politically connected judge is out for blood," he guessed.

"The Honorable Barbara Weaton insists she's simply out for justice, but you can be sure she's not going to take kindly to anyone who is trying to help the woman charged with her son's murder."

He pointed to the thin folder in front of her. "Is that what the other lawyer has done?"

She gave the folder a quick glance. "Over the past ten months."

Despite the evenness of her tone, Jack knew she wasn't only unhappy about the thinness of the folder in front of her. She was angry.

"Why didn't this lawyer do anything?" he asked.

"Earl Payman said Connie wouldn't speak to him. Or anyone else."

"That sounds like a symptom of shock to me. Why didn't he think of that?"

"He brought in a psychologist to examine her a week after her arrest. She wouldn't talk to him, either. The psychologist said he couldn't testify to whether she was legally sane or not. Earl decided the safest thing for him was to plead her not guilty and let a jury convict or acquit her."

"He did nothing else in the intervening nine and a half months?"

"He played a lot of golf with the two senior partners at this firm."

Although Diana's voice remained calm, there was enough contempt in her expression to have sent the incompetent, golf-playing Earl into lockup for life.

"Where has Connie Pearce been all this time?" Jack asked.

"In jail. Earl made no attempt to get her a bail hearing."

"Have you talked to her?"

"Nearly every day since I got her case. But it wasn't until late last week that she opened up and told me what happened."

"And that's when you called White Knight Investigations."

Diana nodded.

He was pretty certain he knew why. "Connie Pearce convinced you that she wasn't the one driving the car that killed Weaton."

"No, she was driving the car."

"She didn't see the guy run in front of her car?"

"She saw him."

Jack let his mind quickly dig through the other possibilities. "It was self-defense," he said as the obvious answer came through. "The guy was coming at her, threatening to do her bodily harm, and the only weapon she had to defend herself was the car."

"No," Diana said. "It wasn't self-defense."

Jack was stymied. He couldn't think of anything else that made sense. "Okay, I give up. What happened?"

"Connie Pearce saw Bruce Weaton in front of her car and she hit him."

Jack was more confused than ever. "If that's what she has admitted happened, then what do you need me for?"

Diana locked eyes with him as she leaned forward in her chair. "I need you to help me get her off."

CHAPTER TWO

JACK STARED at Diana for sixty very long and silent seconds. Did she really have the audacity to ask him to help get a guilty client off?

He understood that most defense attorneys didn't care if their clients were guilty. All they cared about was making sure that the accused was tried according to the dictates of the law. Didn't even matter to them if a guilty client ended up slipping through a legal loophole.

It mattered to Jack. He was a little disappointed to learn that Diana was proving to be one of those attorneys. His father had given him the impression she had integrity. That was one of the reasons he'd wanted the case. Now he had a strong urge to get up and leave.

Only the straight, no-holds-barred challenge on her face combined with the total absence of any apology kept him in his chair. A woman who could face him this squarely didn't strike him as one who would sell out her conscience.

He wasn't going anywhere until he learned what the hell was going on.

"All right," he said, settling back in his chair, "tell me why you want Connie Pearce to get away with murder."

Something that looked suspiciously like surprise flashed across Diana's face. So, she *had* expected him to leave. He found that very interesting.

As she studied him quietly, he returned her assessment, trying to read what thoughts or emotions were going on in that lovely head of hers. But this attorney knew how to keep both well hidden when she wanted to. Damn if she didn't intrigue him more by the minute.

Without warning, she got to her feet. "I'd like Connie to tell you the story in her own words."

"We're going to see her now?" he asked.

"I called early this morning to let her know I'd be stopping by."

Diana grabbed her briefcase and headed toward the door, slipping the long strap of her bag over her shoulder without so much as breaking stride.

"I'll drive you over," he said, hurrying to keep up with her. Most men probably found themselves getting lost in this woman's wake. He had no intention of making the mistake of most men.

"I have my own car, thank you," she said.

"Riding together will give us an opportunity to discuss the case."

"I have to pick up my daughter from class and drop her at home before going to see Connie. You can either follow me or meet me at the jail. Up to you."

A daughter? Damn. His hopes for something personal developing out of this assignment took an immediate and definitive nosedive.

Jack was very particular about the women he dated. And one of the things he was most particular about was that they not have any children.

"I'll follow you," he said.

SIZING UP PEOPLE quickly was an essential skill for a trial attorney, one that couldn't be gleaned from a law book. Diana paid attention to all the signs and made her decisions accordingly.

Jack's good looks and background in the entertainment field had prepared her for the kind of man who presented a convincing image, but who couldn't handle the hard facts of life or come through when it counted.

She had personal experience with the type. For a brief time in her younger and far-less-wise years, she'd been married to a rock musician.

But her openly expressed and brutally honest reservations about Jack's abilities hadn't seemed to bother him a bit. He'd barely even flinched when she told him she wanted his help in getting her guilty client off.

This was not going well.

She had counted on him turning tail and running for the nearest exit. That would have given her the perfect excuse to phone Charles Knight and convince him of the need to free up Richard or David to help her on this case.

Only Jack hadn't run. He was hanging in there, even displaying an open mind. Damn him. She needed an investigator with a proven track record, not some TV star who had decided to play at being a private investigator until another role came up.

She stopped her car in front of the school, feeling the weight of yet another problem she did not have the time to handle. But the moment her daughter opened the passenger door and got in, Diana felt a smile on her lips.

"Hi, Mom."

Definitely two of Diana's favorite words.

"Hi, Cute Stuff. How did astronomy class go?"

"The universe is expanding at an ever accelerating rate," Mel said in her typically matter-of-fact tone as she buckled up. "With all that extra space being created, you'd think we could find a new place to live."

Diana checked her mirrors before pulling away from the curb and reentering the stream of traffic. "We'll resume apartment-hunting tonight after dinner."

"You've given up on finding us a house?"

Diana watched as Jack's car mimicked her actions and moved in behind her.

"Finding a house doesn't look too promising," she said. "I've exhausted every lead from the newspaper and friends alike."

"Grandma did say we could stay with her as long as we wanted to," Mel said, trying to sound nonchalant, but not quite pulling it off.

Diana knew that her daughter hated the idea of moving as much as she did.

"Your grandmother loves us so much she's willing to compromise her privacy and maybe even her chance for happiness with Ray. We have to show her how much we love her by not letting her sacrifice those things."

"We're not going to see Grandma nearly as much now that she's marrying Ray," Mel said, obviously not pleased with the fact.

"Maybe not as much, but we'll still see her. She's not moving away."

"But Ray's moving in. Everything's going to change."

That was true. Diana knew pretending otherwise would be foolish. Besides, she never lied to Mel.

"Everything changes, Cute Stuff. Embracing change—even when we think the change less than ideal—is the best way to handle life if we want to be happy."

Mel thought about that a moment before glancing over at her mom and asking, "Do you suppose the universe is embracing the fact that it's continuing to expand?"

"Only if it's not female," Diana said.

Mel burst forth with a happy giggle.

Ah, to be nine again and able to giggle like that! Women needed daughters if for no other reason than to help them remember those moments of delight.

"You keep glancing into the rearview mirror," Mel

aid, twisting in her seat to look behind them. "Is someone ollowing us?"

"The private investigator who'll be working on Con- ie's case. He's driving the white Porsche back there. ou're never going to guess who he is."

Mel squinted. "I can't see his face, but he can't be Rich- rd Knight or you wouldn't be making me guess. Who is e?"

"Remember that paper you wrote a little over a year go where you contrasted fictional villains from the begin- ing of the twentieth century with their popular counter- arts from the twenty-first?"

Mel nodded. "And concluded that the steady advance f a culture embracing diversity and tolerance had given irth to the creation of an increasing number of fictional illains as three-dimensional characters," she quoted, dis- laying not only her perfect memory, but a mental capacity nd clarity that still frequently left her mother in awe.

Diana had been startled when her daughter had started alking in complete and complex sentences at two. She was loored when she'd later learned that Mel's IQ was in ex- ess of one hundred and sixty.

"How does my paper on fictional villains relate to the rivate investigator following us?" Mel asked.

"He was one of your study subjects, your favorite one."

Mel whirled around in her seat again. "Derek Dementer, rom the soap, *Seattle!*" she yelled, sounding very much ike an excited nine-year-old.

Diana smiled at her daughter's exuberance.

Mel turned back to her mom, her voice still high with er discovery. "Jack Knight is a private investigator ow?"

"Apparently."

"He must be Richard Knight's brother. Richard never aid he had a brother in show business."

Diana nodded as she took a corner. "Richard's too much of a professional to even discuss his personal business, much less brag. If I hadn't taped all those *Seattle* episodes for you, I never would have known his brother was *the* Jack Knight when he showed up at the firm this morning."

"Why did he become a private investigator?"

"I didn't ask."

"I can't wait to meet him. Will he stay for lunch?"

Seemed even her brilliant daughter had been struck by the show business bug.

"No, Jack and I have an appointment to see Connie Pearce as soon as I drop you off. Afterward, I have a ton of work waiting for me back at the office. So, when I take you over to say hello, do me a favor and limit yourself to only one of the zillion questions I know you want to ask him."

Diana could feel Mel's watchful eyes. "You're not happy that Jack is on the case?" her daughter said.

"Why do you ask?"

"You have that frown that pulls your eyebrows together," Mel said as she demonstrated by squeezing the skin on a corresponding part of her face.

Diana put a finger between her eyebrows, making a mental note to work on that. A trial attorney had to be able to control her facial expressions.

"Connie needs the best," she said by way of explanation. "Richard is the best."

"But you still hired Jack?"

"White Knight Investigations has always come through for me. If Charles Knight thinks Jack can do the job, professional courtesy demands I give him a chance."

At least that's what she told herself. But there was a nagging suspicion at the back of Diana's mind that her decision might also have something to do with the fact that she wasn't as immune to Jack Knight's thousand-watt smile as she should be.

JACK FOLLOWED DIANA into the deeply wooded country-side surrounding the city of Silver Valley, finally parking in front of a well-kept Craftsman-style home. He let the car idle as he waited, assuming they'd be leaving right away. But Diana got out of her car and started toward him with her daughter in tow.

Jack let out a frustrated exhale, turned off the engine and got out to stand beside the driver's door.

The girl wasn't bad looking, he supposed, if one liked kids.

Jack didn't. They were noisy, messy and rude, had to be watched every minute, constantly demanded things and were never satisfied for more than ten seconds with whatever they got. He had no idea why anyone would want one.

Nor could he understand what made parents think that other people were interested in getting to know their kids. He'd just as soon be introduced to their pit bulls. At least *they* could be kept on a leash.

Yet here was Diana, like all the other proud mothers he'd met, bringing her kid over to be introduced. He didn't need this. The last kid he'd tried to talk to had sneezed all over him and given him a cold.

He gritted his teeth and diligently tried to keep himself from flinching when this one walked right up to him.

"Hi, I'm Melissa Mason, but everybody calls me Mel. It's nice to meet you, Mr. Knight. Do you mind if I call you Jack?"

He blinked at her in surprise. This kid was articulate, polite, even had a sweet voice. He found himself smiling as he took her offered hand.

"Please do, Mel. You have very nice manners for one so young, or for one of any age for that matter."

"Thanks, but I'm short on tact when I lose my temper. Mom says it's a family failing."

He looked over at Diana as Mel released his hand. "Is that a fact?"

Diana didn't look too pleased with Mel for having shared that.

"Can I ask you something?" Mel said.

"I guess," Jack said cautiously.

"I've read that one of the biggest agonies of being an actor is an endless search for identity. You portrayed a very believable villain on *Seattle*. Did you have difficulty keeping your identity separate from the part you played?"

Hell of a question from a kid this young. Jack gave it a moment's thought before answering.

"When I worked hard and knew I had played the part well, I felt good about myself. I suppose the bottom line is that a strong sense of self develops from doing your best, no matter what your profession."

She tilted her head. "That was a very interesting answer."

"I was responding to a very interesting question," Jack said. "How old are you?"

"I don't like to give my chronological age," Mel said. "It elicits a bias about what I'm like, and I'm not like that at all. Did you know that being aware of a person's age early on in a relationship can actually prevent people from getting to know each other?"

Jack stared at the girl for a moment before turning to address Diana. "Care to help the mentally handicapped here?"

Diana laughed. He felt his insides warm at the bold huskiness of the sound. She stepped behind her daughter, gently clasped her shoulders. "Mel celebrated her ninth birthday a few weeks ago. But she's currently enrolled in schoolwork equivalent to the third-year college level."

"You're a genius," Jack said to Mel, not attempting to hide either his surprise or fascination.

"Not in any widely agreed-upon definition of the term," she answered very seriously. "Genius rarely, if ever, equates to superior intellectual achievement, even when that achievement is blatantly manifested. Most researchers think of it as bringing into existence something original, an inspiration beyond intelligent thinking and clever reasoning. What do you think, Jack?"

"I think I'd better wait for a brain donor before I ask you any more questions," he said, shaking his head.

Mel giggled. "You're funny."

He smiled at the good-natured amusement on the girl's face.

"You'd better go inside now, Mel," Diana said. "We have to be on our way."

"Can't I go with you to see Connie?"

Diana planted a kiss on her daughter's head. "Not without doubling your chronological age and committing a felony."

"My psychology professor said that hearing about other people's pain can help to make you feel better about your own," Mel said.

"Nice try," Diana said. "But not even close to working. Now off with you."

"What's causing you pain?" Jack asked Mel, curious to know, despite Diana's obvious desire to be on her way.

"We have to move out of my grandmother's home," Mel said. "She's really sweet, and she understands me, and I've lived here for as long as I can remember."

"Why do you have to leave?" Jack prodded.

"She's getting married, and her husband's moving in with her, so Mom and I have to rent a place. There are no houses available, only yucky apartments. And Mom's going to have to find someone to stay with me when she's not there. Except I don't want to be baby-sat because I'm no baby.''

''You're certainly not,'' Jack said. Although, as Mel's far too unhappy tone had demonstrated, she was still very much a nine-year-old for all her intelligence.

When Diana had finally succeeded in shooing her daughter into the house, Jack turned to her. ''You could have warned me about Mel.''

''Yeah, but this was more fun.''

For *her* maybe. But he didn't mind. He'd had a chance to hear Diana laugh. That had been a nice surprise. He'd always thought that the deeper a woman's laugh, the deeper her enjoyment of physical pleasure.

Diana's laugh had been so deep he could still feel it vibrating along his nerve endings.

FORTY MINUTES LATER, Diana and Jack stepped through the doorway into the Silver Valley County jail. As they walked through the metal detector, Diana exchanged waves with the security guard who had the latest John Grisham thriller in his hands.

Hustling once again to keep up with her fast pace, Jack followed her into the elevator and watched her punch the button for the next floor.

''Are you as upset about having to move out of your mother's home as Mel is?''

''Just something that has to be done,'' she answered without looking at him.

Jack couldn't tell whether he'd hit on a touchy subject or if Diana's reluctance to talk was due to preoccupation with their upcoming interview. When the elevator doors opened, she was out in a flash.

"Hi, Diana," the prison guard called from behind the counter.

"Hi, Fran."

Jack looked over Diana's shoulder as she signed in, noticing that she entered both of their names. The prison guard buzzed the door to the hallway open and gestured for Diana to go through.

But before Jack could, the guard pointed to a room behind the counter. "Step in there and take off all your clothes."

"I beg your pardon?" Jack said.

"Body search," Fran explained curtly, hands on her sturdy hips, fingers twitching toward the gun in her holster. "Got to make sure you're not taking anything prohibited to the prisoner."

He stared at the serious look on the prison guard's face in growing unease.

"Nice try, Fran," Diana said, "but Mr. Knight's part of the law firm's defense team and not subject to search."

The female guard looked Jack up and down and let out a disappointed sigh. "Rats."

"Thanks," he whispered on an exhale of relief as they walked down the hall.

A smile tugged at the corners of her mouth as she headed directly for a room at the end. She opened the door and gestured for him to step inside. She apparently wasn't the type who waited for men to hold doors open for her.

Jack liked that. He stepped past her into a windowless, eight-by-ten foot room with a Formica table, four scratched metal chairs and an overhead fluorescent light that flickered.

"They'll bring Connie in to meet with us soon," Diana said as she closed the door then and took a seat at the table. "Before she gets here, I need to fill you in on a few things."

He sat across from her and waited. She looped the strap of her shoulder bag over the back of her chair as she began.

"Connie is unnaturally shy. I want her to tell you her story because the emotional impact comes through so much clearer in her words. But she might not talk to you. She offered nothing but minimal information to me at first. It wasn't until I learned she'd lost a daughter that I thought of approaching her another way."

"When you say lost, do you mean the girl died?" Jack asked.

Diana nodded. "Had she lived, her daughter would have been around Mel's age now. I got the idea that Connie might find talking to another mother easier than she would to an attorney. So, on my next visit I stopped asking questions and started telling her about the challenges facing me as a single mom. When she seemed interested, I knew I was making progress and showed her a picture of Mel."

Pausing for a moment, Diana gave her shoulders a little roll as though trying to shake off a sudden tightness. "Connie took one look at Mel's picture and cried. Then she told me about Amy."

"Amy is the daughter she lost," Jack guessed. "How long ago did—"

He didn't get a chance to finish his sentence. The door opened and a guard brought in Connie Pearce, murderess. She walked into the room slowly, as if she was unsure of each step. The instant she saw Jack, she flinched and took a step backward.

Connie not only didn't look like she could run down a man with a car. She didn't look like she could chase down a fly with a swatter.

This case got more baffling by the minute. Jack decided right then that he was not going to leave the room until he had heard this woman's story.

WHEN DIANA SAW Connie's reaction to Jack, she was certain her client was never going to talk to him. But before she could ask Jack to wait outside, he stepped forward, took Connie's hand and smiled into her startled face.

"I'm Jack Knight, Connie. I've been looking forward to meeting you."

His voice sounded very gentle and sincere. Connie's retreat halted.

When Fran seemed ready to take exception to Jack's physical contact with the prisoner, Diana shook her head. Diana and Fran had known each other a long time. The guard trusted her. Fran nodded and quietly left the room.

"You look...familiar," Connie said as she stared up at Jack, a small frown forming.

"Do I?" he asked as he held her hand within his open palm. Smiling one of those devastating smiles of his, he said, "Maybe you recognize me from TV. The soap *Seattle*?"

Connie's mouth opened in astonishment. "You're Derek Dementer! But I don't understand. What are you doing here?"

"Diana tells me you're in trouble. I've come to help."

Keeping her hand within his own, Jack led Connie to the table, held out a chair for her. His facial expression, physical attention and voice all radiated warmth.

He sat facing her, knee-to-knee. "Being an actor was fun for me. But I'd much rather rescue a lady in distress than be the villain causing her distress."

Damn if he didn't sound like he meant every word he was saying, too.

"You really think you can help *me*?" Connie asked, still obviously finding this too good to be true.

"I *know* I can help you," he said with the kind of confidence that brooked no argument. "But first, I need to understand everything that happened. Will you help me?"

For the first time since she'd met Connie, Diana saw her client smile. Jack's constant attention was telling Connie that she alone existed for him. A normal man showing a woman that kind of attention would be hard to refuse. When a charismatic man like Jack turned it on, what chance did a woman have?

"What do you want me to do?" Connie asked.

"Tell me about Amy," he said.

Connie sigh was soft and sad. "Oh."

"I know talking about her is very difficult," Jack said, his voice tender. "But will you try for me?"

Connie nodded. "Okay."

Diana let out a relieved breath. He had accomplished in a couple of minutes what had taken her two weeks. The lawyer in her was impressed, but the woman in her was more than a little annoyed.

Connie inhaled deeply before she began.

Diana knew the story. She focused her attention on Jack, trying to imagine what he would think and feel when he heard it. Was he merely a handsome actor with all the right words at his command? Or was there some substance behind that charm?

CONNIE STRUCK Jack as so childlike and vulnerable that he had a hard time remembering that she was in her late twenties.

"I fell in love with Jimmy when we were seniors in high school," Connie began. "He said he wanted us to get married. But when I told him I was pregnant a couple of months before graduation, he got upset. The day after graduation, he disappeared. I knew then that I'd have to raise my baby by myself."

"Your parents couldn't help?" he asked.

"My parents told me I was going to hell when I told

them. They turned me out of the house and warned me to never come back.''

Jack shook his head. Religion could so easily be perverted into hate when humans turned away from its message of love. He squeezed Connie's hand, urging her to go on with her story.

''A woman who owned a small diner down the street from the high school gave me a job as a waitress and let me sleep in her storage room,'' Connie said. ''The next few months were very hard. But once my Amy was born, I knew nothing else mattered. She was my sweet baby, my total joy.''

He could hear that joy in Connie's voice, see it flooding her face as the memories of her child filled her.

''Amy was the happiest, most loving child. She was the reason I got up every morning and said prayers of gratitude every night. I worked in a day-care center so I could keep her with me. When she got close to school age, I applied to be a teacher's aide. Only then my baby…my baby…''

Connie's head dropped as her voice faltered. She stared down at her lap as her hand clutched his.

Jack would have sworn he was immune to dramatic pauses, but he wasn't immune to this one. Connie didn't know how to simply relate facts. She emitted the complete range of her emotions in full and living color. He now understood why Diana had wanted him to hear the story from her client. No one else could tell it like this.

''What happened to her?'' he asked quietly.

''It was Amy's fourth birthday. I was in the kitchen baking her cake. She was playing on the screened-in front porch. I heard a car, and it seemed much too close. I looked up to see this old car jump the curb and smash through our fence. It plowed into the porch, then sped away. I ran outside to look for Amy and I found her under the wreckage. She was dead.''

Tears poured down Connie's cheeks, large glistening drops of pure grief. Jack had no handkerchief or tissue to offer her. He leaned over and gently rubbed the tears away with his thumbs.

"Did they find the driver?" he asked after a moment.

She tried to speak, but her words were choked by sobs. Out of the corner of his eye, Jack saw Diana answer him with a shake of her head.

Connie wept for several more minutes before resuming her story. Her voice was whispered pain. "I wanted to die. I tried to. But Amy kept coming to me in my dreams. She told me she'd be too sad if I died. I enrolled in night school and earned a teaching credential. They offered me a job teaching third grade. I told them I wanted to teach kindergarten instead."

"So you could be around children Amy's age," he guessed.

She nodded. "Sometimes when they smiled, I saw Amy in their eyes."

Jack let a moment pass before he asked, "When did you meet Bruce Weaton?"

"Over a year ago. Amy had been gone almost four years by then."

"How did you meet him?"

"I worked late one day setting up a classroom exhibit. When I walked out to the parking lot, I saw that one of my tires had gone flat. Everyone else had gone home. I didn't have a phone to call for assistance. I was trying to figure out how to put on the spare when Bruce came by in his car. He changed the flat for me. Afterward, he invited me out for coffee."

"You had coffee with him?"

"Oh, no. He was very handsome and drove a Mercedes. I was certain he was only being kind."

"But you did see him again?" Jack prompted.

"About a week later. I bumped into him while we were both standing in line for popcorn at the movie theater in the mall. He'd come to see some war movie. I was there to see a Disney adventure my class was talking about. I was so surprised when he asked if he could sit with me and watch the kids' movie."

"And after the show?"

"He bought me an ice-cream cone from a concession in the mall. We talked until closing. He kept asking me about myself and seemed really interested in what I told him. When he walked me to my car, he invited me to dinner the next evening."

Jack listened to the amazement in Connie's voice as she described her growing relationship with Bruce. Everywhere they went over the next few months, women gave the good-looking Bruce the eye. But he gave all his attention to her.

Bruce told Connie about his father, Philip, and his brother, Lyle, both of whom were partners with him in a very successful real estate firm. He explained that his mother, Barbara, was a prominent judge. Connie had a hard time believing that this perfect man from a perfect family was interested in her.

After they'd been dating for three months, she finally got up the courage to ask Bruce what he saw in her. To her total amazement, he asked her to marry him.

"What did you say, Connie?"

"I didn't know what to say. He'd been pressing me for weeks for…a more intimate relationship. I'd told him that after Jimmy, I didn't want to be physically intimate with a man again unless I was married. Now he was asking me to marry him. When I told him I wasn't sure, he agreed to give me more time."

At a barbecue the following Sunday, Bruce's seven-year-old nephew had dragged Connie into Bruce's garage to show her the new bike his uncle had bought him for his birthday. As he swung his leg over the bike's seat, the boy's foot caught on the edge of a drop cloth. When Connie had pulled the drop cloth from the boy's foot, she saw a tiny gold locket and chain in the corner. A distinctive blue rose was on the front of the locket.

"I picked up the locket, opened it," Connie said, her voice suddenly nothing but a quivering breath. "I found Amy's picture inside. She was wearing the locket the day the car hit the porch."

Connie lifted her eyes to Jack's. "Bruce had been so sweet to me. He'd asked me to marry him. I couldn't believe he was the man who'd driven the car that had killed my baby."

Jack held firmly onto her hand. "What did you do?"

"All I could think about was getting away. I ran from the garage and got into my car. I started the engine and backed into the street."

"Did you see Bruce?"

Connie nodded. "When I put the car in drive and stepped on the gas, Bruce ran into the street and waved his arms, trying to get me to stop."

"Did you try to stop?"

Connie's chin dropped to her chest. "I tried to steer around him, but I was crying, and I couldn't see him anymore. All I could see was Amy."

"Connie, did you want to kill Bruce?" Jack asked.

"No. I only wanted to get away from him."

Jack gently lifted Connie's chin with his fingertips. The pain on her face bore witness to the truth of her words.

CHAPTER THREE

DIANA ACCEPTED Jack's suggestion to talk about the case over lunch. Normally, she ate at her desk, unwilling to accept the long lines that were inevitable at good restaurants. But talking with him while grabbing a bite would actually be a more efficient use of their time.

Still, she felt uneasy.

She'd worked closely with both Richard and David Knight on cases, even shared an occasional meal with Richard without a moment's unease. Jack's brothers were also very good-looking, but she felt different around Jack, and she couldn't quite put her finger on why.

It probably had something to do with watching him work his magic on Connie. That had been damn scary. Jack knew how to get a woman to talk to him and to trust him with effortless charm. She had no doubt that he could probably make a woman believe anything he said.

How could a woman ever know when he was being sincere?

Diana led the way to a favorite restaurant not far from her office. They got a great table on the second-story terrace that overlooked the street below. The day was dull, as most days in Western Washington were. In the distance the snow-capped peaks of the Olympic Mountains wore dark lumpy hats of cumulus clouds.

But the early summer temperature was mild and the air tasted sweet, reminding Diana that people whose jobs chained them to desks all day needed to get out for a little natural light and fresh air once in a while.

The restaurant catered to business clientele, its patrons appropriately attired. But Jack had taken off his suit coat and tie, opened the collar of his shirt and rolled its sleeves to the elbows. Despite the lack of sunshine, he wore large reflective sunglasses and—what was strangest of all—a false beard.

After the waiter had taken their orders and scurried away, the reason for Jack's altered appearance finally occurred to Diana.

"Do you still get recognized when you go out in public?" she asked.

"Enough that I do my best to avoid it."

"How do fans react to seeing a screen villain in the flesh?"

"Depends on the fan. The nice ones smile and ask for my autograph."

"And the others?"

"They demand to know why I stole my uncle's business while he was in the hospital with a brain tumor, refused to give my nephew part of my liver when he required a transplant, drove my horse-racing competitor to suicide, seduced my sister's best friend when she was in mourning, denied her baby was mine and then tried to murder her husband when he returned from the Amazon—having not been killed in the plane crash after all—only to find he was my long-lost brother who had been raised in the orphanage when we were separated as infants."

She shook her head in amusement. "My, my, you were busy. I must have missed taping a few of the shows."

"I'm surprised you taped any. You don't strike me as a soap fan."

"Mel was writing a paper that involved your TV character, and my assignment was to preserve your performances via the VCR," she admitted. "You might find her conclusions interesting reading."

"If Mel wrote the paper, I might find her conclusions above my reading comprehension."

He was smiling, and Diana suddenly found herself smiling back. She knew few adults—and no men—who would have felt comfortable enough with themselves to admit that, even in jest.

This man had a couple of nice points about him.

The waiter delivered Diana's seafood salad and Jack's sliced roast beef along with their iced teas. Diana realized she was quite hungry and dug in. Her first bite tasted heavenly. This sure beat yogurt and an apple at her desk.

"I understand why you don't want Connie convicted of murder," he said between bites. "That would be unjust."

"I'm glad you feel that way," she said, and she was. But she was cautious, too. "Now tell me why you feel that way."

She studied his face for any sign of the confidence with which he'd greeted her that morning. Or the captivating attention he'd lavished on Connie. But his sunglasses and beard hid so much of his face that reading any expression was next to impossible.

"Connie isn't capable of intentionally squashing a bug, much less a man," he said. "I can't imagine that anyone talking with her for five minutes could think otherwise."

Actually, Diana knew a lot of people too cynical to see her client for who she was. She was relieved to learn Jack wasn't one of those people. That told her something important about him that nothing else could have. He did have some genuine emotional substance beneath the polished surface.

"Have you told the prosecutor what happened?" he asked.

Diana's mouth was full of chunks of tender shrimp and fresh avocado. She shook her head in response.

"I think you should. Any prosecutor who heard Connie's story would understand that she wasn't responsible for her actions at the time she ran over Bruce Weaton."

Diana swallowed before responding. "Any prosecutor in the wonderful world of TV maybe. In real life our Chief Prosecutor has too much time and effort invested in proving Connie's guilt to entertain any thoughts of her possible innocence."

"You don't think he'd care about getting to the truth?"

"All George Staker cares about is arranging the facts in front of a jury so he wins the case. If I told him Connie's story, he not only wouldn't believe me, he'd do everything within his power to use the information against her."

"You've been up against Staker before," Jack guessed.

Diana nodded.

"Tell me about it."

She sipped her tea as she gave his request some careful thought. It would be fair to tell him, she supposed. If he stayed on this case, he would need to know exactly what he'd be up against. Relating the basic facts should be enough.

"My client was a retired military man in his sixties, taking care of his wife who had terminal cancer," she began. "He got up to attend to her in the middle of the night and inadvertently gave her too much medication. In the morning, he found her dead. Staker claimed the man had deliberately given his wife an overdose to collect on her term life insurance that was due to expire. He charged him with murder."

"Are you sure your client was innocent?"

"Positive. I spoke to the hospice nurse. She'd visited the night my client's wife died and administered pain medication without mentioning that fact to my client. He was asleep on the couch, exhausted from caring for his wife. When he was awakened a few hours later by his wife's moaning, he gave her another dose of medication, assuming she hadn't had any. When I learned all this, I went to Staker and asked him to drop the charges.''

"He didn't," Jack guessed.

"And he used what I told him to strengthen the state's case. In his opening statement to the jury, he said the hospice nurse had spent many nights at my client's home, implying they were having an affair. When the hospice nurse got on the stand, Staker cross-examined her about her recent divorce and asked if she was lying because she wanted my client's wife dead so she could be with him.''

"And her denial didn't carry any weight," Jack said, "because the force of the accusation was enough to get the jury to believe the affair was true."

Diana nodded. "I'm always amazed how ready people are to think the worst about someone without a lick of proof.''

"Your client was convicted?"

Diana put down her fork, her appetite suddenly abandoning her. "He took his own life."

"I'm sorry."

Jack had spoken the words softly. Without his impressive array of facial expressions and tonal range, he still sounded very sincere. Diana wondered how he'd managed to do that. Was that ability part of his training, or could it be she was seeing the real him?

"When did this happen?" he asked after a moment.

She hadn't thought she'd share this next part. Now she realized she wanted to.

"Two years ago. I'm still not able to discuss the case dispassionately. Maybe I never will be. My client was a good man who loved his wife dearly. He was depressed over her death and filled with guilt for having had a part in ending her life prematurely, however unintentional.''

''Is that why he killed himself?''

''I think he would have come out of his depression if he hadn't been unfairly accused and tried. He left a letter, thanking me for believing him and asking me to make sure that the hospice nurse was not victimized.''

''What did Staker say when you showed him the letter?''

Diana spoke the words through a clenched jaw. ''He said he wished the guy hadn't killed himself before the jury had reached their guilty verdict because he was robbed of another win. Staker was competing with the prosecutor in a neighboring county for most convictions within a calendar year.''

Jack called Staker a filthy name, so filthy in fact that Diana decided right then that she liked Jack very much.

''Is Staker in another competition?'' he asked, his tone cool with contempt. ''Or does he have a vendetta against Connie?''

''I don't know about another competition,'' Diana said, ''but he never has anything personal against a defendant. They're simply not real to him. Nothing and no one is real to Staker but Staker. The law is something he uses for his own ends. He intends to use Connie's trial to launch his campaign for judge. Her high-profile trial and conviction will give him the media spotlight he craves as the 'hard on crime' candidate.''

Jack chewed for a few minutes before he asked his next question. ''What about the judge who will hear the case? Can you talk to him or her?''

''Him. William Gimbrere. He's a friend of Barbara Weaton's. And he would not be willing to listen.''

''As a friend of the mother of the victim, shouldn't Gimbrere excuse himself from the case?''

"Every judge in the county is a friend of Barbara Weaton's. Earl Payman should have petitioned the court for a change of venue at the time he entered Connie's plea. He didn't. When I did, Gimbrere told me the request had come too late and turned me down."

"I can't imagine that when the jury hears Connie's story, they won't at least opt for the lesser charge of involuntary manslaughter."

"The only option the prosecution is going to give them is guilty or not guilty of first-degree murder. There will be no lesser charge from which they can choose."

"The prosecutor can do that?" Jack asked.

"He's done it."

"But there's no way he can prove premeditation."

"A death doesn't have to be premeditated to qualify as first-degree murder. Paraphrasing Washington State law, a defendant can be found guilty of first-degree murder if he or she manifests an extreme indifference to human life by engaging in conduct that creates a grave risk of death to any person and thereby causes the death of a person."

"Like deliberately running over a guy with your car," Jack said, nodding.

"And you can be sure that Staker will do everything he can to try to prove Connie did that deliberately."

"How can he?"

"By characterizing Connie as a jealous lover. Bruce's nephew said he was showing Connie his new bike and the next thing he knew she was running from the garage. Staker claims that Connie saw another woman's panties lying on the dashboard of Bruce's Mercedes and suddenly realized that Bruce was two-timing her."

"The panties were there?"

"Red lace bikini," Diana confirmed. "Part of the physical evidence in the prosecution's case."

"And the owner?"

"Tina Uttley, an employee at the real estate firm Bruce owned with his father and brother, identified them as hers. She's also admitted to having an affair with Bruce at the time he was romancing Connie."

"Did Bruce's family know he'd proposed to Connie?" Jack asked.

"They said nothing about knowing in their statements to the sheriff's office."

Jack put down his knife and fork, pushed his empty plate aside. "Connie would have said something about Bruce seeing another woman if she'd known."

"I'm certain you're right," Diana said. "But Staker's going to claim that she realized the significance of the panties and that jealousy was her motive for killing Bruce."

"Even though the nephew never mentioned that Connie even looked into the car?"

"All Staker has to do is put Connie in the vicinity and make the idea she saw the panties sound plausible. Without any other explanation for her running out of the garage, he'll count on his suggestion to be taken as fact by the jury."

Jack shook his head. "Connecting the dots so the picture of a lamb turns out to look like that of a lion."

"Pretty scary how well Staker is able to connect those dots, too."

When the waiter arrived to remove their empty dishes, Diana ordered iced tea refills as an excuse to keep squatter's rights on their table. "A trial is basically the telling of two conflicting stories," she said after the waiter had gone. "The story that seems to be the clearest and most believable to the jury given the supporting evidence will be the one they accept. I have to make Connie's story the one the jury will believe."

"How can I help?"

She liked the way he'd phrased that. Not, what is my job? Not, what do you want me to do? But, how can I help?

With every passing minute, Diana became more convinced that Jack really wanted to help.

"First," she said, "you're going to have to put Bruce Weaton in that car at the scene of Amy's hit-and-run five years ago, establish an unbreakable link between him and the locket Connie found hidden in his garage, have every piece of physical evidence analyzed and authenticated by an outside forensic lab and do it without Staker knowing."

"Oh, is that all," Jack said, with good-natured sarcasm.

"No, that's only step one of three."

The waiter refilled their glasses, and Jack squeezed a slice of lemon over his iced tea. "Why an outside forensic lab?"

"One of our strongest weapons will be surprise. Staker and Sheriff Riker have been buddies since high school. What Sheriff Riker knows, Staker knows. We have to maintain complete secrecy about Connie's story until she takes the stand."

"So Staker can't try to twist the facts the way he did in your other case."

"And nearly every other case he's prosecuted. I've watched him at several major trials. His strength lies in knowing exactly what to expect from the defense and putting his own spin on the facts. He can't deal with surprises, which is why he mustn't know that Connie is going to testify, much less what she's going to say."

"If you don't present the evidence of Bruce's involvement in the hit-and-run until after Connie has testified," Jack said, "what will you say in the opening statement?"

"I'm not giving an opening statement. Judge Gimbrere's a firm believer that a jury should base their decision on the evidence, not on a lawyer's interpretation of that evidence, which is what he considers both opening and closing statements by trial attorneys to be. He'd restricted us to one statement to the jury. Staker chose an opening statement. I opted for a closing.''

''Staker will run the show at the onset of the trial,'' Jack said. ''Won't overcoming the jury's early conclusions be difficult?''

''Very,'' Diana agreed. ''The judge will caution the jury not to form an opinion until all the evidence is in, but many will do so anyway. The people who have investigated the psychology of juries say that members place the most weight on what they hear first and last. By the time I'm through, I'm going to shift that weight to Connie's side.''

Despite the confidence Diana put into her words, she knew that her chances were slim. She had an incredibly complex case and was up against the most ruthless and feared prosecutor in the county. And she hadn't even told Jack the most difficult part yet.

''Has Connie given you a description of the car that hit Amy?''

''Not a very good one,'' Diana admitted. ''She doesn't know much about cars and everything happened so quickly. All she could remember was that the headlights were round and close together. There was a vertical grill on the front and the fenders were high above the tires.''

''Color?''

''Just an impression of gray as it sped toward the porch.''

''Age?''

''I showed her a book of old cars. She didn't recognize any.''

''Maybe we're talking about a classic or sports car as opposed to an old one.''

''Quite possibly,'' Diana agreed. ''The fact that Connie

found Amy's locket in Bruce's garage tells me he parked the car there after killing her child. At some point the locket must have fallen off the car and ended up unnoticed in the corner. What we have to do is get a crime scene unit to scour the place for more forensic evidence without Staker knowing.''

''Who owns the property now?''

''According to the county assessor's office, Donald and Joyce Epstein, formerly of Plainfield, New Jersey. The sale included all personal items—furniture, appliances, dishes, flatware, even towels.''

''Which implies that the Weaton family didn't remove much, if anything, before putting the property on the market.''

''That's the way I read it,'' Diana agreed.

''When did escrow close?''

''Last week. I drove by the place yesterday. No one has moved in yet. If the Weatons or Epsteins haven't cleaned out the garage, there might be some evidence left.''

Jack repositioned the Rolex on his wrist. ''Being able to tie Bruce to Amy's hit-and-run will blow Staker's supposed jealousy motive right out of the water.''

''Yes, and that's important. The jury needs to understand that Connie is not the kind of woman who would fly into a jealous rage. If she had discovered Bruce cheated on her, quietly fading away would have been far more in character for her.''

''Speaking of character, the villain I played in *Seattle* was brought to trial on a first-degree murder charge. As I remember, there was a scene where my attorney had to disclose to the prosecutor who he was going to call as witnesses.''

''The writers on your series did their homework,'' Diana said. ''I *do* have to give Staker a list of potential defense witnesses.''

"Then how are you going to keep him from knowing who you're going to call to the stand?"

"My initial witness list will have close to sixty names—few of whom I actually plan to call on to testify. Each week I'll add more names."

"How does that help?"

"All those extra names will camouflage who I'm really going to have testify. Staker won't have a chance to check out all the witnesses. Knowing him, he probably won't bother to check out any since he thinks he's got an airtight case."

"If he sees the names of private forensic lab personnel, he's bound to know that something is up," Jack pointed out.

Diana liked the questions Jack was asking. They told her he had a good mind and was thinking carefully about the case. Despite his lack of experience, he was hitting on some key points.

"I'll be requesting that a lot of the physical evidence evaluated by the sheriff's department be reevaluated at an outside lab," she said. "When I put the names of the lab personnel on my list, Staker will assume they're a smoke screen. Chances are he won't bother deposing them."

"Give him a forest so he won't see the trees," Jack said with a smile. "I've always liked clever women."

Diana shortened the smile she gave him, reminding herself that liking Jack too much wasn't a good idea.

"Once Connie takes the stand and tells the jury what happened, we'll go right to the proof that Bruce killed her child," she said.

"And effectively turn the tables on Staker by putting Bruce Weaton on trial instead of Connie."

"Which is going to bring some immediate questions to the minds of the jurors."

"Such as why Bruce pursued Connie after he'd gotten away with the hit-and-run murder of her child?"

No doubt about it, Jack was very quick.

"Yes," Diana confirmed. "Step two of getting Connie acquitted will be answering that important question as well as others. Even when the law doesn't require motives to be established, juries always look for them. Wanting things to make sense is part of what makes us human."

Jack nodded. "Why we do something is often as important as what we do."

She placed her forearms on the table, aware she couldn't have put it better. "And, for the life of me, I can't imagine what possessed Bruce to do what he did. He was responsible for the death of Connie's child and had successfully hidden his crime. Why would he pursue her? I would think she'd be the last woman he'd want to be around, if he had any conscience."

"Maybe that was the problem," Jack said. "He didn't have a conscience. Or he got some sick thrill out of getting the mother of the child he'd murdered to fall in love with him."

That thought gave Diana the chills.

Jack counted off on his fingers. "First, you want me to prove Bruce killed Amy. Second, you want me to find out about Bruce so the jury understands what drove him to pursue Connie."

"Yes," Diana answered. She could feel his next question coming. She'd been waiting for it.

"That's two things. You said there were three. What's the third?"

"The third thing could be the toughest," she admitted. "I have to be sure to seat a jury who will listen to Connie, understand the shock she was in and believe her when she says that she was only trying to get away from Bruce that day. Because even if we prove to the jury that Bruce killed her child, and help them to understand his motive in pursuing Connie, and they sympathize with the awful shock she must have felt when she learned what he did, they can *still* convict her of murder if they believe she deliberately tried to kill him.''

Jack was quiet a moment. Diana had no clue as to where he might be looking or what he might be thinking. She was beginning to resent those sunglasses that reflected back her own image and nothing of the man wearing them.

''How are you going to seat a jury made up of people with open minds and the ability to recognize the truth when they hear it?'' he finally asked.

''By *your* investigating the hundred and fifty people whose names have been selected as prospective jurors so we can weed out the ones who won't while identifying the ones who will.''

''A hundred and fifty prospective jurors?'' he repeated, his voice rising a full octave from its deep bases.

''The original jury pool was close to seven hundred,'' she added. ''The others were dropped after a preliminary questionnaire established they had either heard or read about the case, had hardship circumstances that prevented them from serving, or were relatives or friends of law enforcement or others connected with the case.''

''How long did that take?''

''Two months. Judge Gimbrere told Staker and me in a pretrial conference last week that we had to select our jury from this panel. He was adamant that he would not call up any others.''

''How long do I have to investigate these people?''

''Formal jury selection starts in six weeks. We have to gather every piece of information we can about these people by then in order to know which twelve we want sitting in the jury box.''

''You want me to investigate a hundred and fifty people

in addition to gathering the evidence to prove Bruce killed Amy and discovering his motive for pursuing Connie, *and* do it all in six weeks?''

''Yes,'' Diana said as if she was making an everyday request. ''Everything has to be done before we go to trial.''

Now he knew. The next move was his.

Jack rested casually against the back of his chair, the index finger of his right hand gliding along the rim of his iced tea glass. Whatever he was thinking was well hidden behind his disguise.

As the silence lengthened, the waiting became more difficult for Diana to bear. She looked away from him to stare at the blur of people passing by on the sidewalk below.

Jack had to know that she'd asked him to accomplish the impossible. A team of professional trial consultants would probably be able to give her a thumbnail sketch on a hundred and fifty prospective jurors in the time available. But not even they could provide the kind of in-depth analysis she required in order to know whom she could trust with Connie's life.

If such an analysis was even possible. Diana had no idea. But she couldn't ask anything less of Jack. Connie's life was at stake.

The Court had approved the expense for only one private investigator. Her motion requesting a trial date extension had both led to an immediate grunt of ''no'' from Judge Gimbrere and an undisguised snicker from Staker.

She was doing what she had to do. And Jack was going to have to do what he had to do. Chances were good he'd be getting up and walking out any minute now.

A part of her wouldn't blame him. And, yet, she acknowledged that another part of her would be very disappointed.

A few hours ago she'd been hoping he would walk out on this case so she could get someone better qualified. But that was before she'd seen him with Connie. He hadn't simply gotten her client to talk. He had listened to her story with compassion.

Diana realized now she'd been overlooking a key ingredient to Connie's successful defense. Jack *had* the most important qualification a private investigator could have on this case—a firm belief in the client's innocence.

What was she going to do if he walked out?

Diana started when Jack suddenly downed the contents of his glass, grabbed the check and stood.

Her heart sank. He was getting ready to run.

Jack whipped off his sunglasses and smiled at her in pure, unbridled enthusiasm. "Come on, Diana. We're wasting time sitting around here. We've got a lot of work to do."

CHAPTER FOUR

JACK COULDN'T BELIEVE what a great case this was.

He had an interesting mystery to solve, some mind-boggling investigative work to do, and he was being given a chance to help a nice woman who was far more of a victim of a crime than a perpetrator. Finally, after enduring nearly a decade of being thrust into villainous roles, Jack had been cast as a hero.

Hot damn. He couldn't wait to get started.

Of course, Diana had given him an impossible task. But what the hell, that was half the fun. The only thing that gave him pause was the fact that they'd be working very closely together for the next six weeks.

She was an alluring combination—strong, smart and sexy. He also liked the fact that she was genuinely committed to helping her client, instead of taking the easy way out as that slimeball Earl Payman had done.

Hard-core morality in a woman turned Jack on big-time.

But his decision not to get involved with women who had children had been based on painful practical experience and important soul-searching. He knew who he was and what he wanted out of life.

Which meant that his relationship with Diana had to remain strictly business. He could handle it. In the past, he'd worked with a lot of desirable women who were out of bounds for one reason or another. Keeping his hands to himself had never been a problem.

He couldn't suppress a smile when he remembered the

surprised look Diana had given him in the restaurant when he'd accepted the case. As he had surmised when they'd met back in her office, she had underestimated him.

In a way, he was glad. There was something so poised about her that being able to rock her erroneous assumptions was irresistible.

He'd agreed to meet with her the next morning to get a copy of the sheriff's report on Bruce Weaton's death and a picture of the deceased, discuss strategy on his investigation and to pick up the list of the prospective jurors. Now he had to see about getting whatever evidence might exist in Bruce's garage into the right hands.

After having listened to Diana's description of George Staker, Jack knew that if he gathered the evidence against Bruce, Staker would do everything he could to make the jury question the validity of both Jack's abilities and the evidence. The fact that Jack had once been an actor would be something Staker would no doubt use against him as well.

But if a sheriff's detective got the evidence, Staker couldn't challenge the findings because he'd be challenging his own source pool.

Diana had agreed with Jack's assessment of Staker. But she'd initially balked at what Jack had planned to do to foil Staker. Convincing her had taken some effort.

Jared, Jack's twin, was a detective in the sheriff's department. Jared had no respect for the elected sheriff, Bernard Riker, whom he considered a politician, not a lawman.

Jack knew that if he gave his twin a lead in Amy's hit-and-run, Jared would track down the truth, no matter where it led.

Jared was his own man. He'd started out as an FBI agent—as their dad had—but chucked the rigidity of the Bureau for the comparative freedom of Silver Valley

County where it was a little easier to apply common sense to law enforcement.

Jack's older brothers, Richard and David, often exchanged information with Jared on a quid pro quo basis when they worked on cases. That sharing had helped Jared make more collars in three years than most other deputies did in a decade on the job.

When he helped his brothers at the family's private investigation firm, Jared insisted on only two things. First, they were to be discreet about his "cooperation." And, second, if he ever had to testify in court about what he'd been asked to do, he had to be able to tell the truth.

He would go out on a limb for family or in the hot pursuit of justice. But he wasn't going to lie under oath for anybody, not even to get himself or a family member off the hook.

Jack was well aware that the confidentiality agreement he'd signed prohibited him from sharing the particulars about Connie's case with anyone not involved in her defense. Ethically, he had no problem telling Jared, since Jack was convinced his brother had to be the one to gather whatever evidence there might be in Bruce's garage. To Jack's mind that made his twin a part of the defense team.

Still, to get his brother's help, Jack had to let him know what had to be done in a way that wouldn't get either of them into ethical or legal trouble. This called for some careful staging.

Jack pulled into the parking lot at Costco, heading directly for the pay phone. This was not a call he wanted anyone to be able to trace to him.

Looking around to make sure no one was within hearing, he dropped some change into the slot and dialed his brother's office. Jared answered with his name.

"Hi, I'm a concerned citizen making an anonymous

call," Jack said. "I have some important information about an unsolved crime."

There was a pause on the other end of the line. He hadn't disguised his voice because he wanted Jared to know who was making the call so that his brother would take what he had to say seriously.

But he had purposely stated the fact that this was to be from an anonymous source so if Jared ever had to explain how he got the tip, he could truthfully say that a "concerned citizen" had called anonymously.

"All right, Mr. Concerned Citizen, I have a pad and pen handy to take down the information you wish to pass me *anonymously*," Jared said.

"About five years ago, a four-year-old girl by the name of Amy Pearce was killed in a hit-and-run," Jack said. "An old car jumped the curb and struck the girl while she was playing on her porch. The driver was never identified. You might find forensic evidence of that old car in the garage once owned by Bruce Weaton."

"Would that be the same Bruce Weaton who was killed last year?" Jared asked.

"Yes."

"The same Bruce Weaton that Connie *Pearce* has been accused of killing?"

Jared had put the pieces together fast. Jack expected nothing less.

"A couple by the name of Donald and Joyce Epstein have recently bought the Weaton property, fully furnished," he said. "If they haven't cleaned out the garage, the evidence could still be there. Connie Pearce was holding a locket on the day she was arrested. That locket and its chain are most likely a part of her personal property being kept at the jail. They, too, could contain important evidence."

"I'm confused as to why you haven't come into the sheriff's office to tell us this in person, Mr. Concerned Citizen," Jared said after a moment.

Jack took pains to word his answer carefully.

"If you decide to reopen this investigation and discover that Bruce Weaton was behind the wheel of the car that killed Amy Pearce, this concerned citizen hopes you will not compromise the defense of Connie Pearce by informing the prosecution of those facts."

"Who do you suggest I inform?"

"The attorney for the defense. If anyone else learns of this connection before she has an opportunity to present the evidence to the jury, her client's right to a fair trial could be compromised."

There was another significant pause on the other end of the line. Jack knew that he'd told his brother he was working for Diana. He had intended to. Jared now knew why he had to contact him anonymously and also whom he could trust.

"Is there anything else you wish to tell me?" Jared asked.

"I advise caution. The sheriff and prosecutor are buddies. Bruce Weaton's mother is well connected. Watch your back. I wouldn't want you to find yourself in a compromising position while trying to clear up an unsolved homicide."

Jack hung up the phone, satisfied that Jared would get hold of Amy's locket and arrange for a team of investigators to scour the garage that had once belonged to Bruce Weaton. If any evidence remained, he'd find a way to let Jack know.

Step one was in motion.

Now on to step two. Jack was going to have to dig up everything he could on Bruce. He knew where to start looking, but he had no idea what he'd find. Not even his fictional character had sunk to the depths Bruce had.

What kind of a man would pursue a woman whose child he'd killed?

"YOU STILL HAVEN'T TOLD ME how dinner with Arnie went last Saturday," Diana's mother said as she ran some hot water over a sponge in the kitchen sink.

Diana stacked the dishwasher with their dinner plates. "That's because my mother always told me if I couldn't say something nice about someone that I should hesitate to say anything at all."

Margaret Gilman switched off the faucet as she turned toward her daughter. "That bad?"

"Oh, yeah."

"I'm so sorry. When Ray said Arnie was going to start dating again now that his divorce was final, I guess I hoped that maybe the two of you—"

"Your heart was in the right place," Diana spoke up quickly. "Unfortunately, he refused to keep his hands where they belonged."

Margaret gave the counter an overzealous wipe with the sponge. "If Arnie made improper advances to you, Ray should be told—"

"—all his efforts to teach his stepson courtesy toward a woman failed? He must know. Why rub his nose in it? Arnie was seventeen when his mother married Ray. No doubt the damage had already been done."

"You're right," Margaret said. "But don't be surprised if I develop a sudden klutzy streak at the wedding and dump a glassful of ice water onto Arnie's lap."

Diana chuckled at the image, although she knew her gentle mother could never bring herself to carry out the threat. "Speaking of the wedding, have you decided where you're going on your honeymoon?"

Margaret squeezed out the sponge and set it at the edge

of the sink. "Ray suggested we fly to Hawaii, but I don't know."

Diana started the dishwasher. The explosion of water and whirling pump had her gesturing for her mom to precede her out onto the porch. She closed the door behind them to shut out the noise.

Margaret eased her trim form onto one of the porch's white wicker chairs and patted the one beside her.

Diana sat, trying to emulate her mother's physical grace, all the while knowing she'd fall short. She'd inherited her dad's big bones and the kind of temperament that *would* dump a glass of ice water on a goon with grabby paws.

She often wished she were more like her mother. Margaret Gilman's smile lit every line in her face with the joy of life. That smile was like a secret fountain of youth. Men were drawn to the wearer in hopes of being able to share in its secret. No wonder she was still turning heads at fifty-five.

Ray was a lucky guy. One of the nice things about him was that he knew it.

"You don't want to go to Hawaii?" Diana asked.

"I'd love to go, but Hawaii is the kind of place you fly to when the weather where you are is cold and icy," Margaret explained. "We wait all year for summer."

Diana inhaled the sweet fragrance as she looked around at the lovely garden her mother's time and talent had created over the years. Red, white and pink roses, all in full and glorious bloom, nodded in the muted evening sunlight. Yes, this was a lovely time of year.

"I was thinking maybe we could drive into British Columbia, find a cute little bed-and-breakfast and spend a few weeks there," Margaret said.

"Some place comfortable and pretty like home, but away from the duties of home," Diana added.

Margaret gave her a smile. "Sometimes I forget what a smart daughter I raised."

Diana smiled back. "Glad I'm around to remind you."

Mel opened the door then, bringing with her the intrusive bumps and grinds of the dishwasher. "I've signed off the Internet, Mom. Be ready to go apartment hunting in about ten minutes. That okay for you?"

Diana nodded in her daughter's direction, and Mel retreated into the kitchen.

"I feel like I'm kicking you out of your home," Margaret said, distress in her tone.

"Don't, Mom. It's time we got our own place. I'll have the last of my student loans paid off in a couple of months. I don't know what we would have done if you hadn't taken us in after Tony took off. Without you there would have been no law school, no—"

"Dear, you've thanked me a million times," Margaret interrupted. "And not a one of them has been necessary. I've loved having you and Mel here."

Diana felt the same tug in her chest that she had first experienced when she finally realized what an incredible mom she had. How blind she'd been as a child—totally idolizing her father and all but ignoring her mother's crucial role in their lives. Kids were so damn dumb. Well, except for Mel, of course.

Thoughts of her daughter brought Diana to her feet. Time she got back to the business of finding them a place to live. One day she'd get a place out in the country like this. But for now, a city apartment would have to suffice.

"Have you told Mel that your aunt Shirley is going to be living with you?" Margaret called out before Diana had reached the door.

"Not yet," Diana admitted.

"Coward."

Diana laughed as she turned around to face her mom.

"We won't be late. I can't be. I have an early-morning meeting with a judge on a plea-bargain, and then I have to see the investigator I've hired on Connie Pearce's case."

"The movie star turned private investigator?"

"I see Mel told you."

"Some actors don't look nearly as good in person as they do on the screen," Margaret said. "What do you think about Jack Knight?"

"I think an engaged lady like yourself shouldn't be asking about handsome men when you have a first-class fiancé to ogle."

Margaret grinned. "Ah, so you *do* think he's handsome."

Diana rested her free hand on her hip in feigned irritation. "Ever since you've gotten engaged you've developed this annoying tendency to try to fix me up."

Her mother's face was full of mischief. "Is that what I've been doing?"

"First with your insurance salesman. Then with Ray's stepson. Now with this private investigator. What gets into brides-to-be? Can't you stand seeing us happy single folk content with unwedded bliss?"

Margaret's grin widened. "Being in love is so wonderful I'm filled with an overwhelming desire to spread that feeling around. Can't think of anyone I'd rather spread it to than you."

"So, DID YOU and Mel find an apartment yet?" Jack asked the moment he walked into Diana's office Tuesday morning.

His simple, conversational question was met with a noticeable pause from Diana. Most women he'd met were more than willing to share news about everyday events. Their biggest complaint was that men were too focused on themselves to ask about a woman's concerns or listen to what she had to say.

But Diana seemed determined not to share much about herself.

Still, she'd let down her guard at lunch the day before. He'd heard the anger and sadness in her voice when she'd spoken of her client's suicide. For a strong woman, she had a soft heart.

A head shake was all he got in answer to his question.

She handed him a folder. "That's the copy of the sheriff's report on Bruce's death and the other stuff you asked for. Is your brother going to investigate Amy's hit-and-run?"

There she was, right back to business. Definitely not the response he was used to getting from women. Did she not find him attractive, or was she too much of a professional to let on?

He told himself the answer wasn't important. She was keeping their relationship businesslike and for that he was glad.

"I contacted Jared as we discussed," Jack said in response to her question. "He'll let us know if and when he finds anything. I also began the search into Bruce Weaton's background. Now that I know where he went to school and who his friends were, I should be able to—"

"How did you find out those things so quickly?"

There was far more challenge than curiosity in her tone.

Jack repositioned himself on her exceptionally uncomfortable guest chair as he set the folder she'd given him on his lap.

"I have no problem indulging your curiosity, Diana. But your question comes across more like a cross-examination of my investigation techniques."

"It was."

Her candor came as a complete shock, which must have been apparent, because a small smile lifted her lips.

She had enjoyed surprising him. Maybe as much as he'd enjoyed surprising her.

"So, you want me to *assume* that you know how to do your job?" she asked.

She was testing him. "As I'm *assuming* you know how to do your job."

That made her smirk. "But you won't take exception to my asking questions purely out of curiosity?"

"I'm always happy to satisfy the curious."

She inched forward on her chair. "Then strictly out of curiosity, how did you find out about Bruce's schooling and friends so fast?"

"His obituary mentioned the schools he'd attended," Jack volunteered easily because he was satisfied that she'd been honest about her motives. "A glimpse at the guest registry at the mortuary where his services were held last year told me who cared enough to show up."

"Doesn't that guest registry go to the family?"

"Smart mortuary personnel keep a copy, knowing that a family in mourning may misplace theirs."

She rested against the back of her chair. "Seems so simple now that you've explained."

"Everything seems simple once you have the answer. Knowing where and how to get the answer is what separates the professional from the amateur."

An amused eyebrow lifted. "Was that another reminder that you are a professional and deserve to be treated as one?"

Jack smiled. "A very gentle reminder. I'm always careful not to inflict any unnecessary bruises."

"As opposed to the necessary ones?" Her brief smile was good-natured.

So, she had a nice sense of humor lurking behind her

formal façade. Getting past this woman's defenses might not be easy. But Jack was becoming more certain by the minute that the effort would be worthwhile.

"Anything else you feel curious about this morning, Diana?"

Damn, he was flirting with her. He hadn't meant to, but those last words had come out full of invitation. Unable to take them back, he carefully wiped the come-hither smile off his lips.

She studied him intently for a minute, then pushed a thick binder in his direction. "Before you get too involved in investigating Bruce's background, I need some quick input on these."

Not only had she not flirted back, she'd completely ignored *his* flirting. Relief vied with an odd disappointment.

Jack picked up the thick binder. "What are these?"

"The preliminary jury questionnaires. They list names, addresses, driver's license numbers and other pertinent information as well as the answers to the basic questions of whether they've heard about the case or know any of the principals who are involved."

Jack flipped through one of the questionnaires. One page listed the names of Bruce, his family members, Connie, witnesses to the alleged crime, as well as Staker and Diana. The next page cautioned each prospective juror not to discuss the case with anyone or allow themselves to be exposed to any news reports.

"What kind of input are you looking for?" he asked.

"I meet with Staker first thing tomorrow to try to agree upon an expanded questionnaire."

"You have the jurors fill that out before you talk to them in the courtroom, right?"

She nodded. "*Voir dire* is the legal term for selecting a jury from the prospective panel. It begins the first day of the trial. Last week, I argued that a more detailed questionnaire filled out in advance would save time. Judge Gimbrere not only agreed to one, he's planning to include a cover letter asking the prospective jurors to be honest and assuring them that their responses will be kept confidential.''

"So Staker didn't fight you on this."

She shook her head. "He wants time to digest the information as much as I do."

"How can I help?"

"If there are questions you want me to ask that will assist with your investigation, I need to know by the end of today."

As attractive and exciting as Diana was proving to be, Jack was thankful that he wasn't planning on pursuing a personal relationship with her. She wasn't even giving him time to complete their business one.

He closed the binder on his lap. "What kinds of questions can we ask a prospective juror?"

"Personal background stuff and whatever else could have a bearing on the specific case for which they are being considered."

"So, if you have a case of spousal abuse, you could legitimately ask prospective jurors if they've been the victim or perpetrator of spousal abuse."

"Both questions would be considered germane," she confirmed. "A prospective juror who has been a victim or an abuser would most certainly be excused from serving on such a case."

"Their experiences having clouded their objectivity."

Diana nodded. "Except that even if a prospective juror has abused his spouse, he's not going to admit it."

No, Jack didn't suppose he would. "The danger is that prospective jurors lie."

"Some lie or omit information to protect themselves or their images. Most will try to be honest."

"The important word here being, *try?*"

"Yes. My biggest concern is that people simply don't recognize their own biases. If they possess a bias that is going to interfere with their ability to see the truth during Connie's trial, I have to know. The judge will ask the prospective jurors if they will decide the case based solely on the evidence presented. If the jurors answer yes, the judge takes them at their word."

"But we can't afford to," Jack said, as he got to his feet.

"Are you going somewhere?" she asked.

"*We're* going to my office."

She remained seated, looking up at him. "Why are *we* doing that?"

"Because my computer is already programmed with what we're going to need to do a quick review of these prospective jurors."

"You could call me later and let me know what you've found."

Yes, Jack supposed he could. But he'd already decided he wanted her sitting beside him while he discovered those answers and developed the jury questionnaire. This was his case as much as hers. He needed her help if they were both to be successful.

"If you want a set of questions by tomorrow, we have to work together," Jack said. "Unless you're looking for an excuse to skip apartment hunting tonight?"

"I can't skip apartment hunting."

"Then let's get going. My schedule's free. I'm prepared to stay with the task until it's done."

"I won't be able to stay past five today," she said, not looking especially happy about the fact.

"When do you and Mel have to move out of your mother's place?"

"Soon."

And that was obviously all she was going to say about that. "If you only have until five," he said, "we'd better get started."

She glanced at her watch. "I have to pick up Mel from school in about thirty minutes."

"I've been meaning to ask. What's a genius like Mel doing in summer school?"

"She's in a special curriculum for gifted youngsters. A former NASA scientist is here this week showing some incredible shots taken by the Hubble telescope, which is why I've been driving her to attend his lectures."

As Jack had suspected, her daughter was the one subject Diana didn't hesitate to discuss. That proud parent syndrome at work. He filed the mental note away for possible future use.

"How does she normally attend class?" he asked.

"Online. The Internet is far more efficient because taking classes by e-mail allows her to progress at her own pace. She'll be back to accessing all of her course work online next week, thus ending my chauffeuring duties."

"So this is the only week she has a chance to interact with her peers."

"The term peer is difficult to define with Mel. The student closest in chronological age to her in this astronomy class is fourteen."

"Does she ever mix with other nine-year-olds?"

"I've put her in several classes with children her own age. She warned me if I ever tried to do it again, she'd report me for child abuse."

Jack smiled.

"There are five other gifted children in the area," Diana said. "Mel seems to feel most comfortable around them, despite their different talents, ages and academic advancement. The leader of the gifted children's program has them performing in a play together in a few weeks so they can interact with one another as children for a change.''

"What kind of play?" Jack asked.

"A murder mystery Mel wrote.''

"Is Mel the heroine or villain?''

"They drew names out of a hat to decide which role they'd play. Mel got the name of the victim.''

"I doubt that's going over well.''

Diana's smile told Jack his comment was on target. She had a really good smile. His reaction to it must have shown on his face because he saw the resulting withdrawal on hers.

"I have to drop some books by the jail for Connie to read before driving Mel home,'' she said, deftly changing the subject.

Jack glanced at his watch, doing the math. That would give him time to talk to Richard. "Then I'll expect you in my office in ninety minutes.''

Before she could think up an excuse why she couldn't, he was out the door.

"DIANA?'' Gail's voice called from behind her.

Diana halted on her way to the back door and turned to see her friend exiting her office. "How did your case go yesterday?'' Diana asked.

"Acquitted, all counts,'' Gail said, smiling.

"Great going. That's five wins in a row. Not that I'm surprised. Your defendants had the superior counsel.''

"The prosecutor's case was flimsy and poorly presented,'' Gail said. "If I know Staker, he'll can that incompetent soon. The dunce actually looked shocked to lose.''

Diana wasn't fooled. Gail was being modest.

Her friend moved closer as she lowered her voice.

"Speaking of surprises, I thought you were going to fill me in on the Pearce case?"

"I came by yesterday afternoon but you were in court," Diana said. "What about over lunch in my office tomorrow? No, wait. Scratch that. I'll be in a meeting with Staker. I might not get back in time."

"How about now?" Gail suggested.

Diana shook her head. "I've got to run, and I'm tied up the rest of the day. Thursday I have to interview a witness on the Pearce case. Friday?"

"Friday?" Gail repeated, frowning. "No, I have something personal to attend to on Friday. How about we grab dinner after work today?"

"Mel and I will be out apartment hunting."

"Oh, right. I forgot."

"How's lunch on Monday?"

"Guess Monday will have to do, but if you're deliberately postponing this to increase the suspense, I think you should know it's working."

Diana smiled as she waved goodbye and headed for the door.

As she darted to her car through a light drizzle, she wished she did have time to talk to Gail about the questions she should be asking the prospective jurors. She consoled herself with the fact that she'd have Jack to exchange ideas with. So far everything he'd suggested they do had been both logical and intelligent.

Developing the questions for the prospective jurors together was a more efficient use of their time, which was why she hadn't fought the suggestion. She had to have her evening free for the dreaded apartment hunting. The night before had been a bust because she and Mel had started too late. Landlords did not like being torn away from their suppers and TV programs to show their properties.

But Diana also knew that aside from the fact that working together was a good idea, she was looking forward to being with Jack. Not because he'd flirted with her. But because he'd immediately stopped.

For a natural charmer like Jack, flirting was probably as ingrained and effortless as breathing. That he had caught himself and was making a conscious effort not to come on to her meant a lot to Diana.

He was treating her like a professional. As far as Diana was concerned, that was the highest compliment a man could pay her.

A good-looking man could turn her head. A smart man could earn her respect. But it was always the considerate man whose company she'd choose.

"YOU SELL YOUR HOUSE YET?" Jack asked his brother as he sat in the chair in front of Richard's desk.

Richard studied him with the same probing stare that their father possessed. The rest of the Knight brothers had tried their hands at other jobs. Richard hadn't needed to. He knew he was a born private investigator.

"Since when did your taste in women change?" Richard asked.

"What makes you think it has?"

"Hell would freeze over before you'd give up your perfect bachelor pad. Your buddies are kindred souls. None of the sophisticated, fast-track females you keep company with would be interested in a small home away from the night life. So who's your new female friend?"

Richard was good all right.

"Diana Mason's mother is getting married," Jack explained. "New hubby's moving in, and Diana and her daughter are looking for a house. They currently live in the country so they're probably used to being awakened by noisy birds instead of noisy neighbors. Chances are good that they'd go for your place."

Richard sat up straight. "Diana told you she was interested in buying?"

"I was thinking you might offer them a lease option for six months, maybe a year."

Richard shook his head, his initial interest fading fast. "A clean sale, okay. But I'm not interested in becoming her landlord. She's a valued client of this firm. Better for all concerned not to complicate matters."

Jack wasn't daunted. Convincing Richard of something was never easy. "How long has the house been on the market now, a year?"

"Eleven months."

"Have you had an offer?"

Richard shifted in his chair. "The real estate agent tells me finding the right buyer takes time."

Jack shook his head. "You could be sixty before the right buyer comes along for that place. Diana and her kid can't find a house. You want them to end up in some dump of an apartment in town?"

"Her personal life is not our concern. Besides, not every apartment in town is a dump. Or have you forgotten I live in one?"

"The image of your place was what brought the dump description to mind," Jack said, big grin on his face.

Jack was trying to get Richard to lighten up and see the opportunity. His brother was never going to sell his small, ridiculously decorated home in the hills. Not unless the Munchkins decided to relocate to Silver Valley.

"Have you talked to her about this?" Richard asked after a moment.

"Of course not," Jack said as though the thought would never have entered his mind. Naturally, telling her about Richard's place had been his first inclination. But after some consideration, he knew that this way had more chance of success.

"I wanted to check with you first to make sure you were comfortable with the idea."

Richard rubbed the back of his neck. Jack recognized the unconscious mannerism. His brother was letting himself think about the possibilities. What he needed now was a little nudge.

"The real estate agent could handle the lease option contract, security deposit, collection of the monthly payments," Jack said. "You wouldn't have to be personally involved. You don't even have to tell her you own the place."

Richard's neck rub became more vigorous. "Let me think it over."

Jack got up to leave. He'd made a good case, but like any expert salesman, he was ready with his closing line.

"What's to think over? You'd be doing Diana and her daughter a good turn and getting some money to cover your expenses on that place. No way you can lose."

When Jack reached the door, he turned back to his brother. "Diana will be working with me in my office today should you decide to tell her about the house."

"You invited her here?" Richard asked.

"Best place for us to work."

"Inviting clients to work in our offices isn't protocol, Jack. Part of keeping their cases confidential is keeping them out of here so other clients don't see them. And vice versa."

How like Richard to spout all the time-honored rules that the ingrained private investigator in him lived by so assiduously. Those rules might fit Richard. But they were way too tight for Jack.

"Couldn't be helped," Jack said. "I need to use my computer programs to generate a jury questionnaire. Be a lot easier for me to follow up on these people later if I have everything in my database."

"Couldn't you have accomplished the same thing by e-mail? Or taken a laptop to her office?"

"We're under a tight time constraint. Besides, my office is a lot more comfortable than hers and affords us uninterrupted privacy. I can have food sent in and there's even a couch to stretch out on."

Richard squinted at his brother ever so slightly. His tone remained even, but the delivery of his warning was no less emphatic. "Please, be careful."

Jack was pretty sure he knew what Richard meant, but he wanted to see if his brother had the balls to say it. "Careful about what?"

"Not to step over the line with Diana."

Yep, he did. Jack almost laughed. Here he was thirty-three and his big brother still thought he had the right to warn him off inappropriate women. That was *really* funny, considering Richard's mistakes with women.

But what the hell. Jack was easygoing enough not to take offense.

"Relax, Richard. I don't date women with kids even if they're interested, and Diana is definitely not interested."

The suspicion in Richard's tone rose a notch. "How did you learn she wasn't?"

Some guys might have been tempted to aim for a brother's chin after being challenged like this. But Jack had learned long ago that humor packed more punch than a fist ever could.

"A woman lets a man know when she's interested," Jack said. "Don't tell me you've been out of the game so long that you've forgotten how it's played?"

Richard shook his head in good-natured defeat.

"The lady's in distress," Jack said, keeping his tone light. "You going to ride in on your white steed carrying a six-month lease and save the day like a real knight or leave her and her innocent child to the nefarious rent hikes of a landlord with larceny in his heart?''

Richard chortled. ''Damn good thing they insisted you only *read* the lines and not write them.''

''Everybody's a critic. Come on, Richard, be a hero. Beats being a villain any day.''

Jack flashed his brother a brilliant smile before leaving his office.

CHAPTER FIVE

AS OFTEN AS DIANA HAD employed White Knight Investigations, she had never been inside their offices. The sign outside the building read, When You Need Help, Call On A White Knight.

She took the elevator to the top floor and followed an arrow that led to reception. The furniture was a tasteful light-oak, the carpet a soft gold, the paintings peaceful landscapes. The view outside the panoramic windows of the busy wet city below was positively energizing.

When she approached the desk, the receptionist stood as though at attention.

"Good morning, I'm Harry Gorman. How may I help you?"

Harry's clipped speech and crisp movements put Diana in mind of a drill sergeant ready to whip some new military recruit into shape. She had spoken to him on the phone many times. Now she had an image to go along with the voice.

"I'm Diana Mason, Harry. Good to finally meet you in person."

Harry executed a quick head bow in her direction. "Likewise, ma'am. Mr. Jack Knight is expecting you."

Harry depressed an intercom key, told Jack that she had arrived and proceeded to lead her down the hall to his office. Harry knocked once, opened the door for her, stepped aside so she could enter and then closed the door behind her.

The office was spacious, full of deep blues lightened by touches of silver. The pictures on the wall were modern art splashes in the same hues. The couch in the corner had clean lines and was man-size, the desk an enormous expanse of stainless steel with a large, flat-screen computer monitor in the center.

Jack's suit coat was off and his sleeves were rolled up. He was in the process of moving a cushioned guest chair next to his. "You'll be able to see the computer monitor better from here. Sit down and I'll show you what I have so far."

Radiating an infectious energy, he retook his seat and started to punch keys. Diana set down her briefcase and bag before slipping onto the comfortable cushioned seat.

As she leaned toward the screen, the first thing she noticed was that Jack smelled good, a combination of clean male skin mixed with sandalwood. With more effort than should have been necessary, she switched her focus to the blinking cursor.

"These are the hundred and fifty prospective jurors' names, listed alphabetically," Jack said as he scrolled down.

"You've already entered all of those names into your computer," she said with a note of surprise in her voice. He had left her office ninety minutes before.

"Harry and I worked on them together," Jack explained. "We've also entered in the other information from their questionnaires. The addresses were helpful in giving me a general idea about them."

"How do you mean?"

Jack faced her. "Market research groups learned long ago that people who share the same socioeconomic background and similar lifestyles tend to live near one another. A kind of birds-of-a-feather-syndrome. Market research groups have classified neighborhoods based on this principle.''

''I'd be interested in seeing an example.''

''Coming up,'' he said as he looked at the monitor once more. ''Let's take Ross Abbott, prospective juror number one. His address tells me he lives in a neighborhood that has been labeled by market research as Silver Power.''

Jack explained that people in this neighborhood had been identified as affluent retirees over the age of fifty-five. They were most likely to be married, have a safe deposit box, take a cruise vacation, own two late-model cars, be a member of AARP, disapprove of graphic violence in any medium, be disappointed in the current education system and vote in favor of any proposition that promised to lower property taxes.

''Where did the market research groups get all that information?'' she asked.

''Census data, real estate data, insurance underwriters, credit reports, consumer surveys. Advertisers know more about us than the FBI ever will. Every time you buy something, someone's database records the sale. Every time you use the Internet, the Web sites you're accessing are tracked.''

''Big Brother is watching,'' Diana said. ''Only George Orwell got it wrong. Big Brother isn't the intrusive bureaucratized state. He's an advertiser.''

''They've studied the makeup of most neighborhoods in the U.S. in order to know who to target their products to.''

''Do another one,'' she suggested.

''We'll try the middle of the list this time and highlight Judy Nolan.''

Diana soon learned that Judy lived in an area advertisers had labeled Young Families. It was generally comprised of four-person families with two adults between the ages of twenty-two and thirty-four and two children under the age of fifteen. They had a large mortgage on their small house and both parents worked. The husband was most likely to be a boxing and basketball fan. The wife belonged to the PTA and a book club. They shopped at Wal-Mart and an SUV was one of the vehicles parked in their two-car garage. They would approve any proposition that increased taxes for schools since they considered their children's education to be of primary importance.

"Scary," Diana said. "I have a feeling I know Ross Abbott and Judy Nolan without ever having met them. How accurate is the information?"

"Fairly, but individuals can and do vary from their neighborhood's established norms. Still, the generalizations can be a place to start when you're trying to get a fix on the basic background and attitudes someone might possess."

"This is great," Diana agreed. "Having the information on a computer database is definitely going to facilitate analysis."

A knock came, and Harry entered with two cups of coffee. He approached Diana, handed the first cup to her. "Nonfat milk, no sugar," he said.

Diana smiled as she took the cup. That *was* the way she liked her coffee. But she'd never mentioned that to Harry.

"Is everyone here a private investigator?" she asked.

"I called your office to check on your preferences when Mr. Knight told me you would be spending some time here," Harry explained.

She couldn't imagine Kelli thinking of doing that for one of their clients, but then Kelli had held only one other job before coming to the law firm seven months before. Harry had close to five decades of experience on her. While he was serving Jack his coffee, she took a sip of hers. Perfect.

When Harry left, she turned to Jack. "Some smart client

with gobs of money is going to lure Harry away from your firm.''

"I used to worry about that, too," he admitted. "I even kidded Harry about it once. He told me he'd never leave. Something about a debt of honor he owed my dad."

"Were they in the military together?"

"Harry was a career military man, but my dad never served. When I tried to question Harry further about the debt, he clammed up."

"Did you ask your dad?"

Jack nodded. "He said it was nothing. And when my dad says that something is nothing, that's his polite warning to back off from his personal business."

Diana understood. She'd always found Charles Knight to be congenial and accommodating. But she'd sensed the hardness beneath his amiable air, as she had sensed it in Richard. She did not sense it in Jack.

What she did sense was a complex man of contrasts. On the one hand, he was easygoing with an ingrained sense of fun. On the other hand, he possessed a remarkable intelligence and sincere compassion.

"So, what do we start with?" he asked, bringing her wandering mind back to business.

Diana had him enter questions about the prospective jurors' marital status, current and past occupations for the past ten years, their spouses' current and past occupations, their children's ages and occupations if any, their length of residency in the community, highest level of education, organizations that they belonged to, magazines they subscribed to, favorite TV shows and the last two books they'd read.

After he'd entered all the questions, he said, "Prospective jurors must feel like they're filling out a job application."

"They are," Diana responded. "They're being considered for one of the most important jobs imaginable—deciding the fate of another human being.''

Jack nodded his understanding. ''Their occupation, education and entertainment preferences should give us some hints as to whether they're intelligent.''

''And hint at those who aren't. Jury selection is often more about deciding who to eliminate than include.''

''Other than smarts, what qualities do you want Connie's jurors to possess?''

''Honesty and open-mindedness. Too bad the market researchers haven't learned to predict those qualities by zip code.''

''I'll see what I can do,'' he said.

''You have some way of checking whether someone is honest and open-minded?'' she asked, aware of the doubt in her tone.

''Finding out if they answered this questionnaire we're preparing truthfully should give us a clue.''

''How do you determine if they lied?''

''When the time comes, I'll show you.''

The look he gave her hinted of friendly mischief. She didn't think he would do anything against the law. He didn't strike her as that kind of man.

''What else do you want to learn about the prospective jurors?'' he asked.

''Everything I can. But learning about the jury isn't the only purpose of *voir dire*. I also take the opportunity to educate the prospective panel. This is the first time most will have sat on a jury. They have to understand that Connie is innocent unless she is proven guilty in a court of law.''

''I thought the phrase was innocent *until* proven guilty.''

''I've always disagreed with that phraseology,'' Diana said. ''Saying someone is innocent *until* proven guilty implies that it's only a matter of time before they are proven guilty. But saying someone is innocent *unless* proven guilty reflects what a trial is really all about.''

Jack sipped his coffee. ''I would imagine that most people think that because someone has been arrested, they must have done something wrong.''

''A very common first reaction. It's yet another hurdle we have to overcome. Most prospective jurors are very busy people, showing up to serve because of duty, not desire. After filling out forms that require them to reveal very private things about themselves, they're made to sit around for hours, waiting to be called into the courtroom. If a defense attorney doesn't acknowledge their inconvenience and show them courtesy in the *voir dire,* she can appear incompetent or inconsiderate or both. That's one way to lose a case before the trial even starts.''

Jack gave her an understanding nod. ''We should have employed you as an adviser when *Seattle* was doing legal scenes. Every courtroom episode pretty much treated the jury as insignificant to the outcome of the trial.''

When the intercom suddenly buzzed, he picked up the phone. ''Yes, Harry?''

As Jack listened to the message Harry was relaying, Diana sipped her coffee and watched him. She liked the questions he asked—and the way he listened to her answers.

''Thank her for the invitation, but tell her I'll be tied up for the next few nights,'' he said into the telephone.

Diana found herself wondering if Jack was turning down a date with some steady lady friend. She rejected the thought. If he had a steady lady friend, he wouldn't be so cold as to have Harry deliver that kind of message.

''Just a minute, Harry,'' he said as he put his hand over the phone's mouthpiece and turned to her. ''Do you want to have something brought here for lunch or have Harry make us reservations somewhere?''

"Here," she decided.

"Any preference as to cuisine or are you willing to leave the menu to me?"

She shook her head. "Last time I let a man order for me I ended up with a hot dog."

He smiled. "I'm not a hot dog kind of guy."

"What kind of guy are you?"

"There's one way to find out."

His expression was so full of dare, Diana couldn't resist. "All right. But I feel I should warn you. Mel's comment about the family failing when it comes to tact goes double in judging food selection."

"Two of my usual for lunch," he said into the phone. "And if anyone else calls, tell them I'm in conference and will have to get back to them tomorrow."

Jack hung up the phone, wearing a pleased smile. As they made eye contact, Diana felt a disturbing quiver of excitement.

The next instant, Jack looked away and scooted his chair closer to the keyboard. Diana felt reassured by his quick return to business, wondering if she'd read too much into the moment.

"What are some of the specific questions you'll want to ask the prospective jurors that pertain to Connie's case?" he asked.

"Sensitive questions that they might find difficult or embarrassing to talk about openly in court," she said. "First on the list would be if they had ever lost a child through disease or accident."

"Staker will want to get them on the jury if they answer affirmatively," he said, "especially since Bruce Weaton's father died after seeing his son killed right before his eyes."

"I'll have no objection to their sitting on the jury. We'll

be presenting evidence that Connie lost her child as well, right before her eyes.''

As soon as he typed in the question, Diana was ready with another.

''Which brings up the fact that we'll also need to ask the prospective jurors if they, their friends, or any of their family members have been involved in a motor vehicle accident and if that accident involved injuries.''

Jack nodded. ''And to make sure we've covered all the bases, the final, related question would be if they've had a friend or family member who was the victim of a violent crime.''

He'd caught on quickly.

''Anything else?'' he asked after typing the last question mark.

''There's a category of questions called juror self-perception,'' Diana said. ''Let's ask the jurors if they consider themselves to be leaders, followers or neither and why.''

''What kind of answer would make you want to eliminate someone from the jury panel?'' he asked.

''I always suspect those who describe themselves as leaders. Too often I've found they're egotists with a need to control others. Get two of those people on a jury and they're bound to be disruptive. They can even end up circumventing its purpose.''

''Too busy fighting over who's going to be leader to get the job done,'' Jack said, a smile almost of amusement drawing back his lips.

Diana was intrigued. ''You sound like you've had first-hand experience with the type.''

''I'm an expert. Enormous egos are synonymous with actors.''

''That hold true for you as well?'' She'd asked the question lightly. Too late she realized that it could be interpreted as a put-down.

But when Jack turned to her and smiled, she stopped worrying. He was not a man who easily took offense. Quite the contrary. Challenges to his abilities and self-image seemed to amuse him. Not many men were that secure in themselves.

"My overblown ego got summarily deflated the day *Seattle*'s producer decided not to renew my contract."

"Dumb move," she said. "Mel tells me that without you the show died a quick death."

"Probably because the writers didn't kill me off with enough gore. After all, I was voted the daytime TV villain viewers most wanted to see boiled in oil."

Jack had an absolutely irresistible smile when nothing but good humor was behind it.

"Did you enjoy playing a villain?" she asked, suddenly very curious to know.

"The part was challenging and certainly paid very well."

But he *didn't* enjoy it. Interesting. "Why no leading man parts after that?"

"My agent told me I was too strongly tied to a villainous image. Audiences would have had difficulty accepting the switch."

She remembered then what he'd said to Connie about wanting to rescue a lady in distress. She was quite certain that he'd meant what he'd said.

"Are you really interested in my acting career, Diana? Or do these questions have something to do with Connie's case?"

She had been thinking about business, but mostly she had been thinking about him. Diana became aware of how close she was to Jack. Slowly, casually, she moved back in her chair.

"I was wondering if we should ask the jurors what TV or movie role they'd choose to play and why," she said.

"To see whether they'd cast themselves as heroes or villains," he said, once again understanding without explanation.

"A fun question for people to think about, and one that could reveal some important self-perception clues," Diana said. "I don't think Staker would object. He's bound to see the benefit. But Judge Gimbrere might consider the question too frivolous."

"Want to put it in and find out?" Jack asked.

"Why not," she decided. "Even if the question gets thrown out, at least we will have tried."

"Speaking of fun questions, want to ask them how they'd change their life if they won a million-dollar lottery?" he asked as he added the other information to the growing questionnaire.

She laughed at the unexpected suggestion. "Their answers could be as revealing, if not more so, than the regular, boring questions prospective jurors are given. Sure, go ahead and put it in."

He suggested a few more unusual questions that she agreed would be great additions before Harry interrupted them to say that their food had arrived. When he brought in the trays, they sat on the couch to eat.

Lunch was baked chicken breast with baby root vegetables and a blend of melted cheeses rolled in a paper-thin pastry. Dessert was slices of fresh strawberries, melon and grapes. The beverage was a tall iced tea.

When Diana was finished, she sunk back against the soft cushions of the couch. "You put hot-dog man to shame."

Jack took a gulp of his iced tea and set the glass on the coffee table, his smile full of self-satisfaction. "You should try me for dinner sometime."

When they maintained eye contact several beats too

long, Diana knew she wasn't misreading the fast-spreading warmth within her.

She stood and went to the window to stare out at the heavy clouds. Cars whooshed by on the streets below. But she wasn't thinking about either the weather or the traffic.

Jack wasn't flirting with her. The heat in his gaze went way beyond the playful stage. She was female enough to be both flattered and fascinated by his interest, but smart enough not to act on either.

Their working relationship could be ruined if she allowed a personal element to intrude. Too much was at stake to chance it.

His face was reflected in the window. He was still watching her.

"So this is your usual lunch," she said as though food had been the only thing on her mind.

"On the Tuesdays that I spend in the office. I've become rather set in my tastes and ways. Comes from being a confirmed bachelor."

A confirmed bachelor. He'd just given her his ground rules in case she decided to pursue this attraction. She appreciated the honesty. Better to know up front that he wasn't available for anything but a fling.

She liked Jack, and she was attracted to him. But casual dating had never been her style. Nor did she want Mel growing up thinking that physical love was inconsequential and relationships between men and women transient.

Human relationships were the most fulfilling part of life—when one selected the right humans.

"Is there anything else you want, Diana?"

Despite the possible double entendre in his words, she heard only a courteous inquiry in his tone. But he hadn't taken his eyes off her.

"I don't want anything else, thanks," she said to his

reflection in the window. It was the right answer to whatever question he'd been asking.

A knock came on the door. Jack called for whoever it was to come in. Diana turned to see Richard stepping inside. She smiled and he nodded in response.

Richard's eyes swept over the empty dishes on the coffee table in front of the couch. "Glad I caught you on your lunch break."

"If you need to talk with Jack I can—" she began.

"I came to see you," Richard interrupted. "I understand that you and Mel are looking for a place to lease."

Diana blinked in surprise. "Yes."

Richard approached, handing her a paper circular. "This house is for sale, but the owner would probably accept a lease option. If you want to check it out, the agent's name and number are at the bottom."

Diana scanned the information on the property. Three bedroom, two-bath, cedar shingles, hardwood floors and only a few miles down the road from her mother's home. This *did* sound good. When she lifted her head, Richard was already on his way out the door.

"Thank you," she called after him.

He paused to turn back to her. "If the house ends up meeting your needs, you're welcome. If you're disappointed, blame Jack. He's the one who insisted I tell you about it."

Richard gave Jack a smile that was a bit too brilliant before closing the door.

Diana looked at Jack, not quite sure how she felt about that revelation. "Why did you—"

"I don't like personal problems interfering with the work I'm trying to do," he said, cutting her off as he stood. "Want to see the place now?"

She was eager to see the house, but it was already after two. "We haven't finished the questionnaire."

"Call the real estate agent and ask her to meet us there," Jack suggested, pointing toward the phone. "I'll drive you over so we can talk about what other questions to ask the jurors on the way. We'll come back here afterward and finish up."

He rolled down his shirt sleeves and slipped on his coat as though the decision had already been made.

"If you wait too long, someone else might snatch up the place," he warned.

She shot him a pointed look as she held up the circular. "You don't happen to own this house by any chance?"

He smiled as he grabbed her bag and slung the strap over her shoulder. "If you still have to ask that question *after* seeing the house, I'll slit my throat."

So Jack would rather slit his throat than be considered the owner of the house? Diana was more eager than ever to see it now.

THE ADDRESS WAS 142 Baby Lane. That alone had been enough reason for Richard's ex-wife to coerce him into buying the two-story dollhouse. Barely fourteen hundred square feet, the dilapidated old place had required a new heat pump, plumbing, floors and roof. It would have cost Richard a lot less to demolish the original structure and build a new one in its place.

But that wasn't what Richard's wife had wanted.

Jack had been to the house once after the repairs had been completed and Richard's wife had finished decorating. That was all he could handle.

Teddy-bear wallpaper covered the kitchen. The small upstairs bedrooms and bath had fawns playing with pink bunnies on the ceiling as well as the walls. The living room was filled with cutesy ducks bouncing beneath umbrellas and skipping over rain puddles.

But the bedroom and bath downstairs had gotten the

worst of it. Wallpaper filled with babies too blatantly sweet even for Gerber ads peeked out of pink and blue blankets.

Jack couldn't make himself follow Diana and the real estate agent into that so-called master suite.

Feeling the need for some fresh air, he headed out the back door, down the porch stairs and walked to the edge of the property, all the while wondering at the insane things a man in love would do.

Thank God he'd been spared.

The half acre that went with the house was overgrown with weeds. Above their waist high tops, Jack gazed out at a small lake. The breeze was stirring the water and someone in a sailboat was braving the waves. Far as Jack was concerned, the view was the only good thing about the place.

A few moments later Diana came to stand next to him. The muted afternoon light fell softly across her cheek. A delicious scent that had been tantalizing him all morning wafted off her hair. The urge to move in closer, bury his face in the glistening black strands and inhale deeply was strong.

That was a bad sign. Not the first of the day, either.

They'd started back in his office when he realized she'd become aware of his attraction for her. Not that he thought she'd do anything about the attraction. But because he'd suddenly and fervently hoped she would.

Jack took a penknife from his pocket and held it out as he asked, "What's the verdict, counselor?"

"You can put the knife away," she said, the amusement at his dramatics lighting her face from within. "Your throat is safe. This is not a house that you would own."

He put the knife back, turning away from her to stare out at the water. "You going to lease the place?"

"Jury's still out," she said. "The real estate agent is

calling the owner to see if the items that concern me can be negotiated.''

Jack wanted to know what her concerns were. He wanted to know a lot of things. He didn't ask any of them.

''I hope they can be worked out,'' she said. ''This is a great spot. The house would fit us quite well. Whatever happens, I want to thank you for talking to Richard.''

Jack allowed himself only a noncommittal shrug in response. He'd already told her that he'd done what he had for purely selfish reasons. He thought he had. Now he wasn't sure. The gratitude in her voice made him feel too good.

''I didn't know Richard had kids,'' she said, almost casually.

''He doesn't.''

Her voice was filled with understanding. ''He and his wife divorced before they came to live here.''

Jack knew Diana was smart. She wasn't disappointing him.

''If you really want to lease this place, I wouldn't let on that you know he owns it,'' Jack said. ''He has this thing about mixing work with anything that could be construed as the least bit personal.''

''We all have that thing.''

The serious note in her voice had him glancing at her. She was looking straight ahead, a small frown drawing her eyebrows together. So, his attraction for her was making her uneasy. He should have known.

The real estate agent pushed open the door to the house and stepped outside. ''Diana, good news,'' she said as she approached. ''The owner has no problem with your requests. Shall we go back to my office and sign the contract?''

''Sounds good,'' Diana said. ''Mind dropping me at my car afterward?''

"No problem at all," the real estate agent assured.

They fell into step together as they headed toward the agent's vehicle.

"What about finishing the questionnaire?" Jack called out to Diana's retreating back.

She stopped and looked over her shoulder. "E-mail it to me. I can complete the rest when I return to my office this afternoon or work tonight if necessary. Thanks to you, I no longer have to go apartment hunting."

Sending him a brief smile, she resumed her course toward the agent's car.

As Jack watched them drive away, he decided e-mailing that questionnaire to her had been a very good suggestion. He'd already gotten a little too close to her today. For her comfort and for his.

But tomorrow, he promised himself, all that would come to an end. He might not be able to control being attracted to Diana. But he sure as hell could stop showing it to her. After all, he was a very good actor.

CHAPTER SIX

"I HAVE A VIEW of the lake from my room," Mel announced happily as she hopped down the stairs. "What's with the decorations? Did a bunch of kids live here?"

"The real estate agent told me the place has been vacant for a while," Diana said, not comfortable telling Mel that Richard owned the place. The wallpaper looked new, its content chock-full of a sad, focused desperation. Discussing the source of that desperation with Mel seemed like an invasion of Richard's privacy.

"Please tell me I don't have to wake up to Bambi and Thumper bouncing around on my walls."

"Not to worry," Diana said. "We're going to paint over the wallpaper."

"Wouldn't removing it be simpler?"

"Spoken like a true innocent."

"That much work, huh?"

"You have no idea," Diana assured her. "And if you're lucky, you never will. Painting has to commence soon. The place will need a thorough airing before we move in. Want to shop for appliances on Saturday after your play rehearsal?"

"I don't have to rehearse falling down and looking dead."

Diana wished she knew how to assuage Mel's continued disappointment over the part she'd drawn. All her daughter's initial joy over doing the play had fled.

"Fixing up this new place of ours will be fun. I'm going to paint my room a light yellow."

"I'll have to ask the owner first," Diana said. "I only got approval for off-white."

"So we have to get the owner's permission anytime we want something different," Mel said with a sigh. "I wish we had a place that was ours."

There was nothing heavier than the weight of having let down a child.

"When Connie's trial is over, I'll check into mortgages," Diana said, as she stepped into the small utility room off the kitchen and began measuring the area where the washer and dryer would go. "Maybe we can turn this lease into a buy."

"Is that a strong maybe or a weak maybe?"

"That's an 'I'm going to do my best' maybe. But between now and then, things are really busy, especially the next couple of weeks what with the wedding, moving in and getting settled. Grandma is going to have to pick you up from school tomorrow, by the way. I'll be stuck in a meeting."

"Are you going to bring a date to Grandma's wedding?"

"A date?" Diana asked, surprised at the non sequitur.

"Arnie asked me when he called Grandma yesterday to say he was coming. I think he wants to sit next to you."

Not even if Arnie were gagged and chained to the chair.

"Dating is so dumb," Mel said with disgust. "I'm not doing it."

I wish, Diana thought. "When your hormones kick in, you could change your mind."

Mel looked up at her mom with a curious expression. "What do they feel like? All those hormones and stuff?"

"Exciting, confusing," Diana said. "Thinking about other things suddenly becomes very difficult. Being attracted to that special member of the opposite sex is one of those things you have to experience to understand.''

''Do you understand why you fell for Dad and married him?''

''All I can tell you is that at the time I was led by love, not logic.''

''So romantic love is like losing your mind?''

Diana laughed as she stretched her tape measure over the counter and took a reading. ''Sounds like a pretty accurate definition to me.''

''You asked Dad to come to the wedding, didn't you?''

Diana nodded. ''He'd already made other plans.''

''He's good at making other plans.''

Diana hated hearing the disappointment in her daughter's voice. ''I'm sorry.''

''I'm not. Things are better when he's not here. I don't have to pretend to love him, and he doesn't have to pretend to love me.''

''He does love you,'' Diana said as she looked over at her daughter.

''I don't like the way he loves me.''

Diana wasn't thrilled with it, either. And she wasn't going to insult Mel's intelligence by pretending otherwise. Nor would she spout meaningless platitudes that things were going to get better.

''This place has a first-rate security system,'' Mel said. ''I know what to do in an emergency. Being with Grandma was great because she loves me. But I don't want someone hired to care for me who doesn't really care.''

''The person who will be here does care. Very much.''

Mel looked puzzled. ''You've found someone?''

Diana steeled herself. ''Your great-aunt Shirley is coming to live with us.''

Mel's eyes widened with incredulity. ''What? Mom, you can't be serious.''

"We need her, Mel. And she needs us. The manager at her apartment complex isn't going to renew her lease."

"Because she's a kook."

"Because she took in a stray cat that no one else wanted and there's a strict no pet rule," Diana corrected. "Other than her somewhat unconventional…quirk, Shirley's perfectly rational. And she loves you. Very much."

"But, Mom, she has no idea what I'm talking about half the time, and I don't care what she's talking about all the time. And she looks so weird, and she keeps calling me by that stupid name. And—"

"Mel, you are brilliant, and I love you dearly, so I'm going to let you in on a little secret. The key to feeling really good about who you are is helping others to feel really good about who they are."

"You mean Shirley."

"She doesn't deserve to be ridiculed or belittled. She deserves understanding and acceptance and love. We all do."

Mel's sigh was full of youthful ennui. "I guess she's better than some tattooed teenager with nothing but boys on her so-called brain."

Her daughter's acceptance of the situation was based solely on its benefit to her. Diana reminded herself to be patient. Emotionally, Mel was still only nine.

"I'm finished measuring," Diana said. "You see everything you wanted to?"

Mel nodded. "The place is great, Mom. I could even walk to Grandma's if I had to. You never said how you heard about it."

"Jack Knight put me in contact with the owner."

"That was nice of him," Mel said as they walked toward the door.

Very nice. The real estate agent told Diana that Richard had contacted the office that morning to say he'd go with a lease option for the right family. Diana felt certain that had been Jack's doing.

He'd said he'd approached Richard because he didn't want her personal problems interfering with getting their work accomplished. She believed him. His commitment to their case was one of the things she appreciated most about him.

But he'd been embarrassed when she thanked him. And he hadn't been quick enough to hide his discomfort over that embarrassment.

Seeing the cool, confident Jack lose his considerable aplomb—even for a second—had been rather unexpected. He'd treated her to quite a few unexpected moments in the past couple of days.

The man got more complicated by the moment. And so did her reaction to him.

"I ALMOST DIDN'T RECOGNIZE YOU without a pack of females draped around your shoulders," Jack said as he slipped onto the barstool next to Jared.

His twin looked over at him, smiling. "I'm trying to cut down to two packs a day."

"Old age will do that to you," Jack said, grinning.

The fact that Jared had been born forty minutes before Jack was an old joke between them.

"Truth is, I only got here a couple of minutes ago myself," Jared said.

"Everything okay?" Jack asked as he signaled the bartender to bring him a beer.

"I was doing some investigative work off the clock. Got a tip about some possible evidence in an unsolved hit-and-run case that I wanted to check out."

Jack nodded his understanding of what his brother was telling him. He glanced casually into the mirror behind the bar, which would reflect the images of anyone who might come within hearing range.

"Did the tip prove to be a good one?" he asked nonchalantly.

"The evidence techs seemed pleased to find the scene caked in enough layers of dust to imply it had been basically undisturbed. They collected a drop cloth and some miscellaneous debris."

"Where did they take them?"

"The items were messengered to the lab for testing, along with other forensic evidence collected on the hit-and-run and a chain and locket belonging to a prisoner awaiting trial," Jared said.

"Local lab?"

"D.C. A friend at the FBI said he'd see everything got priority status."

Jack nodded, understanding Jared wasn't taking any chances that the local lab might leak the information to the sheriff or Staker. He was being as careful as Jack knew he would be.

The bartender delivered Jack's beer. His brother held his hand over his glass. Jack knew Jared would nurse his drink for the rest of the night.

When Jack and Jared were in their twenties, the story had been quite different. Then Jared prided himself on drinking most guys under the table, including Jack. But working at the FBI had sobered Jared in a lot of ways.

Something had happened to him that he didn't talk about—not even with Jack. All Jack knew was that his twin had returned to Silver Valley with a deep scar on his cheek and a serious outlook on life.

"About that hit-and-run," Jared said as he rubbed his fingers on the side of his glass.

"What about it?" Jack asked, instantly alerted by his brother's tone.

"According to the Department of Licensing, the guy who inhabited the premises where the possible evidence was collected didn't own any old cars."

Which meant Bruce was driving someone else's car when he struck Amy.

"Maybe the driver borrowed the car from a family member," Jack suggested.

"Can't find anyone in the family who had an old car registered at that time or since," Jared said.

"The witness to the hit-and-run was pretty shaken up," Jack said. "She also didn't know much about cars. What she thought was old might have been a classic sports car or a foreign car."

"Even so, I doubt she could have confused an old car with the latest Land Rover or Cadillac. The father was the Land Rover fan. The mother and brother only drive Cadillacs."

Then Bruce had borrowed the car, probably from a friend. Those who'd attended Bruce's funeral would be Jack's best leads.

The vibration of Jack's cell phone interrupted his thoughts. He answered and found the caller was Karen, a beautiful blonde he'd worked with on *Seattle*. Karen had been the one who had called the office the other day to invite him to a studio party. The party was currently in full swing, and she was checking to see if he might change his mind and join her after all.

Jack thanked her for the invitation, but said he'd made other plans.

When Jack flipped the cell closed, he found a pretty if somewhat vacuous beautician had come over to say hello to Jared. She had an attractive friend with her who was giving him the eye. Jack paid for his drink and left his brother to fend off both females. Or not.

For the next hour, Jack drove around with no destination

in mind. He liked traveling the mostly deserted roads of the valley at night, windows open, the fresh air in his face. Driving freed his mind from distractions, gave him time to think.

Investigating the prospective jurors would have to wait until Diana had the returned questionnaires. Now he needed to focus on Bruce.

Reconstructing his whereabouts on the day of Amy's death would be Jack's first job. The best starting point would be the police report on the hit-and-run, which would pinpoint time and place. Tomorrow, he'd ask Diana for a copy.

He looked up to find himself at a stoplight a block away from the offices of Kozen and Kozen. Not questioning what unconscious impulse had led him here, he made a turn and drove down the block. The building was dark except for a single light shining through a window on the far end. Even before he caught a glimpse of her car in the back lot, he knew that light meant Diana was there, finishing the questionnaire.

Being with her today had been good. She had a quick, logical mind and a refreshing willingness to accept suggestions. And every time he heard her laughter, he felt the vibrations all the way to his nerve endings. He wished he were in there with her now completing what they had begun.

Jack chuckled at the absurdity of his thoughts. He'd turned down a night of sex with an available, uncomplicated blonde and was now fantasizing about spending it working with a very unavailable, complicated brunette.

Damn, maybe he was getting old. He gunned the engine of the Porsche and headed for home.

GEORGE STAKER EXUDED an air of confidence that some women found attractive. But his icy indifference to the feelings of others had long ago earned him a top spot on Diana's ugliest human list.

He greeted her entry into his office with an irritated frown. "Give me your questions, Mason, and let's get this over with."

"Where are yours?" she asked.

"If you haven't covered the bases, I'll let you know. Come on. I don't have all day."

Diana handed over a copy of the questionnaire and took the chair in front of Staker's desk. The chief prosecutor was his typical, insufferable self today. But his lack of questions told her he was not prepared for their meeting. That wasn't like him.

Was he too caught up in this campaign for judgeship to attend to the case? Probably. He no doubt thought this trial was going to be such an easy win he didn't have to give the details his undivided attention.

Diana rather hoped he kept on thinking that.

Staker plucked at his thin mustache as he scanned through the questionnaire. The mustache plucking was something she'd seen him do in court and was an indication that he liked what he was seeing. Yet when he finished reading the questions, he immediately began with putdowns and petty complaints. He challenged her on the phrasing of nearly every sentence as though she were his bumbling secretary screwing up an assignment instead of a fellow officer of the court.

Diana kept her temper only through an extreme effort of will. She kept reminding herself that if she didn't get Staker to sign off on the questionnaire, Judge Gimbrere would very likely reject it. The jurors would be handed a short, meaningless form on the day they appeared for *voir dire*.

That wouldn't bother Staker much. He considered his case a lock no matter what happened.

But Diana needed this questionnaire. Thanks to Jack, it was the best she'd ever prepared. With it they could learn crucial things about the prospective jurors, which was why she politely agreed to the demands Staker made for rewording, relieved that they did not dilute the original intent.

Three long, tongue-biting hours later, Staker finally signed the document. He then had the audacity to not only instruct Diana to have the questionnaire retyped for presentation to Judge Gimbrere that Friday morning, but also to escort her out of his office implying that her inefficiency had made him late for an important luncheon.

Diana was still seething when she pulled her car into the parking lot at Kozen and Kozen, switched off the engine, grabbed her briefcase and jumped out.

Reaching the back door, she nearly got hit in the face when it swung open and she found herself face-to-face with Ronald Kozen.

Diana nodded politely to him and stepped aside, expecting him to hurry on his way. The exalted Kozen brothers rarely stopped to chitchat with a mere associate at the firm. Their time was too valuable.

But this time Ronald stopped, planting himself right in her path. The left side of Ronald's lip lifted slightly in a perpetual smile that had nothing to do with his mood. A nerve in his face had been injured when he was a child. He couldn't help the half grin, which gave him the benign expression of an indulgent uncle. Adversaries who didn't know him rarely took him seriously until it was too late.

Diana didn't make that mistake.

"Tell me about the Pearce case," he said.

"I met with Staker this morning on the jury questionnaire," she said. "As soon as I make some revisions, I'll get you a copy. I think you'll find the questions to be—"

"I don't care about the questionnaire," Ronald said. "I want to know about the new development on the case."

She stiffened, alert, uneasy. "New development?"

"Gail said you'd found out something new. What?"

Diana's discomfort was both immediate and strong. She considered herself a woman of logic, but she had learned long ago that her body possessed instincts that had nothing to do with logic and everything to do with survival.

"Connie Pearce is talking now," Diana said, careful to keep both her expression and voice from conveying her uneasiness.

"What is she saying?"

Diana sensed that telling Ronald the whole truth would be a mistake. But she couldn't tell him a lie that would later be exposed.

"She didn't intend to hit Bruce Weaton," Diana said carefully.

"You're going to base your defense on lack of intent?"

"Or diminished capacity due to her distraught state."

Behind Ronald's smile was an intense scrutiny. Diana pasted a look of thoughtful concern on her face and hoped to hell she was a good enough actress to be believed.

"Forget diminished capacity," Ronald said. He hadn't made a suggestion. "Judge Gimbrere will be relieved when I tell him you're not going to waste the court's time and money with some stupid temporary insanity defense."

"Excuse me?"

"Parading a bunch of expensive psychiatrists in and out of the witness chair could extend the trial for days. This is a politically sensitive case. Be better for all concerned to get the damn thing over with quickly. No point in offending important people, is there?"

Ronald headed toward his Lincoln Town Car.

Diana stared after him, shocked that the man had had the nerve to say what he had. To call the legitimate presentation of an accused's state of mind to the jury as a "waste of the court's time" or "offending important people" showed a flagrant disrespect for one of the most basic and sacred tenets of the law.

Diana went through the door and stomped down the hallway, her heart as tight as a fist. She charged into her office, skidding to a stop when she saw Gail sitting at her desk, pulling a pad of legal paper out of her bottom right drawer.

Gail got to her feet, sending Diana a sheepish grin. "Kelli missed my office this morning when she came around to replenish supplies. You don't mind?"

Diana closed the door behind her. She'd been remiss in not locking it when she left. "Take what you need."

Even she could hear the ill will that encased her words.

Gail frowned. "Hey, what's wrong?"

Dropping her shoulder bag and briefcase on top of her desk, Diana sank onto the guest chair. "What I told you before about Connie's case was in confidence. Ronald cornered me out in the parking lot a minute ago about it."

Gail's frown deepened as she sat back down. "Ronald is the senior litigator at our firm as well as our boss. He's supposed to know how our cases are going and how we're going to handle them."

"I should have been the one discussing strategy with him."

"I wasn't discussing strategy with him. I was bragging about how sharp you were to uncover something important on the Pearce case after only two weeks when Earl couldn't find anything to offer for her defense in ten months."

Diana heaved a heavy sigh. There was absolutely no way she could find fault with what Gail had done or her reasons for having done it. She reached across her desk and rested a hand on her friend's arm.

"Ronald *told* me not to argue diminished capacity because such a defense would waste the court's time and offend important people. He doesn't give a damn if Connie goes to prison for life. All he cares about is looking good."

Gail shook her head. "Political jerk. I can see why you'd be pissed. Even if Ronald thinks Connie guilty, he's an imbecile to say such a thing to you. If we don't give our defendants the benefit of the doubt, who's going to?"

Diana released her friend's arm and slumped back in her chair. "Ronald has no right talking to Judge Gimbrere about my case, either."

"Hell, Diana, you should know by now that when these blabbermouths get together they violate confidentiality agreements as casually as they recite sports scores. At the firm's picnic last month, I overheard three of our lawyers discussing the intimate details of cases right in front of their wives, kids and anyone else who might have happened to walk by."

That was true. Diana had caught snippets of those lawyers' conversations without even trying.

"But what I can't believe is that Ronald would even think that you'd go for diminished capacity," Gail continued. "What did you tell him?"

"Only that Connie didn't intend to hit Bruce."

"But there has to be more," Gail said, looking at her expectantly.

"The less I tell you about the Pearce case from now on, the better off you'll be. Ronald knows we're friends. If he asks you anything, tell him we haven't talked about the case since you last spoke with him."

"You don't trust me?"

"It's not that. I don't want you compromised because you know something you can't tell Ronald. You have enough problems with Earl trying to steal that junior partnership you were promised. Although why you agreed to come into the firm without getting it up front is beyond me.''

Gail shrugged in what looked like a rare case of embarrassment as she flicked the corners of the legal pad with a nail. ''They talked about the partnership as though it was a done deal.''

Talked. Diana had thought her friend had more smarts than to allow herself to accept employment terms without having them in writing. Still, even the smartest people could make big mistakes.

''Look, I have several good case references where the reasonable doubt defense was successfully argued when the accused actions were not intended,'' Gail said. ''I'll have Kelli get copies to you before the end of today.''

Diana shook her head. ''Thanks, but I won't need them.''

Gail looked at her in sudden concern. ''Wait a minute. Don't tell me you're going for diminished capacity?''

''I'm going for the best defense for my client.''

''Diana, I don't blame you for being upset. Ronald's lower than roadkill for telling you to go with a particular defense simply because he's afraid of annoying his old crony Gimbrere.''

Diana could hear the ''but'' coming. Gail didn't keep her waiting long for it.

''But you'll be making the same mistake he is if you let him goad you into relinquishing your professional detachment on the Pearce case.''

''If caring about a client means that I've lost my professional detachment, then plead me guilty. Connie's a sweet woman facing the possibility of life imprisonment. I don't care who I offend by being on her side. I'm giving her my best.''

''Are you? Jurors distrust anything that smacks of temporary insanity, no matter what euphemisms we use to describe it. Psychologists and psychiatrists get up on the stand and contradict one another so much they end up irritating the jury. As a prosecutor, I always had a great time tearing them apart. And as good as I was at doing it, Staker is even better.''

"He won't expect me to go for diminished capacity,'' Diana said, choosing her words. "You know he's never good at counteracting what catches him by surprise.''

"Even so, I collected a lot of that evidence against Connie before Staker stole the case from me. A surprise or two isn't going to make a difference. And have you thought about what Ronald is going to do when he finds out you went against his direct order?''

"He won't know what I'm doing until the trial is well underway. By then it'll be too late for him to intercede.''

"Diana, you're too damn smart not to know that you're about to commit career suicide. I thought you loved the law?'' .

"I do—especially the part where we're all equal under it.''

Gail shook her head as she walked toward the door. She stopped there and turned to face Diana. "That was a brave and bold ideal, proposed by some pretty brave and bold people. But we both know the reality is that the rich and powerful can manipulate the law as easily as they can manipulate everything else.''

Gail closed the door quietly behind her.

The air in the office suddenly felt oppressive, as if the barometer had dropped. Diana rested her elbows on her desk, staring at the framed law degree hanging on the wall.

She'd graduated summa cum laude, made Law Review, passed the bar on her first try. Despite that, when she had gone looking for a job three years before there'd been three strikes against her—she'd been older than most law school graduates, a woman and a single mother.

The Kozens had hired her after two other firms had rejected her application. She was grateful to the brothers.

But she'd become a Wal-Mart greeter before she'd let them manipulate her.

Diana wearily got to her feet, circled her desk and plopped onto her chair, wondering why anyone in her right mind would choose to become a defense attorney.

She had one hand on the computer keyboard and the other around an apple when Kelli buzzed a few minutes later to say that Jack was on the phone. Diana realized that she hadn't taken off her call forwarding. She did so and asked Kelli to put through the call.

"How did the meeting with Staker go?" was Jack's first question.

"One day Staker will be murdered, and I will represent his murderer cheerfully and without charge."

Jack chuckled. "Did our questionnaire survive?"

"Except for minor rewording. I'm making the changes now. I'll e-mail them to you as soon as I'm through. Staker and I will present the questionnaire as a joint effort to Judge Gimbrere at ten Friday morning."

"Are you eating something?"

Diana swallowed. "Sorry. Lunch is an apple. Was I munching too loudly in your ear?"

"No, it was a nice, soft munch. Do you have a copy of the hit-and-run police report on Amy?"

Only Jack could say her munching an apple in his ear was nice and make the words ring true. "I thought about trying to get the report, but to do so would mean I'd have to request it through the prosecutor's office. That could alert Staker that Amy's case relates to Connie's."

"I'll try my unofficial source," he said.

"Hear anything from that source lately?" she asked.

"Tell you when I get back from following a lead. How late will you be working?"

"Probably six."

"Give me a call on my cell when you're finished."

Diana agreed to, scribbling the number Jack gave her on a pad beside her phone before hanging up.

Being able to share things with him felt good, especially now that talking to her co-workers about the case was out of the question. The gratitude filling her was disturbingly seductive. She reminded herself that maintaining a proper business relationship with Jack was more than prudent. It was an absolute necessity.

"HI, TINA," Jack said as he smiled at the woman slumped in her chair at the Weaton Real Estate Company offices. Jack had waited until Lyle Weaton had left to show a property before approaching Tina.

She looked up at Jack's greeting and immediately pushed aside the multiple listing she'd been browsing through.

"Well, hi, yourself. How do you know my name?"

Jack pointed to the nameplate on her desk.

Tina's lips twitched with disappointment. "Oh." Her tone morphed into a more business one. "What kind of property are you looking for?"

"Something that would appeal to a bachelor. Anything come to mind?"

He gave her a suggestive smile and watched her business façade vanish into a flirtatious squint. "You look familiar. Have we met?"

"You were at Bruce Weaton's funeral," Jack said, knowing she'd jump to conclusions about the comment.

"So that's where I know you from."

"A funeral isn't the right place for introductions. I would never approach a woman at one, not even a woman as pretty as you. But we're not at one now, are we? I'm Jack."

He held out his hand. Tina slipped her hand into his, her inch-long bloodred nails nearly slicing through his flesh. Her grip was like a pipe wrench.

"I've always liked a sensitive man."

"I'll buy you a drink and you can tell me what else you like," he suggested.

Her smile said she thought that a great idea. But a frown followed when she looked around at the deserted office. "I'm the only one on duty now. Got to stay here to man the phones."

Jack looked her up and down suggestively. "Manning phones. What a waste of womanpower."

Tina's eyes darted to her watch. "Oh, what the hell. I'll put on the answering machine. I can return the calls when we get back, right?"

"Right," he said as he finally extricated his hand from hers and reached for the sweater on the back of her chair. "A bit of a breeze out. You may need this."

She looked him up and down. "Honey, with you beside me, I won't be cold."

DIANA CHECKED HER WATCH. Nearly seven. She'd called Jack's cell at six and again at six fifteen, but received a recording both times that said he was not available. She'd left a message, but he hadn't called back.

The depth of her disappointment irritated her.

Well, there was no use waiting around any longer. She picked up the phone to call her mother to let her know she was on her way, but got a busy signal. No doubt Mel was using the Internet. Diana locked the door of the deserted office behind her, got into her car and headed for home.

Traffic was light. A breeze had blown away the clouds leaving the long summer evening warm and clear. Within minutes she was on a peaceful country road, the sun bouncing like a white tennis ball through openings in the heavy canopy of trees.

Most of the other employees at the law firm lived within ten or fifteen minutes and would consider anything beyond that excessive. But Diana was comfortable with the longer commute because she liked living far from the hustle and bustle of town.

Her childhood had been spent in large noisy cities. Every couple of years the dictates of her father's career would have them packing up and relocating to yet another one. Always having to adjust to new schools and schoolmates. No sense of security, permanency.

Diana had promised herself Mel would know a stable environment. Her daughter had lived in the same community and home since she was two. Even after their move next week, her grandmother would still be close by and Shirley would be in their new place to surround Mel with her own special brand of zany love.

But Diana didn't kid herself. No matter what she gave Mel now, it would never be enough. She'd screwed up on the most important responsibility a mother had to her child—the choice of the right father.

Diana turned into her mother's driveway and pushed the remote control button for the garage. As she maneuvered the car forward, she caught sight of a man's figure in her peripheral vision. He was sitting on one of the patio chairs at the front of the house.

As her head swung toward him, he lifted his hand and waved. She was so surprised to see him that she nearly drove into the wall.

CHAPTER SEVEN

"MORE COFFEE?" Margaret asked as she stepped onto the front patio, the pot in her hand.

Jack eagerly held up his cup. "You sure this stuff isn't a love potion, Margaret? I've got a sudden urge to challenge this Ray guy for your hand."

She shook her head as she refilled Jack's cup. "Good looks *and* charm. You must have to fight the women off."

"I have more fun when I don't fight them *all* off," he said, sending her a wink.

Her smile was full of mischief. "I've watched Mel's tapes of *Seattle*. Didn't look to me like you fought *any* of them off when you played Derek Dementer."

Jack chuckled as he sipped more coffee, glad he'd made the decision to come here, if for no other reason than he'd had the chance to meet Diana's mother.

Margaret was a living embodiment of the sweet wholesome homemaker—comforting and bolstering everyone around her, dispensing love and warmth to the weary family who trudged through the door at the end of the day. And even to a stranger like him who had straggled in unannounced forty minutes before.

"Can your daughter make coffee this good?" he asked, wondering why he did as soon as the words were out of his mouth.

"Diana does everything well," Margaret said with a tone full of pride.

As though hearing her cue, the door to the house opened and Diana came outside.

Margaret greeted her brightly. Diana's response was warm, but dropped several degrees when she spotted him sitting comfortably on a lounge chair.

Mel came bounding onto the patio a second later holding the article she'd written on fictional villains he'd asked to read. "Oh, hi, Mom. Jack said he saw you driving up a minute ago."

Diana gave her kid a hug before facing Jack. "I thought you were going to call me at the office?"

"I was late getting out of an interview," he said.

"Problem with your cell phone?" she asked, oh so sweetly.

"Didn't think you'd still be at the office this late," he said. "Figured I'd catch you at home where we could talk about the developments on the case in privacy."

She eyed him silently. He eyed her right back.

"But first we'll have dinner," Margaret said. "Jack kindly accepted my invitation to join us. Will five minutes be enough time for you to wash up, dear?"

"Five minutes is fine," Diana said, stepping inside the house.

A smile tugged at the corners of Jack's lips. She was cool and composed on the surface, but he could tell she wasn't happy with his unexpected presence in her home. She'd chosen not to make an issue of that fact in front of her mother and daughter. Still, he had a feeling he'd be hearing about it later.

"Do you really want to read this?" Mel asked.

Jack realized he'd been staring at the door Diana had disappeared behind a moment before. He took the paper Mel had patiently been holding out to him.

Damn, the thing was at least two inches thick. "I'll start

reading it tomorrow," he promised, batting at a gnat that was buzzing his ear.

Mel's response was a wary stare that reminded him of Diana. He wondered what had happened over the past couple of minutes to cause the kid's easygoing manner to change.

"We'd better get inside before the bugs have us for dinner," Margaret said.

At her urging, Jack went to sit in the small dining room. The walls were painted cocoa and trimmed in cream. The lighting was soft. Mel spread a white cloth over the cozy table for four. Margaret placed a vase of fresh-cut flowers in the center all the while humming to the soft music drifting in from the next room. Navigating the tight corners with perfect synergy, she and Mel set the table.

Jack shook his head in wonder. Guys living together would be shouting at each other to be heard over the ball game blasting away on the tube and bumping into each other on the way to the kitchen for pizza and beer.

Men and women weren't simply from different planets. They had to be from different galaxies.

When Diana joined them, Jack saw that she'd changed into black slacks and a white sweater, both of which revealed lovely curves her formless business suits had completely covered.

Her freshly brushed hair flowed loosely over her shoulders. The soap she'd used to wash with left a hint of vanilla on her skin. When she slipped onto the chair next to Jack's, he realized he should have gotten up and held it for her. He might have, if he hadn't been so preoccupied with his reaction to her.

Tina had hung all over him that afternoon, and there'd been not so much as a twinge. Now just sitting next to Diana he was turned on.

Dinner began with a large salad full of fresh vegetables,

slices of sweet almonds and nectarine, topped with finely grated cheese and a fragrant homemade dressing Margaret mixed at the table. Poached salmon covered in a light dill sauce with glazed carrots followed. Dessert was baked apple covered in dried cranberries and currants.

There were no heavy gravies or breads or fat-laden sweets, and Jack found he didn't miss them. The trim figures around the table were evidence that these females didn't miss them, either.

If Diana ate like this every night, there was very little chance he'd be able to impress her with his selection of dinner—cooked in or out. The fact that he still wanted to was another bad sign.

"That was great," Jack said when he sat back after cleaning his plate. "And not a French fry in sight."

"We're not into foods with bad fats," Mel said as she got up to start clearing the dishes. The standoffishness was still in evidence. "Grandma's taught us how to eat healthy."

Jack turned to face Margaret, his curiosity aroused. "Where do you get your nutrition information?"

"Reading the scientific journals," she said very matter-of-factly.

Margaret might be a sweet little homemaker, but obviously not one of the stereotypical, cake-baking variety. Each generation of female in this family was a surprising original.

When Mel went into the kitchen with the dishes, Jack turned to Diana. "So, what are you doing with all those chocolate bars hidden in your handbag?"

Margaret chuckled.

Diana sent him a look that was slightly less amused as she stood to collect her dishes and his. "Mom's been reading the relevant reports on healthy eating for thirty years. She's better than any encyclopedia on nutrition."

Like Margaret's tone earlier, Diana's was warm with pride.

Most women Jack dated rarely even got along with their mothers. This was a nice change.

When Diana disappeared into the kitchen, Jack remembered the manners his mother had so diligently tried to instill in him and offered to do the dishes. Margaret waved him back into his seat. He sat down, relieved.

"I need to talk to you before Mel and Diana return," she said, noticeably lowering her voice as she cast a glance at the closed door to the kitchen.

Ah, a secret. He loved secrets. Margaret made him wait a few more seconds as she collected her thoughts.

"I'd like you to come to my wedding this Saturday," she said finally. "The ceremony will be an informal affair here in the garden, just family and a few friends. We've asked that no one bring presents. Heaven knows Ray and I already have more junk than we'll ever need. Jack, I realize this is very short notice and you probably have other plans. But if by chance you are free, I would really appreciate your being here."

The invitation had been delivered so sincerely—as well as so clandestinely—that Jack knew there was a lot more than mere politeness behind it.

"Want to tell me what's going on?" he asked.

Margaret sighed. "There's a man who will be coming who is not very nice. I don't want him bothering Diana. If he sees you with her, I'm hoping he'll leave her alone."

"Between you and me, Margaret, I think Diana can handle a bothersome male."

"Normally, I would agree. But this one is Ray's stepson, and what with Ray being so close by and all, well, she…"

"Might feel constrained," Jack finished when Margaret failed to find the right words.

She nodded.

He rested his hand on top of hers. "I'll be here."

Margaret's smile was golden. "Some very fortunate woman is going to rejoice when she gets you for a son-in-law."

"Does this mean you're going to introduce me to your mom?" Jack asked.

Margaret was laughing with delight when Diana entered from the kitchen.

"Do I get to hear the joke?" she asked.

Margaret got herself under control. "Jack's such a lot of fun. I've asked him to the wedding, and he's graciously agreed to come. Will you sit beside him so he doesn't feel uncomfortable among a bunch of strangers?"

"Jack uncomfortable among strangers," Diana repeated, like she thought that could ever happen. "Sure, Mom. I'd be happy to make him feel comfortable on Saturday. But right now I need him out on the porch for a little conference regarding our case. You'll excuse us?"

From the look on her face, Jack didn't imagine the upcoming conference would be a comfortable one. He followed her outside. The moment she'd closed the door after them, she turned to him, folding her arms across her chest.

"What's going on?"

The soft evening light danced through her hair. Her face glowed with annoyance.

"Your mother was kind enough to invite me to her wedding," he said, trying not to stare at her too blatantly. "Something about that bother you?"

Clearly, a lot about that bothered her, but putting the reasons into words seemed to be causing her considerable trouble.

"Why did you come here?" she asked after a moment.

"As I told you, so we could talk about developments on the case."

"We were supposed to do that over the phone."

"Some things are better said in person."

"You could have driven to the office and talked to me there. And speaking of driving, where's your car?"

"I sort of misplaced my keys."

"Sort of misplaced?" she repeated.

"Down Tina Uttley's blouse," he said bluntly.

The startled look in her face was charming. "What?"

"Tina of red lace bikini fame was the witness I was interviewing this afternoon and into early evening," Jack said. "And let me tell you, getting the information I needed ended up requiring more Scotch than anybody should be able to consume."

"Let me get this straight. You'd been *drinking* when you showed up at my home this evening to be with *my* mother and daughter?"

Anger was lighting her now—brilliant, beautiful anger. Jack was beginning to think any emotion would look good on her.

"I showed up here to be with *you*," he corrected. "And, believe me, I was definitely sober and thinking straight. You are not a woman I can trust myself to be around in any other state."

He hadn't intended to be quite so forthcoming. But the desire to see the range of emotions crossing her lovely face made him reckless.

She contemplated his admission for a couple of seconds before confusion lifted, and a pink cloud covered her cheeks. Yep, any emotion.

Getting her poise to slip was dangerously fun.

She quickly regrouped and went back to the offensive. "How many drinks did you have?"

"One's my limit. Always has been. You're looking at a guy who can't hold his liquor. But, boy, can Tina put them away."

"You deliberately got her drunk?"

"She got herself drunk," he corrected. "Which is why I had to drive her home."

"Let me guess. That's when you...misplaced your keys?"

"That's when she snatched the keys out of my hand and dropped them down her blouse. Getting them back didn't seem nearly as important as getting out of her apartment at the time. As it was I barely escaped with my virtue intact."

"Barely escaped," Diana repeated. "Let's see, you're what, six-one? Hundred and eighty pounds of muscle? Tina's bikinis were a size small, which tells me she's probably a hundred and fifteen pounds at the most. Yeah, I bet you were shivering in your shoes."

He tried to laugh lightheartedly, but the sound ran deep with another emotion. On Diana, sarcasm looked so damn sexy.

Some of that must have shown on his face because she was getting that uneasy look again.

Jack strolled toward the edge of the garden, stopping in front of a stone birdbath as he filled his lungs with the clean country air. Time to get back into his *detached* private investigator role. Damn, this shouldn't be that difficult a part to play.

"Why didn't you call?" she asked after a moment.

"My cell phone's in the glove compartment of the locked Porsche."

"There weren't any pay phones?"

"None that worked. Fortunately, I was able to hail an unoccupied cab. I would have taken it to your office, but it was late, and I figured you'd left. Your mother let me use her telephone when I got here. Your office line was busy."

"What are you going to do about your car?"

"I reached my dad. He'll hide a second set of keys to it and my condo underneath the front right wheel."

"And the set that Tina has?"

"Will be retrieved when she's sobered up and not a moment before. Now, do you want to hear what I sacrificed my afternoon to learn or do you want to stay mad at me?"

She eased onto a patio chair. "I'm not mad at you."

He stared at her, not saying anything.

Her lips curled slightly upward. "Anymore."

The emotions that brought a smile to her lips were the best of all. She had the kind of face he could never get tired of looking at. As Jack settled in the chair across from her, he assured himself that at least looking was no problem.

"What have you learned?" she asked.

"First, let me tell you about Bruce's garage."

Jack explained that Jared had found the drop cloth and collected it with other debris, but that neither Bruce nor anyone in his family had owned an old car.

"Still, if there is any evidence that the vehicle that killed Amy was parked in Bruce's garage, it will help immensely," she said. "Did Tina tell you anything of importance?"

"Nothing about his having driven an older sports or classic car. She started at Weaton Real Estate a few months after Amy's hit-and-run and was involved with Bruce romantically for the entire time she worked for him, even after he met Connie and proposed to her."

"Tina knew about the proposal?"

"Bruce assured her his marriage to Connie wouldn't interfere with their affair."

Diana shook her head, disgust flashing across her features. "How did Tina react to that news?"

"She says she didn't care. I'm inclined to believe her. Tina likes to party and isn't all that particular with whom."

"Did you learn anything else?" Diana asked.

"Bruce was a real hustler at the company, brought in the most new clients. Tina described him as charming on the surface, but cutthroat underneath, especially when it came to business. The fact that he didn't drink actually seemed to annoy her."

"But not enough to stop her affair with him."

"As she tells it, he was good-looking, one of her bosses and handy. But she was seeing other men at the same time she was seeing him."

"Did Bruce know?"

Jack nodded. "Didn't matter to him, apparently. Of course, he was dating other women so he could hardly object. But she did keep quiet about the fact that one of the other men she was seeing was his brother."

Diana came forward in her chair. "She was sleeping with Lyle Weaton as well? Did he know about Bruce?"

"According to Tina, not while Bruce was alive."

"A woman sleeping with two brothers—one married and both her bosses—has to be out of her mind. If they had found out—"

"Even if they had known, I doubt that would have caused a big problem between them," Jack interrupted. "Lyle Weaton knows now and he's kept Tina on the payroll. She even hinted that they still get it on."

Diana shook her head. "Where do they find the time to sell real estate? Or the energy?"

Jack shrugged. "It's no big deal. Simply routine sex. Easily gotten, easily forgotten."

"Routine," she repeated, like the word left a bad taste in her mouth. "If the day comes when such an incredibly exciting, intimate act is reduced to the label of routine for me, I hope I'm dead."

Jack stared at Diana for a moment without speaking. He wasn't just surprised at the unexpectedness of her sharing that personal viewpoint. He was stunned at the excitement of his all out-of-proportion response.

Diana rested back in her chair, oblivious to what she had done to him. "I trust you wouldn't be telling me any of this if you weren't confident Tina had told you the truth?"

Jack nodded, making a Herculean effort to pull his thoughts away from the far too exciting images playing through his mind. "The fact that Bruce had no intention of being true to Connie, even if she agreed to marry him, does put his motives into question."

"And we can have Tina testify to that aspect of Bruce's character, or lack thereof. Who will you be talking to next?"

"Jared's getting me a copy of the police report on Amy's hit-and-run. Once time and place are clear, I'll see if I can find out where Bruce was on that day, who he was with and how he came to be driving a car that wasn't his."

"I'd be interested in taking a look at that hit-and-run report myself."

Jack checked his watch. "It should be at the condo. And my dad should have dropped off my keys by now. Drive me to my car, we'll swing by my place, and I'll run off a copy for you."

When she hesitated, he wondered if she were worried about his reasons for inviting her to his home. "I'll bring a copy to you when I come to the wedding on Saturday," he amended. "Call me a cab, and I'll be out of your hair."

"A cab would take too long to get here. I'll drive you to your car."

AFTER DIANA HAD taken Jack to his car, she followed him to the Hamilton Arms, an upscale condo community where the governing board interviewed prospective buyers like they were being considered for entry into a royal family.

Jack swiped his entry key card at the gate and drove through to the secured underground parking. Diana parked across the street and stared at the impressive building of shiny smooth granite, rising five flights into the night sky.

A story about the Hamilton Arms had been circulated the year before around the law office. Seems an affluent couple had filed suit against the managing board when it wouldn't allow them to buy one of the expensive units because their poodle didn't have a pedigree. Diana was never quite sure if that story was meant to be a joke.

She noticed an electronic surveillance camera in the formal entry when Jack let her inside a minute later. They took the elevator to his penthouse condo. He moved aside for her to precede him.

Diana stepped beneath an enormous skylight that showcased the stars. Spotless pale sandstone floors led to a twelve-foot long suede couch the color of bittersweet chocolate. Behind it, the twinkling lights from the city filled a wall of windows.

The rest of the living room's furniture and accessories were amber, black and gold. Healthy plants, with long stems and shiny leaves, waved in the breeze from the air conditioner.

But perhaps best of all was the impressionist mural covering one fifteen-foot wall—a glistening landscape of an enchanted garden that beckoned one to walk along its moss-covered paths, drink in the scent of its swaying wildflowers and touch the leaves of its silvery trees encased in never-ending sunlight.

Jack's home—and it was most definitely a home—shimmered with wit, warmth and welcome. She had no doubt that every woman who'd come here hoped she'd be asked to stay.

"So, this is what an upscale bachelor's pad with weekly maid service looks like," she said, her voice carefully devoid of any and all approval.

"Twice-a-week maid service," Jack corrected in a lighthearted tone as he set his keys on an ebony dish near the entry. "I'm a slob."

No one who lived here could possibly be a slob.

"Feel free to take a look around," Jack said, his voice and grin as inviting as his home. "For a reasonable fee, I'll even let you open the closets and drawers."

"I'll pass, thanks. Where would your brother have left the report?"

Jack eyed her curiously before responding. "When Jared comes by, his first stop is always the kitchen for something to eat."

"Let's go see."

He led the way, darting a look at her. "You're not comfortable here."

Since he hadn't asked a question, she didn't feel pressed to respond. He kept a slight distance between them down the hallway.

She understood he was trying to reassure her. What he didn't understand was that her discomfort had nothing to do with her sense of safety around him. She knew Jack wasn't going to try to seduce her here or anywhere else.

She very much doubted he'd ever tried to seduce a woman. Women he met were probably so willing the thought never occurred to him.

Jack turned on the kitchen lights, revealing a clean expanse of stainless steel appliances, Corian countertops and light maple cabinets. A stack of take-out menus lay on the center island near the cordless phone.

He picked up the sheets of paper lying next to the refrigerator. "This is the hit-and-run report all right," he said as he scanned it. "Happened right after eleven on a Sunday morning, July 5, five years ago."

"The day after the holiday," Diana said as she moved to Jack's side.

He repositioned the report so she could see it more easily. "The small clapboard house where she was living with Amy is in a working-class neighborhood on the other side of town from Bruce's home and business," he said.

"What was he doing driving down her street on a Sunday morning in a car that wasn't his?" Diana asked.

"I may have the answer to half that question. That address is only a few blocks from the park where Bruce used to play softball on the weekends."

"That something else you learned from Tina?"

Jack nodded. "He dragged her out to the park to watch him play once. She told me that looking at a bunch of guys running around a softball field wasn't her idea of fun. The names she gave me of a couple of his weekend athlete buddies match attendees at his funeral. They're on my list of who to see tomorrow."

"Do you have the addresses of these buddies?" Diana asked.

"And you're interested because…"

"I was wondering if they lived somewhere near Connie."

Jack shook his head. "The guys he played with were financially successful businessmen like himself. The Weaton Real Estate Company does a bang-up business. Lyle Weaton is a major player in commercial transactions and his staff has a decent portion of the noncommercial property arena. The death of his father and brother did adversely impact company sales for a while, but Lyle has turned it around."

"This something else you learned from Tina?"

"I checked the company's financial standing before I went to see her," Jack explained.

And got all he needed from another female source, no doubt.

"My copier is in the study," he said on his way out the door. "This will only take a couple of minutes. Feel free to help yourself to a cold drink, or whatever else you might like. The refrigerator's well stocked."

She just bet it was.

Diana walked around the spotless kitchen. She opened a cabinet and saw half a dozen high-quality olive oils, first-rate pasta, Godiva chocolates and imported crackers. In the oversize refrigerator were chilled wine, good aged cheese and an assortment of fresh deli delicacies.

She was certain that if she made a trip to the bathroom she'd find a wide assortment of scented body oils, soft towels and probably no less than a case of condoms beneath the sink.

And there would not be a trace of any other women who had been here. He would have made sure of that.

Diana's chest filled with a disappointment so acute she sighed from the heaviness of it.

When Jack returned a couple of minutes later, she was standing at the exact spot where he'd left her. He studied her face closely as he handed her the copy he'd made.

"Something's wrong," he said.

She folded the papers into her shoulder bag. "Thanks for the report."

As she went past him, he grasped her arm, halting her retreat. His words were a warm brush against her hair. "Diana, what is it?"

The firm grip of his hand, the sudden closeness of his body, and the concern in his voice all invaded her senses so fast she had no time to erect her defenses. Her knees went weak, and her body leaned into his. God, he felt good. She closed her eyes, absorbed the heat and strength of him and struggled for sanity.

"Diana?"

The warmth of his voice was nothing less than a caress. Summoning all her strength, she opened her eyes and shifted her weight off him. "Sorry, I'm a little tired. Normally, I'm not so unsteady on my feet."

She was careful not to look at him, but could feel his eyes on her and the claim his hand still made on her arm.

"I'm not complaining," he said in a tone unmistakably husky with humor and something else. "Diana, come sit down, and I'll get you something to drink."

"Thanks, but it's late, and I'd like to go home. So, if you don't mind…"

He hesitated a moment before releasing her. It took every ounce of her concentration to walk a straight line as she made her way to the front door and let herself out.

Until tonight, she had no idea how deeply attracted she was to Jack. Or how dangerous that attraction was.

Long ago Diana had learned that the energy and enthusiasm she brought to an activity made the difference between living a life full of meaning and one that didn't matter. Nowhere had this proved truer than in her personal relationships.

She gave them her all.

But Jack viewed relationships between men and women far differently. How had he put it? Ah, yes.

Routine sex. Easily gotten, easily forgotten.

CHAPTER EIGHT

THE SIGN OUTSIDE READ Albright's Imports. On the inside showroom floor was a silver Porsche GT2 and an Audi Motorsport racer. Put a supermodel with season tickets to the Mariners in the passenger seat of either one of those cars and most guys would rename the place Paradise.

At least that's what Jack was thinking when he walked in grinning—until the mental image of an unattainable attorney replaced that of the supermodel, and the grin slid off his lips.

A man with the winning smile of a consummate salesman met Jack at the door. "Bud Albright," he said as he held out his hand.

Jack shook the man's hand and gave him his name.

"Recognized you the moment you got out of your Turbo," Bud said, pointing at Jack's Porsche parked out front. "You played Derek Dementer on *Seattle*. Saved me from a lot of boring days when the bad weather scared even the looky-loos away."

"Glad you enjoyed the show."

"All except for the scene when they sent you off the cliff in that brand new Cabriolet." Bud put his hand over his heart. "Man, I still get heartburn just thinking about the waste of that beautiful piece of machinery."

Jack smiled. "A computer-generated stunt. The Porsche Cabriolet is alive and well."

"That's a relief. So, Jack, what's it going to take for me to put you into this GT2?"

This dealership dealt in the kind of vehicles most people could never afford. Dreamers, no doubt, meandered through the showroom on a daily basis. Bud Albright, however, would only expend his energy on those who fit the profile of a potential buyer. Jack knew that the fact the man had met him at the door proved he'd passed that test.

There was only one way he was going to get information out of Bud.

"I'll be keeping the Turbo a while longer," Jack said. "But I do have a friend in the business who might be interested in this little beauty if you can get him a good deal."

"One he can't refuse," Bud assured, rocking forward on his toes in anticipation. "When can he come in?"

Jack's friend was real, but the possibility of his making a trip to the West Sound was not. "He's involved in a shoot at the studio this week. I'm checking out prices and availability while I'm here in the area putting together a project."

A young couple walked in the showroom door. The other salesman took one look at their clothes and wide-eyed demeanor and remained at his desk. When the woman glanced at Jack, her mouth dropped open. She poked the man's arm and began to whisper in his ear.

Bud didn't miss the woman's reaction. He signaled his salesman to distract the couple. The man dropped his car-racing magazine and hopped to.

"Let's do this in my office," Bud said to Jack, nodding toward the back.

Car dealers liked flaunting celebrity clients, but Bud was savvy enough to know that allowing them to be bothered wasn't good business.

Jack followed Bud to a nicely appointed office at the end of the paneled hall. He took a seat on the deep-cushioned guest chair and waved away the offer of coffee.

For the next twenty minutes he let Bud talk about the GT2's options and availability and a delivery price that hovered around the two-hundred-thousand mark, nodding at all the appropriate moments.

When Bud had printed off a list of the vehicle's specs, Jack studied the sheet as though he were really reading what was printed there.

"By the way, what's your friend's show?" Bud asked, obviously trying to sound casual.

"We have an agreement not to discuss each other's projects," Jack said, pocketing the information he'd been given.

"Why's that?"

"We're too competitive to do each other justice."

Bud chuckled. "So tell me about your project."

From the moment Jack had walked into the dealership, he'd been leading Bud to that question. Now he painted a thoughtful look on his face as if trying to decide how much to say. "Something pretty exciting. Of course, it's still in the development stage. You'll have to promise to keep this between us."

"Absolutely," Bud assured him.

Jack sat forward slightly, putting into his body language the subtle nuance that a confidence was about to be given. "The project's based on the actual murder of a real estate agent here in Silver Valley."

"Bruce Weaton?"

Jack feigned surprise. "You knew him?"

"Well, yeah. His father, Philip, was president of our local Chamber of Commerce. Bruce and his brother, Lyle, became active members a few years after me."

"You were close," Jack said. "I'm sorry. This must be painful for you to talk about."

"We weren't that close," Bud said quickly. "Outside of general Chamber business, all Bruce and I really had in common was the Chamber of Commerce softball league. Sixty guys out for a little exercise and some socializing. Bruce was the pathetic center fielder on team three. That's the one I still captain.''

Jack nodded as though remembering something. "I think I have something about the league in my notes. Your teams play at Crisalli Park?''

Bud seemed pleased. "Yeah, only place around with three diamonds. The Chamber pays for the park's maintenance in exchange for use of the fields during the season. We get first pick on the weekends."

"So how long did you and Bruce play together?"

"He signed up when he joined the Chamber of Commerce. Guess that'd be about eight years ago."

Jack settled back in his chair. "Since you knew him for such a long time, maybe you can help me out on something. We're having a hard time with Bruce's characterization."

"This story is about him as well as the woman who killed him?''

"His past definitely will play an important role," Jack said carefully. "His family and co-workers have talked about him as being such a straight arrow, and I'm sure he was a good guy and all, but that makes him sort of boring to a viewing audience. Know what I mean?''

Bud nodded. "You want to know if he had another side."

"Everyone has faults," Jack said nonchalantly and then waited.

Bud shifted in his chair as he gave the request some thought. "This isn't that big a city, Jack. A business like mine, well, I don't sell my cars to the average guy. The goodwill of those with clout can make all the difference in resells and referrals.''

"No one will ever know the information came from you."

That's what Bud had wanted to hear. "Wasn't a secret really. Anybody who knew him could tell you."

"So there was something about Bruce that stands out in your mind?"

"Let's just say I'm not surprised a jealous woman killed him."

"Ah, a ladies' man," Jack said.

Bud snorted. "More like a total lecher. Seemed to think his duty was to try to lay any female in the vicinity. He came on to my wife at one of our softball games. Right in front of me."

Jack sent Bud the expected head shake of disbelief. "How did you handle it?"

"I picked up a bat and told him the next balls I was hitting over the fence were going to be his."

Jack nodded approvingly. "Bet that got his attention."

"Nearly tripped over his feet when he staggered off."

"Staggered?"

"As in drunk."

Jack sat up straight. "I was told he didn't drink."

"He didn't after he joined AA. I'm not surprised his family didn't tell you about his problem. Before he went on the wagon, he was a real embarrassment to them."

"In what way?"

"You mean other than the fact that he had a tendency to overlook wedding rings on ladies' fingers and even husbands standing right beside them?"

Jack nodded.

"Well, once when we were out at the park for some practice, I heard Bruce's father tell him that if he ever took another client to see a property when he was soused, he'd kick him out of the business. Then a couple of months later, both his brother and father had to leave a Chamber meeting to bail him out of some trouble.''

"Jail?''

"Who knows? Lyle got the call on his cell. Then he turned to Philip and said something to the effect that Bruce was at it again. Must have been something serious for Philip to give me the gavel in the middle of an important meeting and go off to get Bruce out of whatever jam he was in.''

"See what you mean," Jack said. "When did Bruce stop drinking?''

"Not long after that incident with my wife.''

"Can you narrow that down for me?''

Bud ran fingers through his wisps of thinning hair. "Let's see. He made the move on my wife toward the end of June, four, no five years ago. It was a couple of weeks later at a board meeting that I learned he'd joined AA.''

"A couple of weeks later," Jack repeated.

"Yeah. Right after the Fourth of July weekend. I remember his brother was at bat that Sunday, and he was next up but nowhere in sight. I found him beneath the bleachers, on his hands and knees, murmuring something about having dropped his car keys. He was loaded. I told him to take a cab home and sleep it off. The following Wednesday night I was in the hall before the meeting, taking down some of the decorations we'd put up for the holiday. That's when I overheard him talking to his father about having joined AA. Far as I know, he never took another drink.''

"Bud, would you happen to have a roster of the guys who played on your team that Fourth of July weekend five years ago?''

"It'd be in the Chamber files. Why?''

"I'd like to talk to some of the guys," Jack said. "But don't worry. I won't tell them you sent me.''

"Give me your e-mail address, and I'll send the roster to you."

Jack wrote out his address and handed it to the man.

"Did you see Bruce a lot after he joined AA?" Jack asked.

"A lot more than before, which wasn't necessarily a good thing. When he started to attend meetings regularly, he got real pushy. Began to think he was a hotshot on the softball field, too. He was even trying to challenge me to become captain. And the women! God, one right after another. But at least when he wasn't drunk, he had the sense to leave the married ones alone. Is any of this helping you with his characterization?"

Jack smiled. "You have no idea how much."

MRS. EDITH LEWANDOWSKI WAS seventy-six, a widow for ten years and cranky as a two-year-old on a rainy day. She had told Diana over the phone that she wasn't going to be dragged down to the courthouse or some law office for any deposition. If Diana insisted on questioning her, she'd have to come to her.

Diana assured Mrs. Lewandowski that taking the deposition at her home was no problem. She not only didn't want to alienate the witness, but she also wanted to get a look at the scene of Bruce's death from the woman's viewpoint so she could have a clear understanding of everything that happened that day.

Mrs. Lewandowski's living room was full of floral furniture with ball and claw legs, rolled armchairs the color of plum and the musty smell that meant she never opened a window.

Figurine collectibles on the mantelpiece didn't look like they'd been touched in years, but the dozen or so books on the shelf near her rocking chair were dust-free and bore the titles of several Pulitzer Prize winners.

Mrs. Lewandowski scowled through a profusion of gray-white bangs as the court reporter asked her if she were going to tell the truth, the whole truth, and nothing but the truth.

"I'm no liar," she declared in a voice that carried into the corners of the room, as though the administering of the oath had been a deliberate attack on her veracity. "Never have been. And you won't get me to lie now."

The court reporter wisely accepted that as an affirmative, took a chair in the corner and tried to fade into the flowered wallpaper.

Diana sat on the settee across from the scowling old woman and smiled. "Thank you very much for seeing me."

When the woman didn't respond, Diana began her questions. "Did you know Bruce Weaton well?"

"He lived across the street from me for more than six years. Waved when he saw me. Persuaded his nephew to weed my garden when my arthritis got so bad I couldn't. Bruce was a fine, upstanding young man. His death was an abomination."

And Mrs. Lewandowski was still mad about it.

"Would you please tell me in your own words what you remember of July 27 of last year?"

"You want to know what I saw the day Bruce was killed."

"Yes."

"I was sitting right here reading when I heard some shouting across the street."

"Do you remember what time that was?"

"Early afternoon as I recall. I looked out my picture window and saw a car backing out of the driveway. Then the car stopped and started forward. Bruce ran in front of it, waving his hands for the driver to stop. The driver didn't stop. The car hit him, and he went down."

Clear. Precise. Not a wasted word. Diana waited until she was certain that Mrs. Lewandowski wouldn't be adding any more.

"Do you mind if I take a look out your window?"

"Be my guest."

The woman's tone remained brisk, but her scowl had relaxed somewhat in the wake of Diana's gentle politeness. Most people responded favorably to being listened to and treated with respect. For an older woman—the bulk of whom were generally ignored—this was particularly true.

As Diana approached Mrs. Lewandowski's rocking chair, she bent to approximate the woman's seated height. The view out the window was unobstructed. Diana could not only see the road but also the front and side yards of the house that had been Bruce Weaton's.

"Do you wear glasses, Mrs. Lewandowski?"

She shook her head. "I had cataract surgery three years ago. They implanted prescription lenses in my eyes."

"Your corrected eyesight is twenty-twenty?"

"Close enough."

"Could you tell what kind of car hit Bruce?"

"A green Dodge Colt. One of my grandkids has one, only his is gray."

"And the driver?"

"I couldn't see her."

"You could tell the driver was a woman?"

"That became obvious when the deputy pulled her out of the driver's seat later."

"What direction was the car going when it hit Bruce?"

"West," Mrs. Lewandowski said as she pointed to the left.

"Where exactly was the car on the street?"

"You mean before it hit him?"

"Did the car change positions as you observed it?"

She nodded. "It started accelerating on the other side

of the street going west like I said. Then when Bruce ran into the street, the car swerved over to this side of the street. That's when it hit him."

Diana kept her excitement from reflecting on her face. This information hadn't been in the original report. Connie had swerved the car as she said. And cranky Mrs. Lewandowski with the good vision and memory could testify to that fact at the trial.

Diana straightened. "What happened after Bruce was struck by the car?"

"Lyle came running across the street toward Bruce. A man who I later learned was their father ran into the house yelling something."

"Did you hear what was yelled?"

"No. I keep my windows closed."

"Did you know Lyle Weaton before this?"

"Lyle is the father of the boy who did my weeding. He'd drop off his son and stop in to see Bruce while the boy worked. Later, he'd take him home."

"At the time Lyle came running across the street, where was the car that had hit Bruce?"

"Stopped on the street."

"Engine running?"

"I don't know."

"What did you see next?"

"A light-blue Cadillac Seville pulled in front of the Weaton house. Barbara Weaton jumped out, ran over to Bruce and Lyle."

"You knew Judge Weaton?"

"I'd seen her picture in the newspaper. A minute later, another woman came running down the front steps of Bruce's house. She yelled at Lyle and his mother."

"Do you know who this woman was?"

"I found out afterward that she was Lyle's wife, Audrey."

"Thank you. Please go on."

"Lyle got up, hurried back across the street to his wife. Judge Weaton stayed on the pavement, holding Bruce's head in her lap. I could see the tears streaming down her face."

A devastating scene for a jury to picture.

"Had the car that hit Bruce moved at all during these events?" Diana asked.

"No. It was parked right in the middle of the street until the deputy arrived."

"When did the deputy arrive?"

"A few minutes after Lyle disappeared into the house. The deputy talked to Judge Weaton. Then he pulled the woman out of the car, handcuffed her and put her in the back of his patrol car. After that, he moved her car."

Diana had read the deputy's report prepared at the time of Bruce's death. His explanation for moving the car was to give the ambulance access to Bruce.

"A couple of minutes later the paramedics came, worked on Bruce a bit then took him away," Mrs. Lewandowski continued. "Another ambulance arrived after that. They carried his father out of the house on a stretcher. I heard he died of a heart attack on the way to the hospital. The prosecutor tells me the case doesn't qualify for a death penalty. It should. That woman doesn't deserve to live."

The angry words were a blow to Diana's ears.

She wished she could explain to this woman what had happened to Connie, but she could say nothing. Not until the trial when all the evidence was presented and her client was acquitted.

If her client was acquitted. Diana didn't kid herself. She and Jack had a hell of a lot to do if they were going to make that happen.

JACK WAS AT THE ENTRANCE when Diana came out of the courthouse late Friday morning. He could have called her, and he told himself the reason he hadn't was that he had something to show her.

But when he saw her, he faced the fact that he'd been lying to himself. The moment she'd leaned into him in his kitchen two nights before, he'd known she wanted him. If she hadn't pulled away—

Jack extinguished the thought. He couldn't afford to dwell on the images that came to mind. Even seeking her out now was probably a mistake. Okay, no probably about it. But knowing that wasn't stopping him.

She wore another shapeless business suit with low-heel pumps. Her blouse was crisp white cotton and her long black hair was drawn to the nape of her neck. As usual, no makeup adorned her face.

She should have looked plain. She could never look plain.

When he caught her eye, she changed direction and started toward him. He met her halfway.

"I was going to call you when I got back to the office," she said.

"I couldn't wait to find out if our questionnaire is a go."

Her smile told him what her answer would be even before her words.

"When Staker and I told Judge Gimbrere that we had agreed on the questionnaire, he didn't even bother reading it, but simply directed his court clerk to send it out with the letter he'd already drafted. We should have the answers back in a couple of weeks."

"This calls for a celebration," Jack said. "Let me take you out to lunch. There's this intimate little restaurant overlooking the water that's—"

Jack stopped himself midsentence when he saw the discomfort spreading across her face.

Yes, she was attracted to him. But she'd made her intent plain when she left his place so suddenly the other night. She didn't want to be attracted to him. And she wasn't going to let herself be led anywhere she wasn't willing to go.

"...or better yet," he said, shifting gears, "we could grab a frozen yogurt at the shop across from the park. Then while we sit on a bench indulging ourselves, we can bring each other up-to-date."

Her frown faded. "That's the place with the fat-free chocolate, right?"

"That's the one," Jack lied, having absolutely no idea. He hadn't been in there in years.

"I'd better follow you," she said. "I'm not sure if I remember where that shop is."

Jack nodded as he started toward his car, hoping *he* remembered where it was.

THEY LEFT THEIR CARS in the parking lot at the yogurt shop and walked across the street to the park. The temperature was in the seventies and the sky impossibly blue—one of those gorgeous days when the rain-drenched green foliage of western Washington finally got a glimpse of the sun.

Not even the fact that Jack had fibbed to her about the yogurt shop carrying fat-free chocolate bothered Diana. The fat-free peach was yummy.

And she wanted to be with him. Damn foolish, but a fact. At least she'd turned down an intimate, romantic restaurant. What could be the harm in eating yogurt in a public park?

The park was deserted except for a guy throwing a stick for a golden retriever and a mother with her twin toddlers sitting on a blanket, catching some rays.

Jack and Diana claimed the bench beneath the shade of a lush white pine. As they ate, she told him about her interview with Mrs. Lewandowski and promised to send a copy to him as soon as the court reporter had it ready.

"You're right, Diana. There was nothing in the crime scene reports about Connie swerving her car to try to avoid hitting Bruce. Mrs. Lewandowski's testimony should put a different slant on things."

"Especially when it's coupled with the fact that Connie had come to a complete stop after hitting Bruce. The deputy reported her car was a few feet from where Bruce had fallen. Doesn't that tell you she had to have been braking at the time she hit him?"

"Seems logical. Was an outside accident investigation specialist called in to interpret the scene?"

"Earl Payman didn't bother—just as he didn't bother to do anything on Connie's behalf. All we have is the brief sketch the deputy at the scene drew after he removed Connie's car."

Jack licked his yogurt. "I have a friend in the insurance business who does this kind of accident reconstruction all the time. I'll give him a copy of the police report and Mrs. Lewandowski's deposition, then take him out to the scene and see what he comes up with."

"Sounds good. The deputy who arrested Connie reported the engine of her car was off. According to Mrs. Lewandowski, no one approached Connie while she was behind the wheel of her car. So Connie had to have been the one to turn off the engine and drop the keys in her lap, even though she doesn't remember doing so. I believe her subsequent shock also supports her lack of intent to hit Bruce."

"What did the coroner's report say was the cause of Bruce's death?"

"He died from the blow to the back of his head that he received when he fell to the pavement. The wounds on his legs from the impact were minimal, again indicating Connie's slow speed. I'll include a copy with Mrs. Lewan-dowski's deposition.''

"The sheriff's report said Lyle Weaton also witnessed Bruce's death.''

"Yes,'' Diana confirmed, "but what he gave the deputy is pretty sketchy. I have a lot of questions.''

"When will you depose him?''

"He's not returning any of my calls. Nor is his wife or Judge Weaton. Technically, they don't have to talk to me until I have them on the witness stand in the courtroom.''

"So you have to wait.''

Diana shook her head. "I can't afford to. If they're going to say something damaging against Connie, I have to know so I can be prepared to counteract it. This afternoon I've arranged an interview with Bob Zucker, a local TV reporter. The interview will broadcast tonight at six and several more times over the weekend.''

"How's that going to help?''

"Bob is going to ask me how the case is going. I'm going to tell him that in order to learn the truth about Bruce Weaton's death, I need to talk to the witnesses who have been avoiding me. When he asks me what witnesses, I'm going to name Lyle, Audrey and Judge Barbara Weaton.''

"Think that will get them to return your calls?''

"The way Bob will conduct the interview, yes. He's never been a fan of Barbara Weaton's politics. When she came out for Staker, that really ticked him off. Bob's been waiting for an opportunity to take her on.''

Jack smiled. "And you're going to give it to him. Very clever.''

Because his smile and compliment felt too good, Diana forced herself to look away. "One of my biggest concerns is that Mrs. Lewandowski paints a picture of Bruce as a caring, considerate man. Staker, no doubt, will elicit those facts from her on the stand. She's a credible witness. The jury's going to like her and believe what she says.''

"But she only knew Bruce as a casual neighbor. Those who knew him more intimately saw a very different man.''

Jack told Diana about his conversation with Bud Albright.

"Bruce joined AA right after the Fourth of July weekend five years ago,'' Diana repeated excitedly. "That Sunday, July 5, was when Amy was killed. Could he have been driving drunk that day he hit Amy?''

"When I realized the significance of the dates, I called Jared and asked him to run Bruce's name through the files to see if he had a criminal record. This is Bruce's rap sheet.''

Jack pulled a folded slip of paper out of his pocket and handed it to her. The sheet had two entries—a drunk and disorderly stemming from a bar fight when Bruce was twenty-one and a DUI conviction when he was twenty-three.

Diana slipped the report into her shoulder bag. "Well, it's something, but I was hoping he'd have a bunch of drunk driving arrests that were more recent. Bruce was thirty-two at the time of Amy's hit-and-run. That's nine years after his DUI.''

"When I checked with the attendees at his memorial service, a couple turned out to be dorm buddies from college. They told me that Bruce was already drinking heavily when he was twenty-one. He most likely had been an abuser for at least ten years before joining AA.''

"Ten years," Diana repeated. "Did getting caught that one time scare him into not driving when he'd been drinking? Or was he simply lucky that he was never caught drunk behind the wheel?''

"Good questions," Jack admitted. "Bruce ended up in the E.R. with a broken arm when he got that DUI. I'll take a look at his medical records and see if there's anything else to learn.''

They were interrupted by the sound of the twin toddlers screeching with delight as they rushed past.

Out of the corner of her eye, Diana caught the grimace on Jack's face. "Let me guess. Not the father type?"

"What gave it away? The hemorrhaging from my ears?"

She chuckled. "Was it fun, being a twin?"

"You don't get to ask any more personal questions until you answer some."

She turned to look at him more fully. His smile was light with humor, but the rest of his handsome features were set with a determination that she was also beginning to know well.

"If you don't like what I ask, you don't have to answer," he said. "Now what could be fairer than that?"

This man knew how to couch his requests so that they were hard to refuse. "Okay, one question," she said.

"Tell me about Mel's...dad."

Diana's eyes returned to the cavorting toddlers, well aware that Jack had phrased his question almost as though he were asking about Mel's past instead of hers. The guy was clever, all right.

"Not much to tell," she said. "I met Tony at a rock concert. The entire time he was performing on stage, he was staring at me. I was staring back, starry-eyed. On our second date he asked me to marry him. It lasted less than three years."

"Why not longer?"

"That's two questions."

"Technically, I think you'll have to admit it's more like a natural extension of the first," Jack said. "You don't strike me as the kind of woman who does anything halfway. So why did your marriage end so fast?"

She kept her eyes on the romping twins as they returned to their watchful mother. "I didn't have a clue what I was getting myself into. Making a marriage work and providing for the needs of a child have to be two of the hardest jobs anyone can take on."

"You'll get no argument from me."

She tilted her head as she looked over her shoulder at him. "I can see that. You made it past thirty without marrying. Good for you."

Surprise lit his face. "I could almost swear you meant that sincerely."

"I did. Of course, it's easier for males."

"Easier?"

"Society encourages boys to concentrate on finding a career and focusing on who they are and what they hope to achieve in life. Girls are brainwashed into thinking that their real value comes from looking good and their real career is getting a mate. Instead of seeking out fulfilling work and getting to know ourselves, our time is wasted in the pursuit of the right clothes, cosmetics and crash diets."

"But you didn't fall for that," Jack said.

Diana snickered at the obvious sincerity of his statement. "I fell for it so completely I got married at the stupid age of twenty-two."

"How long did it take for you to smarten up?"

She shook her head. "I sometimes wonder if I ever will."

"Now that, I don't understand."

"The other day I was waiting outside a judge's chamber. There were three magazines on the table I hadn't read—an *American Bar Association Journal,* a *Lawyers Weekly* and a fashion magazine. And there I was flipping through the fashion magazine, wondering whether I should be investing in wrinkle cream before it's too late. The problem with dumb behavior is it doesn't disappear even when examined and understood.''

He was looking at her with nothing less than admiration. ''Smart, beautiful *and* blatantly honest. Wow.''

For one full, foolish moment she allowed herself to wallow in the sweetness of being a woman admired by a man she admired.

The next moment cold reality had Diana firmly on her feet, distancing herself from the danger that dwelt on that bench. She headed for the trash bin and dropped in her empty yogurt container, silently cursing herself.

Sharing her personal experiences and feelings with a man was an invitation to intimacy. She knew better. And she'd done it anyway. That dumb behavior definitely hadn't disappeared.

She felt him move beside her as he disposed of his empty container. He wasn't even close to touching her, but his nearness was still too disturbing. She retreated to a nearby cedar tree, rested her back against its ancient bark and stared through the gracefully laced branches at the still blue sky.

He followed to within a few feet, crossed his arms over his chest. ''Shall I pretend you're dumb, ugly and insincere? I can, you know. I'm a very good actor.''

She smiled reluctantly.

His returning grin was full of good-natured mischief as he rested the edge of his shoulder on the tree trunk. ''I guess I can tell you now that at high school graduation, I was voted the one most likely to *finally* get his foot out of his mouth.''

She'd needed him to back off and he had. The man was special.

''I should have that medical information for you tomorrow,'' he said. ''Shall we schedule to meet at a particular time and place and synchronize watches or will a call suffice?"

"Do I dare ask how you're going to get access to Bruce's confidential medical records?"

"With wit and charm, of course."

She shook her head, despite an inability to keep a smile off her lips. "Wit and charm notwithstanding, E.R. records aren't kept very long."

"But insurance carriers keep their records forever. And I happen to know which carrier covers the employees at Weaton Real Estate."

"What if the records clerk isn't female?"

The confidence on his face was both dastardly and disarming. "They're always female, thanks to a society that has women trying to track down men instead of a top-notch career."

"You don't have to sound so pleased about it."

"As reprehensible as the reality may be, it certainly makes my job easier. Besides, I love the idea of being pursued by a bold beautiful woman."

Yeah, she bet he'd had a lot of experience with such pursuits, too. Not that she blamed the women.

Diana was chuckling in wry amusement when something caught her eye. For a second she froze in disbelief. The next second, she grabbed Jack and pulled him behind the tree with her.

"Diana, please, a woman normally buys me dinner first."

"Don't make me laugh now," she said, releasing her hold on him while her hands were still cooperating. "Staker's coming up the path right toward us."

Jack moved closer. Diana told herself he had to in order to hide from anyone passing on the other side of the tree. But his hard thigh was suddenly touching hers, and the clean warm scent of him was filling her senses.

He bent near her ear and whispered, "Are you ashamed to be seen with me?"

She raised her eyes to his. The heat of his look went right through her. She clamped down on the excitement building within her and told herself she was stronger than this.

"Jack, I can't become one of your women."

For an instant, he was perfectly still. Then he drew back and a rescuing swirl of cool air bathed her hot skin.

No argument, no charming words, simply retreat. She let out a private sigh of gratitude and relief.

His next whisper was subdued, barely audible. "Tell me why we're hiding from Staker."

"Because of who is with him."

CHAPTER NINE

JACK HELD HIMSELF a half inch away from Diana—not by the strength of the arm anchored on the tree trunk, but by the sense of decency a man held on to when a woman said no.

He'd felt her body quiver when he'd whispered in her ear. She wanted him, and heaven help him, he wanted her. But her message had been unequivocally clear, and the eyes looking into his were cool and controlled.

What's more, she was right. She couldn't become one of his women.

He'd handled a hundred love scenes with beautiful, nearly bare, actresses and had never once lost his focus or been carried away.

But the more he was around Diana, the less he was himself. He wished to hell he knew who he was.

Footsteps could be heard coming up the path, as well as a woman's muffled voice. When the footsteps faltered, then stopped, the voice became more distinct.

Jack peered out from behind the tree. No more than ten feet away stood a tall blond woman and a stocky man with black hair and a thin mustache. Obviously, the guy was Staker. Jack wondered who the woman was.

"…supposed to be on-call so I can't get away," the blonde said. From her voice and business suit he deduced she was a professional.

Staker took her hands in his. "Then we'll spend the weekend at my place."

The ruthless prosecutor sounded a lot more like a man trying to coax a woman into his bed at the moment. From the way the woman looked at him, Jack had a pretty good idea he'd be successful.

"I can't park my car at your place again," she said. "It's too risky."

"We'll put it in the garage."

"Your neighbors might see me driving in. They're starting to notice. One of them even waved at me the other morning. They probably think I'm living with you."

He smiled. "So what if they do?"

"George—"

"You're right. We'll leave your car at your place. I'll pick you up there at ten. Should be dark enough. No one will see you. Okay?"

She nodded.

"Don't wear any panties or bra."

She sighed. "Don't do this to me. I have to get back to work now."

Staker moved in closer. "Give me a kiss to keep me going until tonight."

Her eyes darted nervously around, but Jack ducked behind the tree before she looked in his direction.

"I can't," the woman said. "Someone could see us. I have to go."

Jack looked again in time to see Staker nod and step back. "Tonight then."

"Tonight," she repeated as she turned from him and walked quickly toward the parking lot. When she'd gotten in her car and driven off, Staker pulled out his cell phone and punched in a number.

"It's me. Any messages?"

He stood there listening for a moment. "I don't have time to talk to a reporter about the Pearce case or any other. Blow him off. What? Don't worry, I'll handle her.

She's only pissed because I didn't show her the question-naire before it was sent out. Look, I'm on my way back to the courthouse now. I'll stop by her office and smooth things over. Yeah, right. See you in twenty.''

Flipping his cell phone closed, Staker started toward the parking lot. He hopped into his car and drove off.

"Who was the blonde?" Jack asked as he turned back to Diana.

"My friend," Diana said in a voice Jack had never heard before. Only then did he notice how pale she was.

"You didn't know about her and Staker," Jack guessed.

She shook her head as her eyes went to her watch. "I have to get back to the office. Call me when you learn something. Thanks for the yogurt."

His eyes followed her as she walked back to her car, wanting to do something to relieve her distress, not having a clue what that would be.

"LEROY, HAVE A MINUTE?" Diana asked after she knocked on his office door.

The man scowled up at her from behind packs of case files. His office looked even worse than hers.

"No, but you're coming in anyway, aren't you?"

She stepped inside, ignoring his querulous tone. "Word around the office is that you lost your last case to Staker because of a leak."

Leroy squinted at her. "Why are you here, Mason? To get some new material for yet another joke at my ex-pense?"

She sent him a serious look that matched her tone. "There's nothing funny about a leak in the office, Leroy."

He frowned at her a moment before waving at the chair in front of his desk. Diana figured that was as close to an invitation as she was going to get. She closed the office door and took a seat.

"Tell me about the case," she said.

"My client was picked up in his car seven blocks away from a convenience store that had been robbed of four hundred and fifty dollars ten minutes before. He had four hundred and fifty-one dollars in his wallet and seventy-two cents in his pocket. The clerk at the convenience store said the guy who had robbed him wore a black ski mask and leather gloves. Neither was found on my client or in his car. The clerk said the robber was six-two. My client was five-eleven. The clerk couldn't pick him out of a lineup."

"Did the store have a surveillance camera?"

"Broken."

"Doesn't sound to me like the prosecution had a case."

"They didn't until Staker called to say they recovered the weapon used in the robbery, and my client's fingerprints were on it."

"How did he get the weapon?" Diana asked.

"He claimed an anonymous tip."

"Why do you think there was a leak?"

"When I first interviewed my client, I went through the drill, assuring him that anything he said to me was confidential. He told me he'd robbed the store using a toy pistol. When he drove away, he threw the ski mask and gloves in a trash can, wrapped the pistol in a towel and dropped it in a Toys for Tots collection box sitting on the sidewalk. The donated toys are supposed to be new. Since my client's toy gun wasn't, the collector threw the damn thing in the trunk of his car and promptly forgot it. He retrieved the pistol from his trunk the day the deputy came asking."

"Someone could have seen your client drop the gun in the Toys for Tots collection box."

"At midnight? When it was wrapped in a towel?"

Diana had to admit that didn't sound likely.

"The robbery made the papers when it happened. But there were no follow-up stories around the time when the anonymous call was supposed to have been made. Why would anyone wait six months before reporting what they'd seen to the sheriff's office?''

Good question. ''Could your client have told anyone else about the gun?''

''This guy has no family, no friends, Mason. He'd arrived in state two days before the robbery and had been living out of his car. No one knew he was going to rob the convenience store—not even him. It was a last-minute act.''

''Where did he get the toy gun?''

''He picked it out of a trash bin while scrounging for food that morning. He had no money for bail. I told him not to talk to anyone in jail and he swears he didn't.''

''Why do you trust his word?''

''The regular jail cells were full so they had to put him in an isolation unit. No one was there to talk to. I checked the logs. He had no visitors.''

''Did you discuss your client's confession with anyone at the firm?'' Diana asked.

''Ronald asked about the case, and I told him. No one else. But his office door was open at the time. Someone must have been in the hallway and overheard us.''

''What about your interview notes?''

''I didn't take any notes of the confession. The only way Staker could have known where to look for that gun is if someone at this law firm heard me talking to Ronald and told the prosecutor.''

Had someone? Specifically, had Gail? Was she passing confidential information to Staker about the cases being handled at the firm?

Diana couldn't imagine Gail doing that. But Gail was having an affair with Staker. And Diana would never have imagined that, either.

Staker had been despicable to Gail when she worked in

the prosecutor's office. Stealing cases that came across her desk that would be an easy win. Dumping the ones that should have never gone to trial into her in-basket for no other reason than to make her look bad. At least that's what Gail had said. She'd told Diana that she'd left the prosecutor's office because she loathed Staker so much she couldn't continue to work with him another moment.

But it wasn't loathing that Diana had heard in Gail's tone in the park earlier.

AS MUCH AS JACK CONSIDERED marriage a major mistake, he found the ceremony uniting the two blind souls oddly compelling. Seeing people so gleefully ignoring all the divorce statistics and boldly stepping onto the gangplank of matrimony was a little like watching a couple of full-fare passengers skipping aboard the *Titanic*.

Impending disasters always had a way of riveting one's attention to the scene, whether on-screen or off.

Jack arrived late to the informal ceremony that united Margaret Gilman and Raymond Villareal in her garden full of sunshine. He'd been detained at the insurance company charming a young female clerk into unlocking the office and letting him have a look at the files. He was eager to tell Diana what he'd learned.

As Jack stepped from the house into the backyard, Margaret was finishing what must have been an individually written set of vows for her intended.

''…and lastly I promise that I will never, ever ask you if what I'm wearing makes me look fat.''

There was an appreciative chuckle through the couple of dozen guests gathered around to witness the ceremony. But it was Ray who wore the biggest smile as he took his bride's hand in his.

''Margaret, I can't promise I'll always mow the lawn before it reaches the windowsills, slam-dunk every dirty sock into the laundry hamper and not scorch the walls with curses when the damn Christmas tree lights get tangled. But I *do* promise that 'I love you' will be the first words out of my mouth every morning and the last words I say to you every night and that loving you will be what makes my heart beat happily each moment in between.''

Not bad. Jack had a feeling he could like this guy. As soon as the couple was pronounced husband and wife, Ray kissed the bride with such enthusiasm that Jack found his eyes searching for Diana.

She stood on the other end of the garden. Mel was next to her. Behind Diana stood a big guy, slugging down champagne and trying to look down her blouse.

Jack had no doubt that the creep was Ray's stepson. No wonder Margaret had asked him to be on hand today.

He started toward them but had to come to an immediate halt when a dozen well-wishers surged forward to surround the bride and groom. He was waiting for them to pass when a voice behind him said, ''You're Diana's detective.''

Jack whirled around to see an oddly dressed man. A deerstalker cap crowned his head. A calabash pipe curled out from his lips. Over his dark suit he wore a brown checkered cape.

The strange attire was definitely familiar, although Jack couldn't immediately call to mind why.

He held out his hand. ''Jack Knight. Have we met before?''

The man released the pipe in his mouth and gave Jack's extended hand an impressive shake. ''We share the same profession. I'm Sherlock Holmes, formerly of two-twenty-one Baker Street, London.''

Of course. The hat, the cape, the pipe. Had this been a masquerade party, Jack would have laughed. But guests to weddings didn't come dressed as fictional detectives. What was with this guy?

"I'm retired now, of course," the man said as he knocked the edge of his pipe against a ceramic candy dish on a nearby table to dislodge some nonexistent tobacco. "But do feel free to consult with me if there are any aspects of the case that become confusing."

When the man straightened and replaced the pipe in his mouth, Jack saw a large black cat in the crook of the guy's left arm, previously hidden by the cloak. The cat stared at Jack with large yellow eyes.

"Do you have a card?" the stranger asked.

Jack gave him his card and was about to ask how he knew Diana when Mel sidled up to the man and spoke in a hurried whisper. "Shirley, I've been looking all over for you."

Shirley?

Jack turned back to the strange man beside him, noticing for the first time the missing Adam's apple and the small pores on his face. Well, hell. He wasn't easily taken in, but he sure had been this time. That had been some acting job.

"I had to tell Mr. Knight who I really am, Watson," Shirley said to Mel. "He's a fellow detective. It's professional courtesy to offer my help."

Or maybe *not* such a great acting job. This woman thought she really *was* Sherlock Holmes.

"This is important," Mel pleaded. "You must tell everyone that you're my great-aunt Shirley. There can be no exceptions. Remember, you gave your word to Mom."

"You have made your point, Watson," Shirley said with a touch of annoyance. "No sense in belaboring it."

"And you were supposed to have worn something appropriate," Mel whispered, her embarrassment obvious.

"Dr. Watson is concerned for my safety," Shirley said

as she turned to Jack. "But he asks too much sometimes with this impersonation of his great aunt. A man does not don a woman's clothes."

There was a deep pride in the rebuke that Jack found fascinating. The slight disdain in the tone, the prominent beak pointing upward, the snub of not addressing her critic directly—subtle points of characterizations, all well executed.

Shirley might be crazy, but she did a very creditable job of immersing herself in her role. He was too much of an actor not to appreciate a part well played.

"Concern over Professor Moriarty?" Jack asked soberly.

Shirley's head lifted in immediate and gratified acknowledgment. "Very astute of you to grasp the essence of Dr. Watson's worry so quickly. Diana has not erred in her choice of detectives, Mr. Knight."

He smiled. "Call me Jack."

"And you must call me Holmes, despite the good doctor's concerns." She paused to pet the cat in her arms. "And this good fellow is the Hound."

"A fine fellow indeed," Jack said, happy to play along. He gave the cat's head a cautious pat and was rewarded with eager fur thrusting itself into his palm.

"Once owned by the Baskervilles?" Jack ventured as he indulged the cat's demand to be petted.

"Quite right!" Shirley said, clearly pleased to have found a kindred soul both able and willing to speak her language. "Man's best friend, once misled by human miscreants. I have taken him under my wing."

The cat was purring like a buzz saw when Jack became aware of Diana's presence. He couldn't have said exactly how, except that there was a sweetening of the air. He turned to find her a few steps away.

"I see you've met my aunt," Diana said as she stepped

closer. "Mel, would you like to accompany Shirley to the buffet?"

Mel obediently slipped her hand through her aunt's arm, but Shirley was not to be dismissed so easily.

"Diana, I'm not a fool. This feeble attempt to get me out of the way so that you can tell your detective who I really am is unnecessary. Jack and I have already exchanged professional courtesies. I may be retired, but my powers of observation are still keen. I knew immediately who he was."

Mel shook her head in exasperation, but Diana smiled indulgently at her aunt.

"I very much doubt anyone could fool you. Would you do me a favor and accompany Mel to the buffet? She didn't get a proper breakfast this morning, and I'm counting on you to see she eats a good lunch."

Shirley replaced the pipe in her mouth. "Well, of course. Delighted to be of service. Come, Watson."

Sighing audibly, Mel went along.

As soon as Mel and Shirley were out of hearing distance, Jack turned to Diana. "Your aunt's a charming character."

"Thanks for...indulging her."

"When did she decide she was Sherlock Holmes?"

Diana watched her aunt and daughter at the buffet table. Her voice was soft. "After a car accident that killed her husband and two children. They were her world, Jack. The only way she could survive losing them was to become someone else."

"How long ago was this?" Jack asked.

"Twenty years. Psychiatrists wanted to lock her up in an institution, shoot her full of drugs, but my mom wouldn't let them. The psychologists who tried to talk her back into reality all gave up. Last one told my mom that as long as Shirley is happy being Sherlock Holmes, she'll hold on to her delusion.''

"What do you think?"

"I think Shirley has a wonderful heart. I don't care what name she goes by. She always told me that if I ever needed her, all I had to do was call. I called. And here she is.''

A deep warmth radiated from Diana as her eyes remained on her aunt's oddly clad form. Jack found himself wondering what it would feel like to be on the receiving end of one of those looks.

"So, that's the stupid old broad who thinks she's Sherlock Holmes,'' a nasty voice said, making her visibly flinch.

Jack had seen Ray's stepson approach out of the corner of his eye. Up close the guy was a couple of inches taller than him and at least thirty pounds heavier. He gave Jack a dismissive once-over as he set down his champagne glass on a nearby table.

Diana turned slowly toward the guy, stiff-limbed. "She is my very sweet aunt. I suggest you watch your language, Arnie.''

The noise that came out of Arnie's throat was probably meant to be a laugh. "And you're still acting like you're too good for me with that crazy bitch in the family,'' he said as he grabbed a chip off the snack table and angled it toward the dip.

Jack decided right then that if the guy wanted some dip, he'd give it to him. Hand on the nape of Arnie's neck, he pushed his sneering face into the large bowl. Arnie made a noise that sounded like a squealing pig at a trough as he swung blindly at Jack. Jack quickly released his hold and stepped out of reach. Arnie tumbled backward, the bowl of bean dip following him to the floor.

He was sputtering and cursing when Ray rushed over and went down on his knee beside his stepson.

"What happened?" he asked.

Before Jack could tell him, Diana stepped forward. "I think Arnie may have had too much to drink, Ray. Jack and I will put him in a cab and send him home if you'd like."

Ray looked from Diana to Jack. From the expression of defeat on the man's face, it was apparent to Jack that Ray had no trouble guessing what had happened. Jack leaned toward him and held out his hand. "I'm the Jack Diana mentioned."

Ray grasped Jack's hand and pulled himself to his feet. He looked down at his stepson, who was wiping the bean dip from his face and cursing. "I'm sorry about this, Diana. If you'll call the cab, I'll get him into it. He's my responsibility."

And not a pleasant one. Arnie was in his mid-thirties and still a major pain for his stepfather. Jack shook his head. Becoming a parent—even a stepparent—was a life sentence, served without parole.

Diana left to call the cab. As Jack watched Ray walk his stepson out, he promised himself a man-to-man talk with Margaret's new husband later. He'd better know that if Jack ever caught Arnie around Diana again—

"Thank you, Jack," Margaret said as she approached.

He gave her a little bow. "At your service. Diana told you, I presume?"

"When I pressed her for the truth. My daughter's a tough customer. But she also has the tenderest heart. She's in the library. You'll be careful?"

Not sure if Margaret was warning him because Diana was tough or because she was tender, Jack had no chance to ask because Ray reentered the house then to whisk his bride away for a dance.

Jack went in search of the library. He found Diana inside, standing in front of a bookcase, holding a glass of champagne in one hand and a picture of a man in the other. As he went closer, Jack saw the unmistakable resemblance between her and the man.

"Your father."

She nodded.

He gently lifted the framed picture out of her hand. "What happened to him?"

"Heart attack eight years ago. He was fifty-three."

"Young."

Diana sipped some of her champagne. "Filling his lungs with cigarette smoke every day since he was seventeen made him an old man."

He handed her back the photo. "Was he a good father?"

"He always had a smile and a hug for me. Told me I could do anything, be anything I wanted to be. What I wanted to be was exactly like him."

Despite the accolades in her words, her tone was sad. The combination perplexed Jack.

"You never wanted to be like your mother when you were growing up?"

"My dad earned a salary. She was given an allowance."

Ah.

Diana returned the photo to the shelf. "He had no smiles or hugs for her. He treated her like she was his paid employee because her job was in the home. Since he devalued her contribution, so did I. Took me a while to finally wise up."

Jack understood her sadness now. She loved her father, but the respect she'd once held for him was gone. That was what she mourned.

She finished her champagne, set the glass on the shelf as she continued to look at the picture.

"My dad was a big man, six-four," she said. "Ray is barely five-eight. Yet he stands tall over my dad when it comes to loving my mom for who she is and making her happy.''

''Shame a nice guy like him got struck with such a jackass of a stepson.''

Diana turned toward Jack. ''Nice move with that bean dip. Arnie never saw it coming.''

''Thinking on your feet is mandatory when you grow up with three brothers. Of course with two of those brothers a whole lot bigger and all of them tougher, I learned early on that my funny bone was the only one in my body not likely to get broken in a sparring match. I'm still relying on it.''

She chuckled. ''So *all* of your brothers are tougher than you?''

''I used to think I had the edge on David. But a couple of months ago, that sort of got blown out of the water.''

''What happened?''

Jack sent her an enigmatic smile. ''A lot of things, not the least of which was he decided to get married and raise a family. That's way too brave for me.''

''Now you're the certified wimp in the family?''

''And damn proud of it.''

She laughed with a rumbling huskiness that he felt down in his insoles. He moved closer.

Her voice and smile were full of warmth. ''Thank you for what you did for my Aunt Shirley.''

He'd wondered what it would feel like to be on the receiving end of that kind of look. Now he knew.

''Diana, I did it for you.''

His eyes held hers for a moment before he bent his head. A soft gasp escaped her lips as their breaths mingled.

''Jack, I can't do this.''

He watched the pulse in her neck throbbing.

''Tell me why, Diana.''

For the space of several interminable seconds he waited for her to give him that reason or move away.

She did neither.

He brushed his mouth against hers, tasting cool champagne and something even sweeter that was her.

An eager little sigh escaped her lips. The next thing he knew his arms were tight around her and he was kissing her with a hunger that was deeper than any he'd ever known.

"Mom?"

Oh, God, kid. Not now.

Diana stiffened in his arms, then pushed away. Jack knew she would. A mother's number one priority was always going to be her kid. Best a man could ever do was come in a distant second.

He turned toward the doorway to see Mel frowning at him.

"Everything okay?" Diana asked her daughter in such a calm tone that Jack couldn't believe she was the same woman who had just kissed him with enough heat to burn the hair off his chest.

"Grandmother and Ray are getting ready to pose for pictures," Mel said. "They want us to be in them."

"Okay. Coming, Jack?"

Diana was already halfway to the door.

Jack put his back against the bookcase and concentrated on trying to get his heart to stop punching his rib cage. "In a minute."

Mel stayed when her mother left. She crossed her arms over her chest and stared at him squarely. "We don't want this, Jack."

Great. Exactly what he needed right now. A kid with attitude. He took a deep breath, let it out slowly. "Don't want what?"

"A man messing up our lives."

"You think I'm going to mess up your life because I kissed your mother?"

"You like my mom. And she likes you. I knew it the other night when you kept looking at each other. It'll only get worse from here."

"You really *do* lack tact when you lose your temper."

"I don't care."

"Mel, whatever your mother and I do is between us. You are not involved."

"I *am* involved. Hormones make a woman lose her logic. It happened to Mom before when she fell in love with my dad. She was trying to finish law school. But he wanted a family right away so he got her pregnant, which meant she had to drop out of school. I was two years old when he changed his mind and decided he didn't want us anymore."

So that's how Diana's marriage had ended. He wished she'd told him. "I can understand why that would make her angry."

"She's not angry. I am. She doesn't even know I know."

"How did you find out?"

"He always calls me on my birthday and Christmas, like he's nobly fulfilling some fatherly duty. On my last birthday he confessed what he'd done. Said he was sorry, but he'd screwed up. Thought the family and kid scene were what he wanted. Like that was supposed to make everything all right. I've never had a dad."

"And you want one."

"No, I don't. My mom and I are doing fine the way we are. A man would only come between us."

"I have no intention of coming between you and your mom."

"Ray had no intention of coming between me and my grandmother, either. But he did."

"Not all relationships between men and women have to end in marriage, Mel."

"So you're only fooling around with my mom? You don't really care for her when you kiss her? Does she know that?"

Now what could possibly be the right answer to those questions? Jack suddenly felt like he was facing an irate father who was demanding to know his intentions.

"This can't be a new situation for you," he said. "Your mother must have dated other guys."

"Mom only has serious relationships. She told me any other kind is meaningless. When I didn't like either of the men she brought home for me to meet, she stopped dating them."

"Mel, I think I know your mother well enough by now to appreciate that no one can persuade her to do something she doesn't want to. Not even you."

"But you became her private investigator just recently. I've been with my mom all my life. And I really care about her."

"I care for your mom as well."

"For how long? Until the case is over and you leave her like my dad did?"

Another one of those damn questions for which he had no answer.

"If you really care about my mom, you'll leave her alone. She says you're nice and a good private investigator, and she wouldn't say those things if they weren't true. She needs your help to free Connie. What she doesn't need is for you to mess up our lives. Now, I have to get back to my grandmother."

She stalked out of the room.

Jack should be amused at the audacity of the kid. Or angry. But he was finding that he admired her a little too much to be either. She'd faced him with the same no-holds-barred kind of honesty that her mother possessed.

And she'd asked some questions he should have asked before his brain flatlined and he kissed Diana.

CHAPTER TEN

DIANA WATCHED the local news as she sipped her morning coffee. Her interview had been run four times since Friday. But this was the first time that reporter Bob Zucker had Judge Barbara Weaton in front of the camera, answering the charge of lack of cooperation from the Weaton family. The blazing lights in the background told Diana that Bob had cornered the woman the night before at a much-publicized political fund-raiser for Staker.

"It would be inappropriate of me to comment on the upcoming trial of Ms. Pearce, as you well know," Judge Weaton said in a voice that was very annoyed.

"Is it true that you, your son and daughter-in-law have all ignored Ms. Mason's letters and refused to return her calls?" Bob asked before he thrust the mike back in her face.

"We gave our statements to the police," Judge Weaton said. "The law does not require us to talk to the attorney for the accused."

"So you're refusing to tell her what happened?"

Diana had argued cases before Judge Weaton. The lady was tough. But she was up against a very smart reporter who knew the voting public understood very little about the law, and a whole lot about evasion.

A solid fixture in the local news scene, Bob was somewhere past fifty and long past worrying about offending people in power, particularly the ones who rubbed him the wrong way. Matter of fact, he seemed to thrive on it.

Barbara Weaton's erect shoulders and uncompromising tone radiated an air of no-nonsense authority. "I, and the members of my family, will answer Ms. Mason's questions. In court."

"Where your good friend, Judge Gimbrere, will be able to restrict what she can ask?"

"How dare you imply—"

"Ms. Mason's made a simple request, Judge Weaton," Bob smoothly interrupted. "All she's asked is that you sit down with her and tell the truth. Is that really so hard for you and your family to do?"

"It's not a question of—" she began.

"Are you hiding something, Judge Weaton? Is that why you won't cooperate?"

The woman glared at Bob, fully aware that was one of those loaded accusations for which the wrong response could haunt her the rest of her career. To her credit, she reined in her anger instantly. Her next words were delivered with the kind of even tone that reflected the control Diana had seen Barbara Weaton display on the bench.

"My family and I will be happy to talk to Ms. Mason. All she has to do is contact us." The judge had delivered that message as though Diana had been the one remiss in calling. "Now, if you'll excuse me, I am expected inside."

Diana flipped off the TV with a satisfied smile. She had the home number of Lyle and Audrey Weaton. Right after breakfast she'd call them and set up their depositions. Her first call Monday morning would be to the judge.

Of course, she was going to be in serious trouble when next she appeared in Barbara Weaton's court. But that had been inevitable the moment Connie became her client.

Exposing Bruce Weaton as a criminal wasn't going to ingratiate Diana to the judge. Nor was she making points with Ronald Kozen every time she sidestepped his questions about her defense strategy.

Gail had warned her from the start that this was a case no defense attorney could come out of looking good. Her friend had been right. Even if Diana won the case her career could be over.

Rubbing tired eyes, she tried to look on the bright side of the insomnia that had been plaguing her for days. The extra hours awake were helping her to get the painting and packing done for the move into the new place.

The real problem was the reason she wasn't sleeping well.

She shouldn't have kissed Jack. He'd given her time to back off. But she'd wanted that kiss. And it had been everything she wanted—and more. She hadn't felt so excited by a man since…hell, she couldn't remember ever feeling so excited by a man.

But Jack had disappeared afterward.

Diana figured he'd finally remembered all those very good reasons why they shouldn't be pursuing a personal relationship. Time she remembered them, too.

As Jack waited in the hospital emergency room for Dr. Cummings to come on duty, his thoughts kept turning to Diana. He'd left the wedding reception the day before because he hadn't known what to say to her after that kiss.

The women he dated were simply out for a good time. Showing Diana the very best time she'd ever had was something he most definitely wanted to do. But he understood what she'd meant when she said she wasn't going to become one of his women.

She didn't take relationships lightly. And he wasn't a man who would take them any other way. Nor was he going to pretend to be.

Pretense was fine in front of a camera or in the performance of his private investigation duties. But he didn't indulge in it in his personal life. People got hurt that way.

Mel was right. If he cared for Diana, he'd leave her alone.

Jack was so preoccupied with his thoughts that he almost missed seeing the doctor rushing out of the physicians' lounge. The man charged up to the closed elevator, stabbed the down button repeatedly. Jack caught up with him there, gave the man his name and a picture to identify.

"Bruce Weaton," the doctor said, handing the photo back to Jack. "Yeah, I remember him. A schoolteacher killed him last year. Who did you say you were?"

Jack produced a business card.

"A private investigator." The doctor returned the card and stabbed the elevator button once again. "Medical records are confidential, Mr. Knight. I can't talk to you."

"The man's dead. What are you afraid of, Dr. Cummings?"

The elevator bell binged. "My shift has started. You'll excuse me."

As soon as the doors opened, the doctor stepped inside.

"Been paid off?" Jack called after him.

Cummings sent Jack a look as sharp as a scalpel. "Do I have to call security and have you thrown out?"

Jack gave Cummings the same kind of ruthless stare that had made his TV character one of the most effective villains. "Withholding medical information that relates to a crime is a punishable offense, Doctor. You willing to lose your license?"

The man charged out of the elevator, red blotches staining his hollow cheeks. "I wasn't even on duty the day he was killed. Check the record."

"I have. You treated Bruce Weaton on a Fourth of July weekend nearly five years ago when he was brought in with a head wound sustained in a motor vehicle accident. His blood alcohol level came back from the lab at point two five. That's way over the legal limit. Yet you made no report to the sheriff's office.''

''I did report it, and the time before. Just because he—''
The doctor stopped, appalled at his outburst.

''Just because he what?'' Jack prodded.

The man's lips tightened into a thin white line.

''Look, Doctor. Either you violated the law or the deputy who you gave your report to violated it. Do you want to tell me the truth, or would you rather wait until you and your records are subpoenaed?''

DIANA HURRIED to the courthouse annex early Monday morning for Lyle Weaton's deposition. Lyle was already seated in the interview room when she pushed open the door five minutes after the hour. He looked pointedly at his watch. She apologized.

Although Diana had only seen a picture of Bruce, she recognized the family resemblance in his younger brother's large physique and dark coloring. As the court reporter went about swearing Lyle in, he barely paid attention, instead gazing out the window at the gray day. He agreed to tell the truth in a monotone of indifference.

''Thank you for coming, Mr. Weaton,'' Diana began.

He reacted to the pleasant smile she sent him by studying her like she'd offered him something he'd consider. She stopped smiling.

''Please tell me what happened on July 27 of last year.''

He wrapped his arm over the back of the chair, spread his legs, looked at her with an arrogance she found annoying. ''Why don't you read the sheriff's report?''

''The court reporter and I are ready whenever you are,'' she said pleasantly, ignoring his question and smug tone.

Lyle eyed her for a moment. She lifted her chin and stared right back. His mother had made a promise that her family would cooperate. Lyle had tried to get out of honoring that promise by insisting his schedule for the next three weeks was so tight that he could only meet with Diana at six this morning. When she'd agreed, he hadn't been pleased. This glare game wasn't going to work either.

He finally gave up, his gaze wandering out the window again as he began to describe the family barbecue at his brother's. His wife was in the kitchen with their youngest boy preparing salads and drinks. He and Bruce were with their father outside on the patio getting the steaks on the grill. Lyle's seven-year-old son was playing catch with Connie.

"What time was this?" Diana asked.

"Little after noon."

Lyle was at the grill when he heard his son tell Connie that he wanted to show her the new bike Bruce had bought him. She took the boy's hand and they went into the garage.

"Next thing I know she comes running out of the garage, jumps into her car and hauls out of there."

"Did she say anything?" Diana asked.

"No. Bruce kept shouting at her to tell him what was wrong, but she ignored him. She backed her car into the street, and Bruce ran in front of the car, waving his hands. She gunned the engine and hit him dead-on."

Lyle's description of what happened differed in substantial ways from Mrs. Lewandowski's version. For one, Mrs. Lewandowski said the car was already moving when Bruce ran in front of it. She also said that the car had swerved.

Diana knew now was not the time to cross-examine Lyle on the differences. That would come when Diana got him on the witness stand and pointed the discrepancies out in front of a jury.

"What happened next?" Diana asked.

"My father hightailed it into the house yelling that he'd

call 911. I ran across the street to Bruce. He wasn't moving. I felt for a pulse in his neck, couldn't find one.''

"What about the car that hit him?"

"What about it?"

"Where was the car while you were with Bruce?"

"Couple feet away."

"Was the engine still running?"

"I don't know."

"You didn't hear it?"

Annoyance peppered his tone. "I was concentrating on my dying brother."

Even so, Lyle had witnessed Connie hit his brother with her car and he went in front of that car without first checking to be sure the engine was off and the keys were out of the driver's hands.

That told Diana one thing very clearly. Lyle hadn't feared that Connie was going to hit him.

"Please describe what happened next," she said.

"My mother arrived, ran over to Bruce and me. I told her how he'd been hit and that my father was calling 911. She knelt down, talked to him, tried to get him to respond. He didn't."

"And then?" Diana prompted when he stopped.

"My wife came out the front door and yelled that my father had collapsed and she needed help. My mother told me to go, said she would stay with Bruce. I grabbed my son and followed my wife back into the house."

"Mr. Weaton, where was your son when you grabbed him?"

Lyle leaned toward her. "He'd come out of the garage to see what was going on, and I had to tell him. For a week afterward, he woke up with nightmares. You leave him out of this. Do you hear me?"

"Mr. Weaton, I'm a parent as well, with an appreciation for the trauma an incident like this can cause a child. I've read the statement your son gave to the sheriff's office. Since he was in the garage at the time Bruce was struck by the car, I have no intention of questioning him. Now, could we please continue?''

Lyle squirmed about in his chair for the next minute, as though he couldn't quite get comfortable. Diana waited patiently for him to get himself back under control.

''What happened when you went inside Bruce's house?'' Diana asked after what she deemed to be an appropriate interval.

''When I entered the kitchen with my son, I found my father on the floor, barely breathing. I did what I could, but he died on the way to the hospital.''

''From what, Mr. Weaton?''

Anger scored deep lines around Lyle's mouth. ''From the shock of seeing my brother murdered right before his eyes.''

Diana knew she was going to have to get a copy of Philip Weaton's medical records. If Lyle repeated those words while on the stand—and she was sure Staker would see he did—the jury would be trying Connie for two deaths.

''Mr. Weaton, are you acquainted with the woman who lives in the home across from the one your brother owned?''

''I've seen her a few times.''

''Have you had occasion to speak with her?''

Lyle shook his head. ''Bruce talked my older boy into weeding her front yard. Place was getting to look like a trailer park. Embarrassed the hell out of Bruce to have to live across the street from that old woman's mess.''

Apparently Bruce wasn't the kind neighbor Mrs. Lewandowski had taken him to be. His motives had been selfish. Diana was going to make sure that Lyle repeated his last comments in front of the jury.

"Mr. Weaton, did it surprise you when the red lace panties belonging to Tina Uttley were found on the dashboard of your brother's car?"

He shrugged. "My brother was a player."

"Meaning?"

"He slept around."

"What was his relationship with Connie?"

"She was nothing but one of his broads."

Either Lyle didn't know about Bruce's true relationship with Connie or he was lying.

"Did your brother generally invite his female partners to family barbecues?" she asked, careful to keep her tone even.

"Sometimes."

Diana felt certain he was lying now. "What are the names of some of the other female partners who attended a family gathering where you were present?"

"He went through them so fast I never bothered keeping track of their names."

"How fast was that?"

"None of them lasted more than a few weeks."

"How many weeks had he been seeing Connie?"

"A few."

"So you don't know for certain?"

"I wasn't my brother's keeper."

Wrong guy to be quoting from the Bible if one wanted to be believed.

"How long had your brother been seeing Tina Uttley?" Diana asked.

Lyle first crossed then uncrossed his legs before answering. "You'll have to ask her."

"She's your employee. You haven't asked her?"

"I don't get personal with my employees."

According to Tina Uttley, that was a whopping lie.

Diana felt certain that this guy had told her quite a few this morning.

DIANA WAS BACK in her office, busily filling in Vincent's ridiculously complicated billable-hour time sheet when Kelli buzzed to say that Jack had left a message on their voice mail. Her stomach gave an excited flutter as she reached for her phone. Punching in his cell number, she was uncomfortably aware she'd memorized that number the moment he'd given it to her.

"I've learned some things you need to know," he said as soon as she had identified herself. "I'll be by in five minutes."

His tone was strictly business. She told herself she was relieved.

"I have a luncheon date with a co-worker in about an hour."

"This is important, Diana."

"All, right, I'll reschedule. But I'd rather we not discuss the case here. That could be…unsafe."

There was a moment of quiet on the other end of the line. "I'll pick you up out front."

Diana hung up the phone and gathered her papers, shoving them into her briefcase. She hadn't been looking forward to lunch with Gail anyway.

The thought of talking to Ronald about Gail's clandestine relationship with Staker crossed her mind. But she'd decided that would be wrong. There was no proof that Gail was leaking information to her lover.

A person was innocent unless proven guilty. So far, all Gail was guilty of was hiding a romantic relationship with Staker. And incredibly bad taste in men.

She had decided to ask Gail for the truth today. But her friend's door had been closed when she arrived at the office. That door was still closed as Diana walked by now. She stopped at Kelli's desk and asked her to tell Gail that she'd had to go out and couldn't make lunch.

"Ms. Loftin didn't come in today," Kelli said. "Her mother died. Sorry, she told me to tell you but I forgot."

Shock and sadness hit Diana with a one-two punch. "Did Gail say how it happened?"

"A stroke. In her sleep. Apparently there was no warning."

A blessing it was quick. A curse there was no time to say goodbye.

"Her mother lived in Eastern Washington," Diana said. "Is Gail going there?"

Kelli shrugged. "She only told me that she wouldn't be in for the rest of the week and to be sure Ronald knew. And to tell you."

"Kelli, would you get her on the phone for me now?"

The receptionist punched in Gail's home number and handed over the receiver. Diana held the phone to her ear through seven rings before she returned the receiver to the receptionist. "No answer. I hope to hell she doesn't have to go through this alone."

"Do you have a key to Ms. Loftin's office?"

Diana sensed Kelli's discomfort at her show of emotion and accepted the change of subject. "No, why do you ask?"

"I thought I'd take the chance to replenish her supplies. Every time I try to, she's either on the phone or her door's locked."

"We're all supposed to keep our offices locked."

"But no one else is as paranoid about it. She locks hers even when she's going to a meeting in the conference room."

That was true. Diana had even watched her do it. Was Gail simply being cautious? Or was she hiding something?

Damn, she didn't want to be suspicious of her friend. Especially not now.

"Don't worry about replenishing her supplies," Diana said. "It's not like she'll be needing anything until she returns. You can catch her then."

Kelli frowned, looked down at her hands. "I tried to bring stuff in when she was on the phone one day, and she cuffed the receiver and told me to get out of her office."

That didn't sound like the Gail Diana knew.

She was beginning to wonder if she knew her friend at all.

"YOU WANTED TO TELL ME something?" Diana prompted after she and Jack had been driving around for a couple of minutes in silence.

"Some things about Bruce you should find interesting," Jack said.

Actually, he wanted to talk about the kiss first. But finding the right words was difficult. He couldn't remember feeling this tongue-tied since very early adolescence.

"I caught your TV interview," Jack said, picking a more neutral subject. "And Judge Weaton's response. Your strategy worked well."

"I took Lyle Weaton's deposition this morning," she said. "I'll send you a copy."

She paused to turn toward him. "Before we get into the case, I'd like to clear the air. Things got a little out of hand the other day. What do you say we put the kiss behind us and get things back on a business basis?"

The fact that she had taken the initiative was so much better than if the suggestion had come from him. For the first time since Jack had picked her up, his hands relaxed on the wheel.

"If you think that best, Diana," he said soberly.

She surprised him by laughing. "Your attempt not to sound relieved isn't working."

Damn, his acting skills must really be slipping if she could read him so well. When he glanced over at her and saw the good humor that lit her face, he suddenly found himself laughing.

"How were you going to approach the subject?" she asked.

"I was going to ask if we could be friends."

"The old 'let's be friends' routine? I thought that was the woman's line."

He tried to sound innocent. "Is it?"

She laughed again. "I guess the women you meet always want to be more than friends. Why am I not surprised?"

Her compliment was open, unexpected, nice.

"But using the 'let's be friends' line is somewhat prosaic," she said. "I would have thought that with your dramatic background and daunting communication skills you would have come up with something a bit more imaginative."

"Imaginative, yes. Honest, no. After kissing you, no man with blood in his veins could go back to simply a business relationship."

The playful look vanished from her face. She stared out the passenger window. This wasn't so easy for her after all. That shouldn't make him feel good. But it did.

"I've never had a female friend under fifty before," he said. "We're going to need to establish some ground rules."

"Like what?"

"You have to promise to refrain from pulling me behind any more trees and letting your mother invite me to any more of her weddings."

Diana's lips lifted. "Anything else?"

"No, other than those, I'm pretty much a tower of strength. Anything you have to stay away from?"

She pretended to give it serious thought. "Champagne."

"Domestic or imported?"

He could see her smile growing. "Both, I'm afraid."

"Fear not. I shall slay any brute who dares to offer you either."

Her laugh was lovely and deep.

They were telling each other bold-faced lies and having fun doing it. Being with her was special.

"What have you learned about Bruce?" she asked after a moment.

Jack stopped stealing glances at her and watched the road. "You wondered whether he had the sense not to drink and drive after his early DUI or simply hadn't been caught doing so. The answer is neither."

"Meaning?"

"Twice over the past seven years he was brought into the emergency room from injuries caused in driving accidents. Both times his blood alcohol level was far in excess of the legal limit."

"You got that look at his medical records," she guessed.

"And talked to the E.R. doctor who treated him. Bruce denied being the driver of the car. He was backed up both times."

"By whom?" Diana asked.

"The E.R. doctor said it was his father the first time. But despite the fact that his father claimed that it was he and not Bruce who had been driving, Bruce sustained an injury to his chest that could only have been caused by impact with a steering wheel.''

"What did the E.R. doctor do?''

"Only thing he could,'' Jack said. "Treat Bruce's injuries and release him.''

"You said there were two times.''

"And the second one is crucial to our case. A woman brought Bruce in for treatment of an open gash on his forehead that required stitches. She told the doctor Bruce had hit a tree.''

"What did Bruce say?'' Diana asked.

"Nothing at the time. He was too drunk. When a blood alcohol test came back showing Bruce was over twice the legal limit, the doctor called the sheriff's office to report the incident and a deputy came down to arrest Bruce.''

"But there was no such arrest on his record,'' Diana said.

"Because the woman pulled the deputy aside and changed her story. After talking to her, the deputy returned to the doctor and told him that the woman, not Bruce, had been driving.''

"Didn't the doctor suspect something when the story was changed?''

Jack nodded. "Especially after having treated Bruce for that other accident the year before. But the most important thing about the second incident is the date and time it took place. The records show that the woman brought Bruce into the E.R. approximately forty minutes after Amy's hit-and-run.''

Diana sat straight up in the passenger seat, her voice rising with excitement. "He must have driven to the E.R. afterward. Or been driven. Who was the woman who went with him?''

"The doctor didn't know. Her name wasn't noted on the medical record."

"Could he give you a physical description?" Diana asked.

"It's been nearly five years so the doctor's memory of the woman is sketchy at best. All he could call to mind was that she displayed no signs of being under the influence of alcohol and he had the impression she was somewhere near Bruce's age."

"Does the doctor remember the deputy's name?"

Jack shook his head. "The E.R. doctor is eager to testify for you, though. He's rather upset that Bruce got away with driving drunk on those two occasions."

Diana's sigh was both frustrated and sad. "He's not the only one. Bruce's father covered for him in that first accident. If he hadn't, Bruce could have been stopped, and Amy would be alive today. Hell, they'd probably all be alive today."

Jack knew Diana was right.

"Bud Albright said Bruce was drunk at the ballpark that day," Jack offered after a moment. "Someone must have had an old or classic car there that Bruce used. It might have belonged to the woman. She could have even been with Bruce when he hit Amy."

In his peripheral vision, Jack could see Diana nodding. "I'll get a subpoena for the E.R. doctor and Bruce's emergency room medical records so they can be admitted as evidence. Unfortunately, this means I have to tell Judge Gimbrere how those records relate to Connie's defense. Staker's going to know the moment I do."

"And Staker will also realize that we believe Bruce was the one driving the car that killed Amy."

"Can't be helped," Diana said. "We need those medical records to prove Bruce's involvement in Amy's death.''

''Do you think Staker will give Judge Weaton a heads-up?''

''Probably. She's been his chief supporter politically. But if it comes out that she knew her husband was keeping their son's drunk driving a secret, Staker may want to distance himself from her. Otherwise, he'll be tainted by association.''

''Can you put off requesting the subpoena until right before the trial?'' Jack asked.

''That's a thought. The judge knows I got the case late so he won't be surprised at last-minute requests. Staker will be livid, of course, but who cares? The less time we give him to react, the better.''

She arched her back as she rolled her shoulders. Finding the motion too provocative, Jack wisely shifted his eyes back to the road.

''After talking to the woman in the E.R., the deputy must have written up an accident report,'' she said after a moment. ''Maybe even given her a ticket.''

''Jared's going to check the computer for citations issued on that day. He's agreed to give me a list of what he finds.''

She became quiet, and Jack glanced over to see a troubled look on her face. ''Want to tell me about it?''

''The woman, Jack. I can understand a father lying in the mistaken belief he was protecting his son. But why would she lie about being the driver? Tina, Bud Albright, Lyle—all of them describe Bruce as going through women with little if any caring. Who was she that she'd lie to a deputy for Bruce and cover up his crime?''

''I'll let you know when I find her.''

She sent him an appreciative look. ''Yes, I do believe

you will. For someone who's only been at this private investigation stuff for a short time, you're very good.''

"I may have only joined the firm a year ago, but I've been in training for the profession since I was a kid. When both of your parents are private eyes, the conversation around the dinner table is all about the best surveillance methods, interview techniques, tailing, disguise, equipment and how to gain access to the most reliable information sources.''

"I didn't know your mother was a private investigator.''

"Before any of us. White Investigations was the name of the firm when she ran it with my grandmother. My dad became part of the business when he left the FBI and they got married. That's when they changed the name to White Knight Investigations. Every Sunday we still get together for dinner at my parents' place and discuss cases.''

"Has Jared mentioned anything about the materials collected from Bruce's garage?''

"Only to say that the results could take a while. Unfortunately, this is not TV where by the next scene all the forensic fibers and fingerprints have been identified and the cops are hot on the bad guy's trail.''

He heard her soft exhale.

"Something wrong?''

"Merely a little tired. You know how it is.''

He knew. She'd kept him up for two nights in a row with X-rated dreams.

"You'll feel more alert after we have something to eat,'' he said. "Do you have a preference, or are you willing to let me choose?''

She laid her head on the seat rest. "I'm in your hands.''

Jack took the next corner fast, trying hard not to dwell on the literal image her words invoked.

He picked a French restaurant that offered seating on its

tree-lined patio. He hadn't missed the fact that Diana had chosen to sit on the terrace of the first restaurant they'd gone to. Since the temperatures were mild, staying indoors seemed a waste.

Only too late did he remember that she was careful about what she ate and probably wouldn't consider French food a good choice. But she surprised him by her enthusiasm when she ordered several items from the menu.

"Don't tell me French food is healthy?" he asked when the waiter had left.

"I think the French have the right idea," she said. "A small amount of something truly rich and satisfying is far superior to a large quantity of something that never satisfies."

He'd always been a firm believer in that himself—and not only about food.

"Ah, so I might actually find a chocolate bar in your shoulder bag."

She smiled.

The waiter delivered their food. Jack ate what was normally one of his favorite dishes, but it was the memory of her taste that filled him. He reminded himself that retreating from a physical pursuit of her had been the decent thing to do. But his body didn't like the decision.

Their plates were clean and their coffee served before he broached the other subject she'd alluded to earlier.

"Tell me about the unsafe office problem."

She took a sip of her coffee. "Gail Loftin was the woman who was with Staker in the park last Friday. She's a lawyer at Kozen and Kozen."

"And you think she might be telling her lover things she shouldn't."

"I don't want to think that. But several of the firm's lawyers have unexpectedly lost cases to Staker over the past few months, and one is convinced someone at our law offices passed on privileged information to the prosecutor.''

She paused a moment to drink some more coffee. ''We don't always win, of course, but lately Gail is the only one who *has* won. Not that she isn't a dynamite litigator. But even though her cases have been important capital offenses, Staker has assigned other people to prosecute them. Normally, he takes those cases on himself.''

''He doesn't want to go up against his lover in court,'' Jack said in understanding. ''Does she know about Connie's case?''

''I've told her very little and even partially misled her on my defense approach. Nothing she might pass on to Staker would matter.''

''Are your files safe?''

''What I don't carry with me in my briefcase is on my computer. And, thanks to Mel's expertise with password encryption, virtually inaccessible to anyone but me.''

She was being very careful. He expected nothing less.

''The thing is, I can't bring myself to believe that Gail would do this.''

But the suspicion was eating at her.

''Diana, would you like me to find out if there is a leak?''

She looked at him in surprise as she put down her coffee cup. ''I've already given you far too much to do on Connie's case. I can't ask you to—''

''You didn't ask. I offered.''

''No, you don't understand. I haven't even told the senior partner at my firm about my suspicions, much less gotten funding for an investigation.''

''Consider it a favor from a friend.''

She rested her hand on his forearm. ''Thank you, Jack.

But as a friend, I would never take advantage of you like that.''

She was giving him one of those smiles again. His hand closed over hers before he realized it. "Diana—"

He never finished the sentence, because the waiter appeared with the bill. Jack quickly released his clasp on Diana's hand, wondering what in the hell he thought he was doing.

When they were back in his car, she asked him what he had begun to say to her back in the restaurant.

"Not important," he said and then drove her straight to her office.

CHAPTER ELEVEN

"HAVE YOU SEEN Jack lately?" Mel asked her mother.

"He's been too busy trying to find a witness for me. Would you hand me that roller?"

Mel followed Diana's pointing finger and passed over the paint roller. "So you haven't seen him since the wedding?"

"We met briefly on Monday. Any reason you're asking?"

"I just wondered."

"About the kiss?"

Mel nodded as she pushed her paintbrush over the wall. "You really like him?"

Diana watched the groove deepen in her daughter's brow. The frown had become a frequent feature this week. Mel always got nervous when Diana showed interest in a man.

"I wouldn't have kissed him if I didn't really like him. You know that about me, right?"

Mel's nod was grave.

"Jack's a good guy, Cute Stuff. But he's not my guy."

"Looked like you two were fitted together."

That's exactly how Diana had felt being in Jack's arms.

She gave herself a mental shake as she concentrated on edging her roller against the door trim. "Attraction between men and women is a natural part of life. How we handle that attraction reflects our emotional intelligence or lack thereof."

"How are you handling it?"

Diana picked up a brush to paint what the roller had missed. "Jack said he'd like to be my friend. I like that idea as well."

"What do men and women friends do together?"

"Don't know. Never had a male friend before. I doubt we'll be getting together to braid each other's hair or do any body waxing, though."

Diana sent her daughter a smile. Mel didn't smile back. This wasn't going well.

"The Hound and I have successfully applied the third coat to the kitchen," Shirley said suddenly.

Diana looked over to see her aunt standing beneath the arch that led into the living room. She brandished a wet paintbrush in one hand, a can of paint in the other and a big smile on her face. The enormous black cat stood at her feet.

"What's next?" Shirley asked.

"Sit down for a while and let me get you something to drink," Diana offered. "I have a thermos of hot tea, one of milk and some cold drinks in the ice chest."

"First the work, then the refreshments!"

"Okay, Holmes. The upstairs bathroom needs a second—and let's hope final—application of white."

Her aunt beamed as she marched toward the stairs. "I'm your man. Come, Hound." The black cat swished its crooked tail and followed in her wake.

When Shirley had disappeared up the stairs, Mel asked her mom, "Why is she so excited about painting?"

"Makes her feel needed."

"We're just painting."

"One of the great things about Shirley is that she never *just* does anything. Hang around her long enough and you might even learn to appreciate that."

Mel didn't look convinced. For the umpteenth time in

the past week, Diana reminded herself that emotional maturity took time.

The familiar sound of the William Tell Overture rang through the empty room. Diana stepped over the drop cloths to get to her shoulder bag, dug out her cell phone and answered with her name.

"It's Audrey Weaton. I can't make our appointment tomorrow."

This was the third time Audrey had called to cancel her scheduled deposition. Diana's long pause must have conveyed her annoyance because Audrey's voice held a contrite tone as she rushed to fill the ensuing quiet.

"It's a busy time for me and a customer called a moment ago to say she's flying in tomorrow. I have to meet with her early."

"A customer of the real estate agency?" Diana asked.

"No, I don't work with my husband. I have a business of my own making jewelry. I can talk to you at my home now. Lyle will be at the office late with some clients, and my oldest son is spending the night with a friend. It's the best I can do."

Diana knew getting a court reporter on such short notice wasn't going to be easy. Or inexpensive. But maybe worth the try to get this matter resolved.

Putting Audrey on hold, Diana punched in the number of one of the single moms she knew could use the extra money. When the court reporter agreed to come, Diana went back to Audrey, telling her she'd be arriving in forty minutes.

After hanging up the phone, Diana turned to Mel. "I have to go out. I'll leave the cell phone and a number where I can be reached with Shirley. This shouldn't take more than an hour or two."

"Where are you going?"

"I have to see someone regarding Connie's case."

''Jack?'' Mel said, another furrow appearing on her forehead.

''No, a witness,'' Diana corrected as she slung her bag over her shoulder and headed for the stairs. She was getting a little concerned about Mel's worries over Jack. Normally her daughter accepted her assurances.

Looked like you two were fitted together.

Maybe that was why Mel wasn't convinced. And maybe that's why Diana hadn't been too convincing when she told her daughter that she and Jack were only going to be friends.

JACK WAS BLEARY-EYED after going over the reports that Jared had secured for him. Thirty-two women drivers had been cited for traffic violations in the county on the day Amy was killed. Jack had compared the women's last names with those from the softball teams. None of the names matched.

If Bruce had driven away from the game with a woman, she wasn't one of the other guy's wives. That meant she might have been another guy's date. Or a sister or daughter with a different last name.

Including the three Weaton men, there were sixty guys who'd played at the park that day. It had taken Jack four days to track down and interview the seven men who had been on the guest list for Bruce's memorial service. They all told the same story about Bruce's drinking before AA, his killer business instinct beneath a charming façade and his womanizing ways. Jack had learned nothing knew from them.

There had to be a quicker way of locating the woman Bruce had been with and the car he'd been driving on the day of Amy's hit-and-run.

Jack punched in Jared's cell number. His brother answered after two rings, the background music telling Jack that Jared was out somewhere. He checked his watch. Eight o'clock. He hadn't realized it was that late.

"I need a favor," Jack said.

He heard a woman giggling in the background as she asked for another drink. "You'd better not need that favor now," his brother warned.

Jack grinned. "Bright and early tomorrow will do. Vehicle registration checks on sixty names."

"You're joking."

"Current records aren't as important as what they were driving five years ago."

Jack could hear his brother's irritation over the phone. "Do you have the foggiest idea the amount of time it would take to check on that many vehicles belonging to that many people over that period of time?"

"Give me your access to the Department of Licensing records and I'll be happy to search them myself."

"You know I can't do that."

No, Jack was sure he couldn't. Jared would bend the law but not break it. "I hear the county commissioners have finally agreed to add a Chief of Detectives to your unit. When you solve Amy Pearce's hit-and-run, you'll be a natural for the new position."

An exhale of frustration came through the telephone line. "If you weren't my brother..."

Jack grinned. "I'll drop the names off at your place tonight. I'll even bring over a chilled bottle of imported wine and a box of chocolates for the lady."

"Your tail better be out of there in forty minutes. If tonight's going to be my last free night from work for a while, I'm damn well going to make the best of it."

Jack laughed as he disconnected the line. The thought occurred to him that there was still time for him to make a call and spend the night in the same kind of fun as his brother planned to engage in.

Except that he'd lost his taste for that since he got this case. Or, more accurately, since he got a case of Diana Mason.

He'd stayed away from her all week, diligently rejecting all the flimsy excuses that came to mind to see her. Except every time he remembered the taste and feel of her, she was right back in his arms, melting into him. And he was—

The ringing phone jarred Jack out of his fantasies. With the conflicting emotions of relief and irritation, he answered with his name.

"Glad I caught you in, Jack," Shirley's voice said. "Need some help here."

Diana's aunt was the last person Jack expected to receive a call from. He sat up, feeling a sharp stab of unease. "What's wrong?"

After listening to Shirley's explanation, Jack relaxed back in his chair, wearing a big smile that should have bothered him. "Sure, Holmes. Happy to be of service."

THE WEATON HOME WAS on the end of a cul-de-sac in a hilly part of the city, sheltered beneath four-hundred-year-old western hemlocks. Plush honeycomb-colored carpet, crisp white linen drapes and spotless glass shelves full of lovely handpainted Lenox vases reflected a carefree woman with relentless good taste and ample time for housecleaning—not a harried working mother with two young boys.

Diana always wondered what genes enabled some women to pull off such feats.

Audrey showed Diana and the court reporter into the living room where an assortment of delicate finger-sandwiches waited.

At least she was being civil. That was a nice change

from her husband. Still, she was clearly tense as she sat on the couch, bouncing a two-year-old boy on her knee.

While the court reporter munched a sandwich and wrestled with her uncooperative machine, Diana took advantage of the delay to try to relax Audrey.

"Is that a sample of the jewelry you make?" she said, pointing to the bracelet that the woman was wearing, a delicate gold filigree with turquoise and diamonds.

Audrey nodded. "Yes, it's one of my designs."

"It's beautiful," Diana said.

Audrey picked up a brochure from the end table. "This is the latest catalog, hot off the press."

Diana accepted the catalog with the name *Farrell's Originals* embossed on the cover, flipped through the glossy pages. The pictures were professional, highlighting the delicate intricacy of design and pleasing symmetry of an assortment of beautiful rings, broaches, pendants.

The prices weren't listed, but Diana was certain that whatever they were she couldn't afford them. "Very nice," she said.

"I make most of the jewelry right here," Audrey volunteered proudly. "Lyle had the attic converted into a workshop when we moved in here after the wedding."

"So jewelry making was your business before you married?" Diana asked, as she took a bite of one of the finger sandwiches. It was also very good.

"My mother's and mine. Still is. We're co-owners, although she relies on me to make most of the jewelry now that her sight isn't the best. Our clients are from all over the world."

Diana could believe it after seeing the beautiful bracelet on Audrey's wrist and the samples in the catalog. "A successful businesswoman, a perfect housekeeper and a full-time mom. If you tell me you made these sandwiches, too, I'm going to start hating you."

Audrey laughed, a nice sound. "My cook made them before she left this evening. I also have a housekeeper. Am I forgiven?"

Diana smiled. "Your membership in the 'real woman' world has been reinstated."

Audrey's shoulders relaxed as she rested back on the sofa. "This week has been a madhouse because my sitter quit," she confessed. "Can't watch the kids and get anything done. But Jason is a good boy. He'll be quiet while we talk. Won't you, honey?"

Audrey's voice was a hopeful plea. Jason squirmed on her lap and stuck a chubby finger up his nose.

The reporter nodded to Diana that she was ready. Diana acknowledged the message and beckoned for the court reporter to swear Audrey Weaton in. The chitchat was over. Time to get down to business.

"Please tell me what happened on July 27 of last year," Diana began.

"Bruce invited all of us for a barbecue at his place."

"All of us?" Diana repeated.

"Lyle, me and the boys. And his parents, of course. Bruce said it was so we'd have a chance to get to know Connie."

"Had he done this with other women he dated?"

"No, that was a first. Family get-togethers were always restricted to family."

So much for Lyle's earlier contention that Bruce had included other women he'd been seeing.

"Had you met Connie before this, Mrs. Weaton?"

"None of us had."

"When did you arrive at Bruce's that day?" Diana asked.

"Little before noon, I think. Connie was already there and Philip, Lyle's dad, arrived soon after we did. We were all standing around the barbecue. Lyle Jr., my oldest, was playing catch with Connie. When he dragged Connie into the garage to see the bike Bruce had got for him, Lyle told me to take Jason into the kitchen and start getting the salads and drinks ready while the men of the family made the fire.''

"Real caveman approach, huh?'' Diana coaxed when Audrey paused.

"I wanted to wait until Barbara got there,'' Audrey said. "But Lyle obviously wanted to talk to his father and brother alone.''

"Was that usual behavior?''

Audrey shrugged. "When they talked business or shared dirty jokes, they generally made sure the kids and I were elsewhere.''

Diana nodded. "What happened next?''

"I was in the kitchen a few minutes later when I heard shouting outside.''

"Could you tell who it was or what was said?''

"No. I looked out the kitchen window, but the shrubbery hid the view of the street. Then Philip burst through the back door and said a car had hit Bruce. He ran over to the phone and dialed 911.''

"And what did you do, Mrs. Weaton?''

Audrey's eyes seemed to glaze over. "I picked up Jason and hugged him.''

Like she was hugging him now? So tightly that the little boy was wiggling and starting to complain?

"Sorry, honey,'' Audrey said, as she seemed to come to her senses and loosened her hold on her child. "I guess I was in shock.''

"What happened next?'' Diana asked.

"Philip hung up the phone, said something about the ambulance being on its way and then collapsed. His breath was labored like he wasn't getting enough air. I sat Jason in his chair. Then I dug the bottle of nitroglycerin tablets out of Philip's pocket so I could put one under his tongue.''

"How did you know to do that, Mrs. Weaton?"

"It had happened before. When Philip continued to have trouble breathing, I called for another ambulance, explaining his medical condition. Then I ran outside for Lyle. He came in and rolled Philip onto his back to try to help him breathe better.''

"Was Philip a big man?" Diana asked.

"Six-three and more than two hundred and fifty pounds, most of it around his middle. He was a smart man about business, Ms. Mason. But he could be so stupid about his health.''

"How so, Mrs. Weaton?"

"He'd had two heart bypass operations, yet refused to stop smoking and overeating. His doctor had warned him to cut back on work, too, but he ignored that as well.''

"Did your husband know this about his father?"

"Of course. Lyle was always trying to get his dad to quit smoking and to start exercising.''

And yet Lyle had mentioned nothing about his father's medical problems in his deposition. He'd tried to put the blame of Philip Weaton's death on Connie. Diana had no doubt he'd try to do that on the stand as well. Only now she had confirmation that Philip Weaton was a walking time bomb. And Audrey could testify that Lyle knew that as well. He wasn't going to appear too credible to a jury.

That was exactly what Diana wanted.

"Mrs. Weaton, were you surprised to learn that Tina Uttley's underwear was found in Bruce's car?"

"Truthfully, no. Bruce...played the field, and he wasn't what you'd call a sensitive man. The moment I met Connie and saw how shy and unsophisticated she was, my heart went out to her.''

"Did you think Bruce would hurt her?"

"He couldn't help but hurt her, Ms. Mason."

Audrey sighed, feathering the fine hair on her son's head. "He was my brother-in-law, and I know what she did wasn't right. But I kind of understand it. Bruce had no idea how to treat a nice woman. He should have left Connie alone and stuck to the Tina Uttleys of this world. Those women have no heart to hurt."

"Do you know Tina Uttley well?" Diana asked.

Audrey's mouth tightened. "Well enough."

"How long was Tina involved with Bruce?"

"Ever since they met in real estate school."

"They met in real estate school?" Diana repeated, surprised. "When was this?"

"About a year after Lyle and I were married, must be eight years ago now. That was when Bruce's father gave him the ultimatum that he either learn the business or get out. When Tina got kicked out of her real estate job, Bruce hired her and resumed their affair—if you can even dignify calling what they did together an affair."

There was considerable anger in Audrey's voice when she said that. Did she know about Tina and her husband? Is that why she had such contempt for Tina?

And why had Tina given Jack the impression that she'd only become acquainted with Bruce when she went to work for him, a few months after Amy's death? Was she hiding something?

Diana made a mental note to tell Jack. This had been a very interesting deposition.

WHILE JACK LOOKED for the woman who had been with Bruce on the day of Amy's death, he also continued to complete his background investigation into Bruce.

One of the things Jack had learned from his parents was that talking to a person's enemies could prove as helpful in getting to know them—and sometimes even more helpful—as talking to their friends. He'd made use of that knowledge many times in his career. He was about to make use of it again.

A perusal of the county's civil lawsuit records had revealed that Edgar Pettibone had sued Bruce for destruction of property. The suit had been settled out of court and the particulars hadn't been revealed. But the original filing was still on the record, along with Edgar Pettibone's address.

When no one answered at the Pettibone house, a friendly neighbor volunteered that Edgar had gone out on his boat and should be back soon. Jack waited in his car to avoid getting soaked by the relentless drizzle until he heard the telltale putt-putt of the boat's engine.

A few minutes later, Jack was making his way down the long boat ramp.

The smell of the sea and the dark gray water were heavy beneath the weight of the overcast day. A man tying up his boat looked over his shoulder as Jack approached. "Help you?" he asked in a slightly high voice.

"Edgar Pettibone?"

The man got to his feet, pulled a white cloth out of his pocket and began to wipe his hands. "Yeah. And you'd be?"

Jack gave the man his name and business card.

"Private investigator, huh? Who you after?"

"I'm collecting background information on Bruce Weaton."

Edgar flipped Jack's card between arthritic fingers. "This for the trial of that woman?"

"Yes."

"You for or against?"

Not sure what Edgar meant by that, Jack decided to play it safe. "For the truth. Against any lies. I could use your help."

Edgar thought about it a moment. "Let's get up to the

house and out of the wet. My joints don't do so well in this weather.''

Edgar's house was a small cottage—from the water markings on the rocks below, probably no higher than six feet above extreme high tide. Inside was a compact three rooms with a small kitchen to one side and a bath at the back.

Jack sat on a threadbare plaid couch while Edgar retrieved two beers from his small refrigerator, the loud motor of which reminded Jack of an old lawnmower his dad had once owned. Edgar handed one of the beers to Jack and then eased himself onto the padded wicker chair across from the couch.

"Cheers," he said as he flipped off the tab and took a swig.

Jack followed suit out of politeness.

"What do you want to know about Weaton?" Edgar asked, after a couple of thirsty swallows.

"You filed suit against him a while back. What was it about?"

"Part of the settlement agreement was a promise not to discuss the particulars."

Not many out-of-court civil settlements went in for gag clauses. Jack's curiosity upped a notch. "I can understand why you'd be concerned about living up to your promise while he was alive. But now that he's dead…"

Jack waited. If Edgar hadn't been ready to talk, he would never have invited Jack into his home.

"He killed my friend, H.G."

Jack came forward in his seat. "How?"

"With his Mercedes."

"When was this?"

"If you've looked up the records, then you should know that it was seven years ago."

"I know that's when your suit was filed. But no date of

the actual incident was in the records. Do you remember the exact date?''

''Not likely to forget the day H.G. died. A month before I sued.''

''Mr. Pettibone, I'm confused. Wouldn't a homicide be something for the criminal court to handle?''

''H.G. was my African gray parrot. Been with me for twenty-five years.''

''I see. I'm sorry for your loss, Mr. Pettibone. Will you tell me what happened?''

The older man took another swig and was silent for a moment as he stared into space. ''I put H.G.'s cage on top of the mailbox right before eleven. The postman would open the cage and let H.G. collect the mail in his beak. Watching for the postman to arrive was the highlight of H.G.'s day. I kept a lookout from the window. That day Weaton arrived before the postman, drove his car into the mailbox and tore it to pieces. H.G. didn't have a chance.''

Edgar swallowed hard, seeming to fight down his sorrow. A moment later he went on to explain that he had gotten the license number of the car and called the sheriff's office. They showed no interest in coming out to investigate a dead parrot. Edgar contacted an attorney who traced the black Mercedes to Bruce Weaton and filed a civil suit against him.

''He killed H.G.,'' Edgar said. ''I couldn't let him get away with it.''

''But you settled out of court.''

''Lawyer said we had to. Said a jury wouldn't understand about me and H.G. They'd think me a crazy old fool. H.G. would only be a parrot to them. He wasn't only a parrot, Mr. Knight. Every morning he'd fly off his perch, land on my bedpost and mimic a trumpet doing reveille to wake me up. He'd eat his seed at the breakfast table with me and recite the alphabet without missing a letter. When the cat next door would sneak through the fence to stalk the birds at our feeder, he'd drop twigs on its head and laugh. He could sing the first stanza of the Star Spangled Banner. He could…''

Edgar bent his head and sobbed.

Jack knew there was nothing he could say. A background check on Edgar had revealed that the man had worked as a machinist at the Bremerton Naval Shipyard until his retirement eight years before. He'd never married or had children.

H.G. hadn't only been his friend; he'd been his family.

Edgar pulled the cloth out of his pocket and wiped his eyes. Jack was waiting until the man had himself back together before asking him if he'd agree to testify to what he'd told him.

"He came back," Edgar said suddenly. "The bastard came back."

"Bruce Weaton came here?" Jack asked in surprise.

Edgar nodded. "Two years ago. Out of the blue he knocked on the door, asked me if I remembered him. Like he was someone I could forget."

The man's arthritic hands clutched the handles of his chair.

"What did he want?" Jack asked.

"He was holding a cage with a parrot in it. Idiotic smile on his face. Said he was replacing the one I lost."

Edgar's jaw clamped shut, the muscles in his cheek twitching.

"What did you do?" Jack asked after a moment.

"I slammed the door in his face. Any man who thought giving me another parrot was the way to make amends would never understand what he'd taken from me. Never."

Jack was certain that Edgar was right.

Could Bruce's actions in this case be the key to understanding what made the guy tick?

CHAPTER TWELVE

Shirley answered the door before Jack even had a chance to ring the doorbell. Her short-cropped black hair was slicked back, yellow sweats under her brown cape, the black cat in the crook of her arm.

"Heard your footsteps coming up the drive," she said. "Firm step. Good you brought a van. Come inside."

"I parked the van at the back of the garage. How did you see it?"

"Didn't. Distinctive engine noise. The rest of the household isn't up yet."

Jack enjoyed how well Shirley had adopted Sherlock's detection skills. Maybe that was the secret to happiness, deciding who you were going to be and being your best at it.

Stepping between the neatly stacked boxes arranged by size, Jack noticed their typed labels listed not only precise contents but also directions for exact placement within the new house.

"Someone's either compulsively thorough or thoroughly compulsive," he said.

"Diana's current bout with insomnia has its productive side."

Diana wasn't sleeping well, either. He was perversely glad.

"Let us start out our day's task with a hearty breakfast," Shirley said.

Sounded good to him. Been a while since he'd pulled

himself out of bed at four-thirty in the morning. When he followed her into the kitchen and smelled the freshly brewed coffee, he began to consider adopting her as his aunt. He could get used to having a home-cooked breakfast prepared for him.

"I was about to feed the Hound," she said.

As he poured himself a cup of coffee and added cream and sugar, Jack watched Shirley open a can of tuna fish and dump the contents into a bowl. No matter what she called the animal, on some level Shirley knew her hound was a cat.

Fascinating how far parts of the human mind could happily soar with delusions while other parts remained firmly anchored in reality. Jack began to wonder what delusions he might be harboring of which he was unaware.

"There are fresh eggs and butter in the refrigerator and the frying pan is in the cabinet to the right of the stove," Shirley directed. "I'll slice the cantaloupe."

Jack chuckled to himself as he headed for the fridge. Appeared one of those delusions he'd been harboring was that his breakfast was going to be prepared for him.

DIANA WOKE a half hour later than she'd planned. Dragging herself out of bed, she donned her sweats and walking shoes, then tied her hair into a ponytail on the top of her head. As she trudged past Mel's room, she could see her daughter was flat on her back, still fast asleep. Diana decided to let her snooze a while longer.

From the smells wafting through the hall, Diana could tell the coffee had already been made, fresh bread was browning in the toaster, and Shirley was scrambling eggs. What a terrific aunt she had.

But when Diana entered the kitchen, she blinked, certain she was seeing things.

Over the past week, her sleep had been frequently disturbed with dreams of Jack. But none of them had been of him bent over a stove cooking, her mother's flowered apron tied around his neck and waist.

"Hi," he said. "How do you like your eggs?"

This was too much to take without a good dose of caffeine. Diana staggered over to the coffeepot, got a mug from the cupboard and filled it. Without a pause, she yanked open the refrigerator, added milk and started to gulp.

"Not a morning person," Jack said, a damn smile on his face. "I'll make a note."

"Mmmph," she managed through her drinking.

"Please, your language. We're not alone."

Diana followed Jack's admonishing look to see her aunt sitting at the kitchen table. Shirley was concentrating on stuffing a fork full of egg into her mouth while rubbing the purring cat's back with the sole of her shoe. She waved a hand in greeting. Diana's arm came up in an automatic response.

When she saw Jack was still grinning at her, she went back for more coffee.

He put the eggs he'd been scrambling onto a plate and turned off the burner. Moving closer, he lowered his voice. "Are you always this wonderfully frazzled in the morning, or am I correct in assuming that Shirley forgot to mention I'd be the one helping you move today?"

"When did this happen?"

"Couple of nights ago. The guy who was supposed to come by in his truck hurt his back and apparently begged off. Since you were out, Shirley called and asked if I could help."

"You have far more important things to do than to waste your day carrying boxes."

"Waste? Hardly. This is an investment. I fully expect you to be there when next I face the chore, especially now that I've gotten a look at your labeling skills. So, what will it be, poached or scrambled?''

''Coffee's all I want.''

Taking the cup out of her fingers, he wrapped her hands around the plate of scrambled eggs. ''You're going to need all your strength if you hope to keep up with me.''

He refaced the stove and removed a couple of eggs from the carton. With an expert flip of the wrist he cracked them, dumping the contents into a mixing bowl.

Not only handsome, smart, sexy and sweet, but he could cook, too. Life was not fair.

As she walked toward the table, Diana could still feel the warmth of his hands where they'd held hers. He was right. She was going to need all her strength today.

JACK SAT down on the back stairs of the house on Baby Lane, pleasantly tired after a long day of moving. The physical activity felt good and reminded him he needed to spend more time with the weight machine at the gym. The females in this family were in astonishingly good shape. Even Shirley hadn't let up all day.

If it had been up to Jack, he would have unpacked only the essential stuff. These ladies not only had all the beds made and dishes in the kitchen cabinets, but books were placed on shelves, linens in closets and pictures hung on the clean white walls. Even the hummingbird feeders had been filled and twirled in the breeze off the porch eaves.

In less than a week Diana had accomplished what Richard hadn't been able to bring himself to do in eleven months. She'd given this house a much-needed face-lift and turned it into a home.

Only Mel's quiet, watchful face had brought a cloud to the day.

When the door opened, Jack turned around to see the kid coming toward him. She plopped down next to him and rubbed her palms across the knees of her sweats as she stared up at the tiny birds fighting for position at the feeders.

He had the feeling there was something specific she'd come to say. But as the quiet stretched between them, she seemed to have trouble finding the words. Not a problem he would normally associate with this kid. Maybe she was going to tell him to get lost. Again. He sipped his soft drink and waited.

When she did finally speak, her voice held none of the combative tone she'd displayed at the wedding reception. "Shirley told me a minute ago that she was the one who asked you to help us move."

Mel must have thought it was her mother's idea. No wonder she'd been giving him the cold shoulder all day.

"No consulting detective could possibly turn down a request from the inestimable Sherlock Holmes to be in on the action," Jack said.

"She doesn't do the character right," Mel said. "When Sir Arthur Conan Doyle wrote about Sherlock Holmes, he never once described him as wearing a deerstalker cap. Nor did he smoke a calabash pipe."

Didn't surprise Jack that the kid had read the stories. But it did surprise him that she showed such little affection for her great-aunt. Was it because Shirley insisted on calling her Dr. Watson?

That had to be annoying when you were nine, an age when the search for identity began to take on monumental importance. Jack could remember the rebellion he'd felt every time someone confused him with his twin while he was growing up.

"Sidney, the original illustrator of the Holmes character, drew the cap," Jack said. "And William Gillette, one of the early actors who played Holmes, selected the pipe as the prop that would neither interfere with his arresting profile nor perfect articulation.''

Mel shot a glance at him over her shoulder. "You seem to know a lot about Sherlock Holmes."

"Being aware of the backgrounds and understanding the traits of popular characters played on TV or in the movies was all part of acting."

"Why did you leave acting?"

"Because the only parts I was being offered were those of villains, and I didn't want to be labeled a villain all my life. As fun and challenging as acting can be, I need to be seen and accepted for who I am. I suspect we all have that need."

She tilted her head toward him curiously, but offered no comment.

Jack knew that the best way to put someone at ease was to introduce a subject that let them display their expertise. "About that paper you gave me to read," he began.

"I know. You've been busy."

"Actually what I was going to say is that I'm curious why you never entertained the possibility of an inborn factor being at core of Derek Dementer's villainy. He did have an institutionalized psychotic twin that you must remember my playing on several occasions."

She squinted up at him. "Derek's behavior was antisocial in many ways, but never psychotic."

"You feel confident of that?"

She nodded. "He selected highly competitive roles in society where his outward charm and inner ruthlessness would be rewarded. He was a successful politician, corporate CEO, even horse owner and racer. A psychotic— like his twin—was too out of touch with reality to be able to function at that high a level. Derek's definitive character trait was his lack of conscience."

"An inability to emotionally bond with others that left

him without remorse for his actions," Jack said, once again awed at the kid's mental acuity and communicative skills. "And you believe that formed out of his being rejected and neglected as a child. You made a compelling argument. I doubt the writers who created the character even considered him that thoroughly."

Her voice reflected surprise. "You really did read my paper."

"I told you I would. Didn't you believe me?"

She looked down at her feet, her toes wiggling beneath the soft fabric of her tennis shoes. "Sometimes people say they'll do something because they don't want to hurt your feelings or simply want you to go away."

"You get a lot of that from adults?" he asked.

She nodded. "Most adults avoid me. I make them nervous."

"They don't always know as much as you do, Mel. That scares them."

"Doesn't scare you."

He smiled. "I grew up in a pretty smart family. Got used to feeling dumb."

"You're not dumb. That's why if I know something you don't, it doesn't bother you."

Jack figured anyone that astute deserved a swig of his soft drink and offered it to her. She took a healthy gulp before returning the bottle.

"You got good grades in school, didn't you?" she asked.

"I wasn't a natural athlete like my brothers. Had to try to excel somewhere."

"In gym class last semester, all the other kids called me the klutzy geek freak. They never picked me for any of the teams."

The sadness in her tone was unexpected, as was the anger that burgeoned inside him.

"Screw 'em, Mel. Those kids are nothing but ignorant brats. You only have to look at the stupid music videos and television shows they watch to know the best they can hope to grow up to be are annoying telemarketers. You're going to grow up to be an astronaut, nuclear physicist, Nobel Prize winner—hell, absolutely anything you damn well want."

She looked at him quietly and very seriously for a moment before she smiled. "Mom sort of told me that, too, except she left out the screw 'em part."

Jack chuckled, a combination of relief, amusement and amazement at himself for having gotten so angry. "Sorry. I'm not used to talking to kids."

"Me neither."

He studied the small lift to her youthful chin, the sharp intelligence in her eyes. No, he didn't suppose she was.

She gave him a discerning look. "Do you really want to be just friends with my mom?"

That was what she had come out here to ask him.

Her concern over losing her closeness with her mother had gotten a lot clearer to Jack during the past few minutes. She had no ties to kids her own age. Her father wasn't in the picture. She no longer lived with her grandmother. And she hadn't yet—and might never—bond to her wacky great-aunt. Way she saw it, her mother was all she had.

He returned her look. "No, I don't want to be *just* friends with your mom. But I'm going to try."

After a moment she broke off eye contact and stared down at her shoes. "Thanks."

A profound sincerity echoed from the simple word. Jack felt oddly touched, although he could not have said why.

Some movement or sound caused him to glance around. Diana stood at the back door. How long she'd been there, he couldn't guess.

"A somewhat thrown together—but hopefully tasty and healthy—dinner awaits the day's intrepid workers," she said. "Anyone hungry?"

Mel jumped to her feet, more animated than he'd seen her all day. "Starved. Coming, Jack?"

"No, thanks," he said as he stood. "I'll be heading for home. Call me when you get some time on Monday, Diana. There are things we need to go over on the case."

Jack didn't wait for a response. He headed toward the driveway where he'd parked the van. Slipping onto its seat, he started the engine, then drove away without once looking back.

Because if he had looked back, he'd see Diana and change his mind about staying. That wasn't an option, not if he was going to keep his word to a worried little girl.

"THE JURY QUESTIONNAIRES ARE BACK, Jack. Do you have time to meet with me and go over them?"

Diana waited through the pause on the other end of the line. She hadn't seen Jack in more than a week. He'd sent over his time sheets and investigative notes by special messenger, keeping her apprised of his progress. But the only time they'd talked even by telephone was when she called.

She understood that he was trying to find the car Bruce had been driving on the day Amy died as well as the woman who was with him in the E.R.

She also understood that Jack was avoiding her.

"Do you want me to come there?" he asked.

"Be easier than my trying to lug all the paperwork elsewhere. We can use the conference room here to sort through them. It's free today. What's your schedule like?"

"I'll be over in fifteen minutes."

Diana hung up the phone, trying not to be excited at the thought she would soon be seeing him.

No, I don't want to be just friends with your mom. But I'm going to try.

That's exactly what he was doing, too.

Diana had overheard everything Jack had said to Mel on the porch steps. His kindness and consideration for her daughter had touched her heart. The fact that his words had not been empty but that he was living up to them meant a lot.

And made her wish he wasn't living up to them quite so well.

Shaking her head at her confusing emotions, she stacked the questionnaires onto the mail cart she'd borrowed from Kelli and wheeled it down to the conference room, trying not to spill the two cups of coffee on top.

Jack arrived a few minutes later wearing light blue jeans, a sleeveless dark blue T-shirt, a baseball cap and dark glasses. Other than the loose sweats he'd worn to help her move, Diana had only seen him in suits.

Unfortunately, these formfitting clothes gave him an even sexier look. After an appreciative moment in which her stare traveled from his flat stomach to the well-defined muscles in his exposed arms, she finally managed to lift her eyes to his.

"Casual day at the office?"

He smiled in response. "I had an early breakfast with one of Bruce's old girlfriends this morning."

Diana didn't like her reaction to that news. She sat down, infused her tone with a professionalism she did not feel. "Have a seat. Tell me all."

Taking a chair two down from hers, he removed his sunglasses and immediately reached for the coffee. Since he claimed to have had breakfast, she would have thought he'd already gotten his caffeine fix for the morning.

Then it occurred to Diana that food and drink might not have been on the breakfast menu—inasmuch as it involved one of Bruce's old girlfriends. Unaccustomed jealousy clouded her heart.

How foolish she was to feel this way. All she and Jack had ever shared was a kiss. She had no claim on him. No woman would ever have a claim on him.

"This is the ninth old girlfriend of Bruce's I've met with outside of Tina Uttley," he said. "Four of them were from the days in which he barhopped, five after he joined AA. Each tells the same story. Although he diligently pursued them, once the conquest was over, so was his ardor."

Was Jack like that as well?

Diana gave herself a mental kick. Her preoccupation with Jack's love life wasn't only stupid. It was distracting her from the case.

"Two of the women from his drinking days were married," Jack went on. "They were the most bitter when the relationship ended since they felt they had taken a big risk to be with him. Still, married or not, they both struck me as women with wandering eyes. And not even they accused Bruce of being cruel, merely emotionally uninvolved."

"Are you saying you don't think he was being cruel when he went after Connie?"

"His pursuit of Connie was cruel, but I'm beginning to doubt he meant it to be. You remember my telling you last week about Edgar Pettibone and his parrot?"

Diana nodded. "Bruce tried to give Edgar another parrot as an apology for having killed his."

The implication of what Jack was getting at hit Diana. "You can't think that Bruce intended to marry Connie as some sort of apology for having killed her child?"

"As wild as that sounds, I'm beginning to wonder. I've talked to several AA counselors while trying to track down where Bruce attended meetings. I've learned that one of the Twelve Steps in the program is to list all persons you've harmed and make amends to them.''

''But to pursue and propose marriage to Connie without loving her and with no intention of ever being faithful to her…that wasn't making amends, Jack. That was sick.''

''I agree. But Bruce might have seen it as atonement. You read Mel's paper on the character I played. Remember how she characterizes him as totally oblivious when it came to understanding the impact of his actions on others?''

''You think Bruce was like that,'' Diana guessed.

''I believe he could have been. Ever since reading Mel's paper, I've been seeing a correlation between the character I played and Bruce. Bruce may have followed the Twelve-Step program's precepts, but I seriously doubt he internalized them. He was too emotionally distant from the feelings of guilt, compassion and love to understand the impact of his behavior on others.''

Remembering Bruce's callousness toward women both drunk and sober and his ruthlessness in business, Diana thought Jack might be right.

''Did you ever find out about a history he might have had with Tina prior to her coming to work at Weaton Real Estate?'' she asked.

''When I retrieved my keys. Audrey Weaton was correct. Tina and Bruce did meet in school and both got kicked out and lost their tuition when some drunken practical joke Bruce pulled misfired. Wasn't a big deal for Bruce. His parents coughed up the fee and got him into another class. But Tina had to wait tables for another year to get enough money to reapply.''

Diana shook her head. ''Then he sobers up years later and gives her a job at his company where she becomes his handy mistress. And that's how he apologizes to her for getting her kicked out of school?''

"In his warped way, that might have seemed perfectly fine to him."

"Warped is putting it mildly."

"Diana, if you give the facts we've uncovered about Bruce to psychologists with even half of Mel's mental acuity, I think they're going to come up with the same conclusion and be able to testify to Bruce's twisted psyche on the stand."

"Your brother, David, recommended a very good psychologist to me a year ago. I've already put his name on my witness list and sent him what you've given me so far on Bruce. I'll pass along the rest and see what he says."

Jack smiled. "Should have known you'd already be on top of it."

Trying to ignore his smile and light compliment, she pushed on. "I assume you have written documentation on your interviews with Bruce's ex-girlfriends in case we need to call them to the stand?"

"Harry is typing my notes as we speak. They should all be in your hands by the end of the day."

She couldn't resist repeating his words back to him. "Should have known you'd already be on top of it."

What she read on his face made her heart race. She broke off eye contact, telling herself that he'd probably spent the night and morning with another woman.

Reaching for his coffee cup, Jack downed its contents. "Anything interesting in the returned questionnaires?"

She pushed the stack she'd already seen toward him. "I've reviewed about thirty of them. Their responses to the questions we asked about what character they'd like to play on TV or in the movies and what they would do if they won a million dollars are the most interesting."

"Any concerns?"

"The thirty-two-year-old guy who picked Hannibal Lecter as the character he'd most like to be. He didn't elaborate on the reason, but his selection of a flesh-eating psychopath is enough for me to want to disqualify him.''

''What's your favorite answer so far?'' Jack asked as he picked up the first and started to flip through it.

She sent him a grin. ''The seventy-year-old widower who says he'd like to be Derek Dementer because he got to sleep with every gorgeous female character on the show.''

Jack laughed, a wonderful hearty sound filled with such good nature it could only have sprung from a very good heart. And suddenly Diana found herself laughing along with him, no longer caring with whom he'd spent the night or morning.

She was in serious trouble.

WORK WAS what Jack needed to concentrate on for the next few weeks—if he had any hopes of keeping his cool around Diana. Seeing her after seven long days of diligently staying away made him realize how much he'd missed her.

And after seeing the way she looked at him when he arrived, it was all he could do not to take her into his arms and make love to her right on that conference table.

But he couldn't make love to her. What was nearly as depressing, he had absolutely no desire to make love to anyone else and hadn't in weeks.

''You haven't been your scintillating self lately, Jack.''

He looked over at his dad, sitting to his right at the Sunday dinner table. ''Damn. Don't tell me I forgot to take those scintillating pills again.''

Charles Knight chuckled. ''The murder case getting you down?''

Jack hacked off a piece of his steak and stabbed it with his fork. ''You kidding? This criminal stuff's a breath of fresh air. A victim I've no desire to mourn. An accused who should be getting off. It was all those civil cases you had me on that lacked civility.''

Charles watched Jack while he chewed. ''And, yet, something's turned down the dimmer switch on that light-hearted repartee you're normally regaling us with.''

''Comes from putting in a lot of hours,'' Jack said after swallowing.

''Good try, but not going to fly. You've kept me laughing through an entire dinner after twenty hours of standing out in the freezing rain filming a scene. Is it Diana Mason?''

Jack shoved more food into his mouth as a way of stalling for time.

His dad's eyes didn't move from his face. ''Richard told me she spent the day in your office.''

Jack glared at his oldest brother who was in deep conversation with their mother on the other end of the table.

''Richard's got sex on the brain, Dad.''

Charles's eyebrow raised ever so slightly. ''I was wondering whether Diana was proving difficult to please. I wasn't trying to imply there was anything between you. But since you did, there must be.''

Damn. Opened mouth, inserted foot. Guilty conscience will do it every time.

Jack put down his fork, reached for the Cabernet in the center of the table. Normally he never touched red wine because it gave him a headache. Tonight he'd welcome a headache to take his mind off another ache.

He gestured toward his father's empty glass. When Charles shook his head, Jack filled his wineglass. ''For the record, there's nothing unprofessional going on between me and Diana.''

''And you want there to be,'' his dad said without a pause.

Jack took a sip, let the warm wine slide down his throat.

When the game was up, the best thing a man could do was gracefully admit defeat. "Oh, yeah."

"Good luck, son."

Jack didn't know what he'd been expecting his dad to say, but that definitely hadn't been it. He stared into his father's quiet face.

"What, no congratulations on keeping things all business?" Jack challenged. "No cautionary tale about the dire consequences of what happens when a private investigator gets personal with a client?"

"You've kept things businesslike for your sake, not the business," his dad said astutely. "As for the dire consequences…"

Charles Knight paused to gesture down the table toward Jack's brother, David, and his new wife, Susan. "The dire consequences are staring you right in the face. You don't need me to point them out."

Jack watched the newly married pair, smiling at each other as only two mindless idiots madly in love could. A shiver shot down his spine.

When a hand clasped his shoulder, he jumped.

"Whoa, Jack," Jared said. "It's me."

Jack made an effort to sound normal. "You're late. We thought you weren't coming."

"Got tied up with a few things," his twin explained.

"Better get some food while it's hot, Jared," their dad said.

"In a minute. I need to talk with Jack first. Let's do it in the library."

Jack read his brother's pointed look and words. He excused himself from the table and followed his twin into the next room, closing the door behind them.

"I faxed the report on all the vehicles belonging to those sixty guys to your office before coming here," Jared said.

"Wasted effort, Jack. None of them owned an old car that came even close to the one Connie Pearce saw."

"You know what kind of car it was?"

"The FBI lab found a microscopic fleck of gray paint on Amy's chain that matched a fleck of paint on the drop cloth found in Bruce's garage. It's a rare paint. Only one car in their database was a fit."

"Come on, Jared. The suspense is killing me."

"A 1932 Duesenberg SJ. Nothing less than a marvel in its time. A two-and-three-fourth ton bomb that took only seventeen seconds to reach one hundred miles an hour. No doubt about its ability to rip through a flimsy front porch like the kind on Connie's Pearce's house."

"Can't be many of those cars still around," Jack said, already planning how he'd go about finding this one.

"There's more," Jared said. "Both the chain and locket had minute traces of skin and blood. The DNA matched the sample I sent from Amy Pearce's forensic evidence file. The locket Connie was holding in her hands on the day of her arrest was definitely the one Amy was wearing when the car hit her."

Jack's voice bristled with excitement. "This forensic evidence proves that the car that hit and killed Amy as well as her locket were both in Bruce's garage. Jared, this is great. We've got what we need to tie Bruce to Amy's death."

Filled with relief at the findings, it took a moment for Jack to note that his brother's expression remained solemn.

"What?" he prodded.

"When Ms. Mason puts me on the stand, I'll be able to testify to everything I've told you. But, Jack, I can't keep this under wraps any longer. I've got to tell the sheriff what I've been working on come Monday."

"Why?"

"Because this is no longer an old case that's going to

be closed and relegated to the solved file because the perp is dead. According to that E.R. doctor, the woman who was with Bruce told a deputy she was driving.''

"But that was a lie," Jack protested.

"Whether she lied is not the issue. The possibility that she was involved in the hit-and-run means she has to be found. To do that I have to openly question the deputies to see who was called down to the E.R. that day.''

Jack shook his head. "You can't. As soon as the sheriff learns what you're doing, Staker's going to know.''

"I understand this puts you in a bind, but—"

"It's not me in a bind, here. If you don't find the woman and make her tell the truth in time for Connie's trial, all we'll have is the E.R. doctor's statement. The deputy obviously believed the woman, which is why Bruce was never charged. Staker has what he needs to convince the jury that the unidentified woman was the one driving.''

"Jack, I'm not working on your case. I'm working on a hit-and-run.''

"Which you wouldn't know about if I hadn't told you. If Staker convinces the jury that Bruce wasn't responsible for the hit-and-run of Connie's child, he can spin the facts to make Bruce look like an innocent victim of Connie's revenge.''

Jared exhaled tiredly. "Look, there's a woman out there who's either committed a crime or is an accessory to one. It's my sworn duty to bring her in.''

"All I'm asking is that you do it without telling the sheriff.''

"I can't. My sending that evidence to the FBI lab for evaluation can be interpreted up to this point as simple dabbling into an unsolved crime on my free time, using friendly sources willing to do me a favor so as not to tie up our local lab. But the results of that forensic evidence coupled with the E.R. doctor's statement have changed this into an official investigation. It's my badge if I don't inform the sheriff and openly pursue this case according to the book.''

Jack told his twin where he could put his damn badge and left the room. A moment later he slammed the front door to his parents' home behind him.

As he drove away, he accepted the fact that he wasn't being fair to his brother. He didn't care.

From the first he'd seen Jared as an important extension of the defense team, which was why he'd talked Diana into putting the investigation of Amy's hit-and-run into his twin's hands. But now Jared was going to be helping the prosecution.

And it was all Jack's fault.

CHAPTER THIRTEEN

DIANA SMILED when she saw Jack waiting for her outside the jail Monday morning.

"How's Connie?" he asked as they started toward their vehicles in the lot.

"In good spirits. I dropped off some tapes of *Seattle* so she could watch them. Fran is going to set them up on the VCR and watch them, too. You have a couple of fans there."

When he shrugged without comment, concern overrode her pleasure at seeing him. "What's wrong, Jack?"

Opening his passenger door, he beckoned her inside. Once they were seated, he related the details of the conversation with Jared the evening before.

As disappointed as she was with the turn of events, she knew Jack was more so. "We'll find a way to work through it," she said simply.

"I shouldn't have brought Jared in on the case. You had reservations from the first about sharing things with him. I didn't listen."

"You did the right thing, Jack. Without Jared's help, we might not have an unbreakable chain of evidence linking Bruce to Amy's death. Nor would we have gotten the forensic information so quickly and unequivocally verified."

Jack continued to stare out the windshield, the muscles in his jaw working. "Staker's going to use that quick, unequivocal information against Connie. This gives her a much stronger motive for killing Bruce than jealousy over another woman.''

Diana hated hearing the disappointment Jack was directing at himself. She put her hand on his arm. ''If you want to know the truth, I never expected to be able to keep the facts surrounding Amy's hit-and-run from Staker even this long.''

He looked at her. ''That's not what you said at lunch the first day we discussed the case.''

''You're right. I asked you for the sun, moon and stars that day. And damn if you didn't jump to your feet, rush out and start to round them up.''

His hand closed over hers. ''You're the kind of woman who can do that to a man.''

A long moment passed in which Diana forgot everything but the man sitting beside her.

The sudden blast of a car alarm nearby dropped her back to earth. She swung toward the noise and saw an obviously frustrated man several cars away, punching on his remote control, cursing as he tried to deactivate the device.

By the time Diana turned back to Jack, his hand was no longer holding hers and he was once again looking out the window. She slipped her hand from his arm.

''You're going to have to remind me what we were talking about,'' he said.

She let out a sigh. ''As soon as I remember.''

His chuckle was riddled with far more discomfort than mirth. ''Something tells me the next few weeks are going to be the longest of my life.''

Hers, too.

''What next, counselor?'' he asked.

Cool, calm and right back to business. He had no idea what an aphrodisiac his continued restraint had become to her. Or how tempted she was to test the limits of that restraint.

"I've known all along that the real key to getting Connie acquitted is selecting the right jury," she said, forcing herself to focus on the case. "That's what we have to put our efforts on now. Tell me what I can do to help you check out the information the prospective jurors put on their questionnaires."

"Do you really have the time to assist?"

"I'll make the time. And if it requires computer searches, Mel can also lend a hand. She's a whiz on the Internet."

"What about her schoolwork?"

"Very light this summer, and she will grab at any excuse to avoid thinking about her role in the upcoming play."

"Okay, pick her up and meet me in my office with your computers. You're about to learn how to find out most anything about anyone."

"I'VE RUN the prospective jurors through the Credit Bureau, Jack," Mel said a few hours later. "There are twenty-seven with really bad credit histories. Some of them are already among the fifty-one names Mom put in the questionable file. Do you want me to cross-reference them?"

Jack glanced over at Mel sitting on the couch in his office, her computer comfortably positioned on her lap. Diana hadn't overstated her daughter's skills.

"Cross-referencing is a good idea," he told her. "Print out the file when you've finished."

Mel nodded.

"Three have criminal records," Diana said.

Jack scooted his chair next to her to read the information off her monitor. When she brought her laptop and set it on the other end of his desk, he accepted the fact that he was going to be tortured all day by having her within reach—and so unreachable.

"Ralph Montgomery's a surprise," Jack said, pointing to the record on the seventy-year-old widower who'd said he'd like to be Jack's soap character.

Ralph lived in an area the advertisers had dubbed, *Older Eclectic Intelligentsia.* As the advertisers predicted, Ralph subscribed to the *Christian Science Monitor, The Smithsonian* and drove a vintage Jaguar. His favorite books were mysteries, his favorite TV shows were *Jeopardy* and Boston Pops specials, and if he won a million dollars he'd donate it all to the local animal shelter.

Jack read over Diana's shoulder. "He yanked a rifle out of a hunter's hand and broke it over the guy's back. Seems the hunter was trying to shoot a doe and its fawn on Ralph's property two springs ago. Ralph pled guilty to assault. Was fined and given a six-month suspended sentence."

"I'm getting to like Ralph more by the minute," Diana said.

"Doesn't bother you that he answered 'no' to the question asking if he'd ever been convicted of a felony?" Jack asked.

"I doubt Ralph considered what he'd done a crime. And from a moral standpoint, I'm on his side. But this guy has me worried."

Jack followed Diana's pointing finger. "A DUI two years ago he didn't own up to? I see what you mean. He's going to identify with Bruce. And he also lists himself as a strong leader, which probably means he's a loudmouth."

"I'm adding him to the list we want excused, as well as this one," Diana said as she picked up another questionnaire. "This woman has a drug selling conviction from eight years ago she conveniently forgot to mention."

"How are you going to weed out the ones you don't want?"

"Those I catch in a lie I can get excused by the Court for cause. In addition, I have twelve peremptory challenges, which means I can get a prospective juror excused without giving a reason."

"With a hundred and fifty prospective jurors, twelve peremptory challenges don't seem like a lot."

"Which is why I have to maneuver Staker into using his peremptory challenges to excuse the others that I don't want sitting on the jury."

"Care to share how you're going to do that?"

"Give me a sec." Diana sifted through the stack of returned questionnaires until she found the one she'd been looking for. "Take this prospective juror. She's twenty-eight, collecting unemployment, doesn't read, her favorite TV shows are cartoons, and if she won a million dollars, she'd have her boobs and butt done."

"Not a lot of wattage in that light bulb," Jack agreed. "Staker's going to love her."

"But four years ago, she was a teacher's aide in a kindergarten. When I question her in *voir dire,* I'm going to ask her lots of questions about that job. And Staker's going to excuse her because those questions are going to make him worry about the possibility that she'll identify with Connie."

Jack smiled. "I'm glad you're on our team."

Despite her attempt to be cool, he knew she wasn't immune to his compliment.

In the quiet moments when she wasn't looking, he studied her, like a lovely piece of art he wanted to know very well. He could read every small lift to her lip now, every nuance in her most casual glance.

"Even with all this information, a lot will depend on luck," Diana admitted. "The court clerk draws the first sixteen names from the prospective hundred and fifty when *voir dire* begins. Those sixteen people will be the twelve regular jurors and four alternates unless they are excused for some reason.''

''What you're saying is that if the clerk draws the names of people who we feel will be good jurors, they'll be less work to do. If she draws mostly losers in the first batch, then your job will get a lot tougher.''

''In the proverbial nutshell.''

''Any other way to get an inappropriate juror excused?'' Jack asked.

''Maneuver them into admitting in court that they can't be fair. Unfortunately, the ones I'll want to remove can't— or won't—admit they're predisposed to be unfair. Some people love the sense of power that comes with judging others and deciding their fate.''

Yes, Jack had met a lot of those people. ''We've only begun on the background checks available through the Internet organizations our firm belongs to,'' he said. ''We still have professional license, education, military and employment verification, plus a dozen others before we get down to the footwork.''

''I'm finished,'' Mel said. ''What would you like me to do next?''

Jack looked at her bright, eager face. He could get to like this kid. She'd been at it for hours and not one complaint.

''Go back to the menu options and check the home and business phone numbers the prospective jurors have given us, Mel. See what name those numbers are actually listed under.''

She nodded as her fingers started to fly over the keyboard.

Jack shook his head as he turned back to Diana. ''I feel like I'm violating the child labor laws.''

''When they come to arrest you just remember to invoke your right to remain silent,'' Diana said. ''With a good attorney, you won't get more than five, six years.''

Her smile was full of fun. And to think he once thought she was lacking a sense of humor. Seemed like a century ago.

''What do you want me to do next?'' she asked.

He was very tempted to tell her. Damn good thing she'd brought Mel along. Maybe that's *why* she'd brought Mel along.

DIANA EAGERLY READ the accident reconstruction report from Jack's insurance company contact. Several days had passed since Jared had told Jack he'd have to tell the sheriff about his investigation. Yet, Staker had not notified her about the new development in his case against Connie.

The law required him to disclose such information. Clearly, he was stalling. Was he afraid that since Connie had such a very good reason to kill Bruce the jury might sympathize with her? Or was he waiting to spring the information on her right before they went to trial?

Shuffling her speculations aside, she reminded herself that the important thing was she already knew. Whatever games Staker played, she'd be prepared. In the meantime, two very good investigators were working to find the woman who had been with Bruce in the E.R. Even if Jared was unsuccessful, Diana had full confidence in Jack.

Strange, that. Jared was the trained sheriff's detective with all the power of his department behind him. But it was Jack she counted on to come through. The more she was with him, the more she was certain that he was everything he presented himself to be.

And even when she wasn't with him, he was constantly in her thoughts—interfering with her concentration. With a discipline that became more difficult to rely on with each passing day, she refocused her attention to the accident reconstruction report.

In addition to an overall summary, several diagrams had been drawn of the scene of Bruce's death from the different viewpoints of the two eyewitnesses—Lyle Weaton and Edith Lewandowski.

From the position of Bruce's body and the vehicle, the preparer's conclusion was that Connie's car had hit Bruce at an angle, showing she had tried to avoid hitting him. And in order for Connie to have come to a stop so quickly, the report also concluded that she had been braking at the time she hit Bruce. Neither of those points had been mentioned by the investigating officers.

Diana was impressed with the credentials of the man who'd prepared the report. He'd worked on the accident reconstruction team for the Las Vegas police department for fifteen years before moving to the Pacific Northwest and joining a local insurance company's staff. Staker was going to have a very hard time disputing the man's conclusions or impugning his ability to make them.

A knock sounded on the door. Diana called for whoever it was to come in. Gail poked her head inside.

"Hey, stranger."

"You're back!" Diana said, smiling as she slipped the accident report into a folder. She went to her friend and gave her a hug, only too aware of the recent emotional wear on Gail's face.

"Yeah, I know I look like hell, Diana, but I'm okay. Thanks for the flowers and the card. Can you spare some time to talk?"

"Of course. Sit down."

Gail did.

"You were the one in the family who was closest to your mom, weren't you?" Diana asked as she retook her seat.

Gail nodded. "My brothers and sister were always too busy with their families to spare much time for Mom. Last time I saw her, she asked me when I was going to start a family. I laughed and reminded her that she had nine grandkids, but only one devoted daughter. You know what she said?"

Diana shook her head.

"She said I needed to have a daughter because that's the only way I'd understand how special I made her feel."

A tear trickled out of Gail's eye. Passing a tissue to her, Diana kept one for herself.

"I'm going to have a baby."

Gail's shocking words pulled Diana straight up in her chair. The unbidden figure of a chubby, two-foot-high Staker look-alike with a thin black mustache running around the courthouse in a sagging diaper flashed through her brain. She desperately wiped the appalling image from her mind's eye.

"You're pregnant?" Diana asked with a voice somewhere in the stratosphere.

Gail shook her head. "No, but I'm going to be." She paused to let out a long, heavy exhale. "I can't believe I said that. Thirty-seven years old and not once in all that time did I ever even consider marrying, much less having a baby. My career and my freedom have always meant too much to me. But now…"

"Now you are in the throes of grief," Diana reminded in the most gentle voice she possessed. "Making such a major life decision may not be…such a wise thing."

"It's what I want," Gail said in a tone that meant the subject was closed.

Diana let out an internal sigh. Gail was the least maternal woman she knew. Not even houseplants survived in her care.

"What about the father?" Diana fished. "Have you decided who he'll be?"

"I've been seeing someone for...several months now."

"Tell me about him."

Gail squirmed on the chair. "He can be sweet. And he makes me feel so feminine. For a woman my size, believe me that's some trick. But he can also be so damn irritating and distant and annoying..."

Diana didn't need convincing.

"Thing is, I don't know what he's going to do when I tell him I want to have a baby. He and his wife didn't have any kids. Work is everything to him. No doubt the reason she divorced him a couple of years ago."

"He told you that?"

"Not in so many words. He doesn't like to talk about his marriage or himself. Rarely shares anything personal."

"Are you...comfortable with that?" Diana asked.

"What the hell. Most men are emotional clams." Gail paused to look at her sideways. "You haven't asked who he is. That would have been my first question."

"I was afraid you'd lie to me."

Gail's eyes widened as she read the expression on Diana's face. "You can't know."

"That it's, Staker?" Diana said gently.

Gail exhaled hard. "You're right. I was going to lie my head off and tell you it was an old boyfriend from college. You must hate me."

"Do I seriously question your sanity when it comes to choosing men? Most definitely. Do I hate you? Not possible."

"You're so damn nice."

"Damn nice of you to notice," Diana said smiling.

Gail sank back in her chair, looking a hell of a lot better than when she'd first knocked on Diana's door. Getting rid of an ugly secret could have an amazing effect on a woman's complexion.

"How did you learn about me and George? We've been so careful."

"You knew he had political aspirations and that you were next in line for chief prosecutor should he be elected judge. And yet you left the prosecutor's office to take a position here at Kozen and Kozen without even getting the junior partnership they promised you in writing. There had to have been a compelling reason for you to have thrown away such an important career opportunity."

Diana had deliberately implied that she'd figured all this out independent of seeing Gail and Staker together in the park and overhearing their conversation. The last thing she wanted to do was admit to having eavesdropped and embarrass Gail by the other things she'd overheard. What lovers did together was private.

Gail sighed. "Do you know how strict the county guidelines have become against colleagues dating?"

"No, but I figured you were caught in something like that."

"When George and I first realized what we were feeling for each other, we knew if we did anything about it, both of us would be in danger of losing our jobs."

"And you left so he'd no longer be your boss."

Gail nodded.

"But you're on the other side of the legal fence now. Isn't it hard not discussing cases?"

"Since I don't get to choose my cases, George agreed to hand off the prosecution on any case I'm asked to defend."

Diana had already noted that trend. But the other possibilities still nagged at her since the question of the leak had yet to be resolved. "Aren't you tempted to pass on things you overhear about other cases at the firm?"

"We decided from the beginning not to talk shop. If we hadn't, we would have broken up long ago. George can be so rigid. Once he gets an idea in his head, there's no reasoning with him. Even when we used to be on the same side of a case, he drove me up the wall."

A frustrated honesty rang from Gail's words. Diana no longer worried that her friend was the leak at Kozen and Kozen—if indeed there was a leak at all.

"I worked for George for nearly nine years, Diana. If you had asked me how I felt about him during most of that time, I would have said he was nothing but an arrogant SOB. But something happened a little over a year ago when we were working together on a case. I can't explain it. I only know that now...now I love him."

Diana wanted to ask what she could possibly find that was lovable about the man. She didn't. Love wasn't something that could be explained. She'd fallen in love with Mel's dad—a self-centered bastard if there ever was one.

"How does Staker feel about you?" she asked.

"He's told me he loves me and that I'm the only woman he'll ever want."

Remembering Staker's preoccupation lately, Diana began to wonder whether his personal life with Gail might be at the core.

"Of course, the Kozen brothers are never going to give me that junior partnership when I get pregnant."

"They can't discriminate against you because you decide to have a baby," Diana protested.

Her friend's head shake was that of the wise, experienced woman. "They'll find another excuse. These good old boys always do. But you know what? I don't care. From the day I got here I've worked nearly every night, volunteered to be on call every weekend, billed more hours than any other attorney at the firm. And all for the promise of that partnership. Now I'm putting the baby first."

Gail ran her hands through her short hair. "You know what surprises do to George. This one is going to blow him away. Any suggestions on when or how I should tell him?"

Diana was delighted Gail was asking for her advice on this. "How about in the courthouse right before he's ready to prosecute the Pearce case?"

For the first time since Gail had come into her office she laughed like her old self.

"WHY ARE WE DOING THIS, Jack?" Mel wanted to know.

For several days, Diana and Mel had spent most of their free time assisting him on Internet searches to gain background on the prospective jurors. They'd learned everything they could through electronic means.

"Because we've come to the hands-on part of our investigation," Jack said.

"I didn't know part of being a private investigator was becoming a trash collector," Mel said, her nose twitching as though she already smelled something bad.

Jack could see Diana's smirk as she stuffed envelopes.

"White Knight Investigations has had a long-standing agreement with the City of Silver Valley," he explained. "Periodically, we substitute for the regular trash collectors and perform a recycling service. All it takes is labeling the sides of our van with the words, *Neighborhood Recycle*."

"And you actually drive around and pick up trash?"

"Even wear a uniform. Of course, since we do it at no cost, we get to select the neighborhoods where we pick up the trash."

"I don't understand how this is going to help Connie's case," Mel said.

"When I collect the trash from the prospective jurors next Tuesday morning, I'll learn things about them available through no other means."

Mel thought about that a moment as she folded a circular and handed it to Diana for stuffing into the next envelope. "You're going to go through their trash?"

"Every scrap," Jack said as began affixing another roll of pre-printed labels on the next set of envelopes. "What people throw out can tell you things about them that not even their best friends know."

"It's not against the law to snoop into their stuff?"

"First of all, we're not snooping," Jack said as he handed the finished envelopes to Diana to keep their production line going. "We're investigators trying to ascertain whether someone possesses the necessary intelligence and understanding to decide the fate of another human being—a very nice human being, I might add. Second, according to the law, whatever someone throws away is no longer 'their stuff.' It's trash and, as such, can be picked up and used by someone else. I'm going to use it to find out about them."

"But aren't you misleading them when you say that you want them to separate out their paper so it can be recycled?" Mel persisted.

"Not at all. Once I'm finished looking through the important stuff, I'll be taking the trash to the dump and the recyclable items to the recycle center."

"What if they don't separate their trash as the circular asks?"

"Then I'll know two things," Jack said. "One, they are not the kind of people who will take the time to help clean up the environment. And, two, I'm going to have to wear a really thick mask and gloves going through their trash trying to obtain more clues about them."

Mel's lips curved into a smile at the image. "Can I help you pick up the stuff next Tuesday and go through it?"

Last thing he expected was that. Jack glanced at Diana

for some clue as to how to answer Mel's question, but she was giving all her attention to stuffing envelopes.

"I won't simply be picking up trash on Tuesday, Mel. I will *be* a trash collector. To be believable, I have to immerse myself in the part. Trash collectors—even those involved in a neighborhood recycling project—don't have nicely combed hair or respond to questions in well-formed sentences. I'll have on a scraggily wig, long sideburns, be unshaven and wearing overalls that have old stains on them. But more importantly, I'll be projecting the attitude of a simple man whose greatest joys in life are a six-pack of cold beer, watching sports on a big-screen TV and one day bowling two-fifty."

"You could be married, and I could be your daughter. The man you're portraying would want his child involved in doing something good for the community, right?"

"What makes you want to pretend to be a trash collector when you balk at performing a far more sophisticated role in the gifted children's program?"

"All I do is die in the play. Here I can be part of the action and do something that's real and important."

She didn't give up easily. Jack appreciated a tenacious spirit—and a kid who went after what she wanted with logic, not whines. "You'd have to wear stained overalls, old shoes, gloves that fit and be ready to really work."

"I have old clothes and gloves. I'm not afraid to work."

No, she wasn't. "Can you be ready to go at 5:00 a.m. Tuesday?"

Mel nodded eagerly.

"When you pass out from garbage fumes, are you going to get your mother to sue me?"

She giggled as she shook her head.

He shrugged with all the dramatics at his disposal. "Well, all right. But if I decide to drag you to a fast-food restaurant for lunch afterward, you don't squeal on me to your mother, and I get to eat your French fries with all the bad fat in them. Deal?''

Mel's smile was the biggest he'd seen. ''Deal.''

He nodded, looked down at the labels in his hands, concentrated on affixing them to the next batch of envelopes. Out of the corner of his eye, he could see the smile on Diana's lips. It warmed him in places he never realized existed.

CHAPTER FOURTEEN

JACK FOUND Craig Sutherland at the city's Maintenance downtown courtyard, eating lunch. The man was visibly startled when Jack showed him his private investigator's business card. His unease grew with Jack's first question.

"A person in AA has a strict right to privacy, Knight," he said with obvious irritation. "How did you even know about me?"

"You've told your boss and all your co-workers you're in AA. You've petitioned the court for joint custody of your kids based on nearly five years of sobriety. Didn't strike me that you were trying to keep your membership a secret."

Sutherland shoved his runny jelly sandwich on moldy bread into the brown paper bag on his lap. "What do you want?"

"To start with, some general information," Jack said. "Step Five in the Twelve-Step recovery program is admitting to another the exact nature of an alcoholic's wrongs, isn't that correct?"

"Why are you asking me if you already know?"

Jack ignored the man's irritated tone. "I understand that when most alcoholics get to Step Five, they select someone within the program in whom to confide rather than a psychologist or counselor because they believe that only another alcoholic can truly appreciate what they're going through. Is that how it was with you?"

Sutherland wiped his sticky hands on wrinkled jeans. "That's my business."

Jack had hoped the man would cooperate. Now he knew only a hard line was going to work. "You were Bruce Weaton's confidant and he was yours."

"No, you're—"

"There's no point in denying this, Sutherland. You and Bruce attended meetings on the same night, sat together, left together. I not only know you were his confidant, I also know you're back to drinking. I showed your picture to the clerk at the liquor store around the corner from your apartment. He tells me you've become a regular customer over the past three months."

"Please, you can't tell my ex-wife," he said in the voice of a man suddenly ready to sell his soul. "I'm begging you. I'll give you anything I have. My kids mean everything to me. I can't lose my chance to be with my kids."

"You threw away that chance when you started drinking again."

"No, you don't understand. I've got it under control. I only drink a little at night to relax me when I get home."

"You're lying to yourself, Sutherland. No alcoholic ever has his drinking under control. You're going to lose your kids, your job, everything you worked so hard to get back."

Sutherland's head and shoulders drooped. The brown sack fell out of his lap onto the ground. He covered his face with his hands and sobbed.

Jack felt like a schoolyard bully beating up on a sick kid. Still, for Sutherland's sake—as well as everyone else's—he had to do this. He waited until the man had regained some composure before continuing.

"You have one chance."

Sutherland's head lifted. The defeat on his face was so oppressive, Jack flinched inside.

"What do you want?"

"You're going to tell your boss that a family emergency requires you leave immediately and take the two weeks vacation coming to you," Jack said. "As soon as you've talked to your boss, you're going to call this man at this number and give him your name."

Sutherland took the card Jack held out to him.

"The man is my brother and is a trained psychologist. He's going to get you into a very private and intense alcoholic recovery program that takes place out on a secluded island in the West Sound. The boat for that island leaves this afternoon. You'll be on it."

"I can't afford a—"

"All of your expenses in the program are covered. During the next two weeks, you *will* live the life of a sober man. You will also learn things that not even AA has been able to teach you. When the two weeks are up, you'll attend AA meetings for the rest of your life and remain sober. Because I'll be keeping tabs on you. And if you so much as sniff another drink, I'll contact your ex-wife and give her everything she needs to make sure you never see your kids again."

Sutherland looked at the card in his hands and then at Jack. "You're not going to tell her I went back to drinking?"

"Not if you grab this opportunity to get sober for good."

The man stared at Jack in disbelief. "Why are you doing this for me?"

"I'm part of Connie Pearce's defense team."

Sutherland started.

"Yes," Jack said. "I'm fighting for that young woman's life. Bruce told you all about Connie when he confessed the wrongs he had done to her. By keeping silent, you have harmed her as well. You're going to come forward now and make that right.''

''I can't. We pledge never to reveal—''

''Your pledge to Bruce died with him, Sutherland. You're on Step Eight now. It's time to make amends to your kids by getting sober and giving them back their father. And it's time to make amends to Connie Pearce by telling her attorney everything Bruce told you.''

''You mean now?''

Jack stood. ''Right now. We'll meet with Connie's attorney as soon as you see your boss and make that call to my brother.''

Jack bent down to pick up the leaky sack at his feet. He dumped its disgusting contents into the nearby garbage container where it belonged. ''On the way there, I'll buy you a decent lunch.''

As soon as Diana had received Jack's call that he was on his way to his office with Craig Sutherland in tow, she grabbed her briefcase and headed there to meet them. When she arrived, she found that Harry had set up a video camera in Jack's office. She appreciated Jack's foresight in arranging for a visual and auditory record.

To make sure Sutherland understood the gravity of the situation, Diana brought along a Bible and asked him to place his hand on it. When he did, she swore him in exactly as a court reporter would have done in a formally recorded deposition.

Sutherland raised a shaky hand and promised to tell the truth. She asked him to repeat his name for the record, and he did so.

''Mr. Sutherland, please describe your relationship with Bruce Weaton.''

''We met nearly five years ago at a general AA meeting. You only give your first name at the meetings, but I recognized Bruce. He'd sold my sister and her husband a house. I sat next to him, glad to know someone. We talked, helped each other out.''

''In what way?'' Diana asked.

''I joined AA because the court ordered me to if I wanted to see my kids again. But it was…hard. Dropout is highest in the first few weeks. Admitting to the problem, putting it in the hands of a higher power—none of that stopped the cravings. You have to distract yourself. Bruce and I, we…used the same distraction.''

''What was that distraction?''

''Women. Bruce knew a lot of them. When things got rough, sometimes we'd talk, but most of the time, he'd get on the phone and have a couple come over. They weren't prostitutes. At least they never asked me for any money or anything.''

''You used sex as a way of keeping your mind off alcohol?''

Sutherland nodded. ''It worked.''

''Other than that…distraction, did you and Bruce do anything else together?'' she asked.

''Not much outside attending the AA meetings a couple of nights a week,'' Sutherland said. ''Truth is, he could be downright cold at times. Not that I was always in the best of moods.''

''How do you mean cold?''

''Well, like the time I told him how hard it was for me when my wife walked out and took the kids. He laughed. Said I was being stupid. Said there were plenty of other women out there that I could have kids with if I wanted.''

''He expected you to forget your feelings for your wife and children?'' Diana asked.

Sutherland shrugged. ''Some guys don't have the stomach to listen to another guy spilling his guts. Maybe Bruce wanted me to shut up. Which I did. Anyway, when the time came for Step Five, we were comfortable enough with each other to get into that baggage.''

''Would you explain Step Five, please?'' Diana asked.

''It's the one where we're supposed to admit to ourselves and another human being the exact nature of our wrongs.''

''What were the things that Bruce told you?''

''He admitted to having wronged several people, Ms. Mason. The biggest wrong was to Connie Pearce.''

When the man paused, Diana leaned forward as encouragement for him to go on. ''Please tell me what he said.''

Sutherland exhaled a long breath as though he were releasing something buried deep inside him. ''Bruce was driving drunk five years ago. He lost control of his vehicle, went over the curb and killed Connie's little girl.''

''Bruce admitted he was drunk, he was driving and that he killed Connie's child?'' Diana repeated, careful to make sure all points were clear.

Sutherland nodded. ''Of course, he didn't know whose kid it was at the time. He lit out of there fast. Later, when he listened to the news report, he learned her name.''

''Did he mention if anyone was in his vehicle with him at the time he killed the girl, Mr. Sutherland?''

The man shook his head.

''Did he say anything about where he'd gotten the vehicle he was driving?''

Again, a shaking head. ''Bruce didn't share a lot about the specifics, only related the bare facts. Whatever feelings he had, he kept to himself. But he did say that killing the little girl was what had forced him into joining AA.''

''Forced him?'' Diana repeated.

''Someone else knew what he did. He never told me who or how they knew. But I got the impression that if he hadn't joined AA and stayed sober, that someone would have turned him in for having killed that girl.''

"Once you knew about the crime, didn't you feel an obligation to report what Bruce had done?''

Sutherland squirmed in his chair. "You've got to understand, Ms. Mason. Step Five in AA is like talking to your pastor. Everything that's said is secret. Keeping that secret is like a sacred thing. If it weren't, no one would be honest and confess their wrongs. Even now that Bruce is dead, I still feel like I'm betraying a solemn oath by telling you.''

Diana nodded, letting the man know she understood and sympathized with his discomfort. Giving support to a person's feelings cost nothing.

"Mr. Sutherland, I understand that Step Eight in the program is listing all persons who have been harmed and making amends to them. Do you know how Bruce Weaton planned to make amends to Connie Pearce for having killed her child?''

"No, but I do know he was never going to turn himself in,'' Sutherland said.

"He told you that?''

Sutherland nodded. "Said that would be stupid because it couldn't bring the kid back. I didn't argue with him. Each of us has to make restoration in our own way. But, I swear to God, the last thing I ever expected of him was suicide.''

"Suicide?''

"Well, what would you call romancing the woman whose child you'd killed and then letting her know what you did?''

But Bruce hadn't let Connie know. He'd kept it a secret from her.

Unless he left Amy's locket in his garage so Connie would find it? Unless he deliberately ran in front of her car trying to get her to kill him? Had Bruce set Connie up to kill him in retribution for killing her daughter?

No, Diana rejected the idea. Everything she'd learned about Bruce revealed a man out of touch with feelings of real remorse. He was too cold and ruthless for her to buy the suicide theory.

Jack's suggestion that Bruce had planned to marry Connie as a way of making amends made more sense in light of the guy's twisted psyche. Except, that didn't feel quite right to Diana, either.

She had the strong sense she was missing an obvious explanation. What in the hell was it?

Well, at least she now had confirmation that Bruce—not the woman who had brought him into the E.R.—was driving the vehicle that killed Amy. Sutherland's testimony along with the forensic evidence would be enough to convince the right jury, no matter how Staker tried to twist the facts.

Finding Craig Sutherland had been integral to establishing that aspect of her case. Jack had come through for her, as she knew he would.

"SO, TELL ME ABOUT this role you don't want to perform," Jack said as he and Mel drove toward the first address on their trash pickup list Tuesday morning.

"Five of us are panelists on this TV game show, only we're not people. I'm Matter. The other four represent the fundamental forces of the universe—the strong Interaction force, Electromagnetic force, Weak force and Gravitational force."

"Interesting. You wrote this play, Mel?"

"The idea and basic content, but the director has made a lot of changes."

"They always do. What's the plot?"

"During Act One, we panelists answer questions about

ourselves that are actually clues to who will be murdered, how and by whom. Since I'm Matter, my answers hint at my being created out of unstable elements. I collapse at the end of the first act. The really good part comes in Act Two when the murderer is unmasked, and I'm not even on stage.''

Jack understood her disappointment. He'd felt it more than once himself.

''Mel, have you ever wondered why storytelling is so popular?''

She shook her head.

''Whether writer or performer, we have the power to create an imaginary world so full of interesting ideas and feelings that others can't wait to share it. When you're able to entice an audience into entering your world, you connect with them in a way that's magical.''

''You've felt that way?''

''Even with some of the smallest roles I was given.''

''How?''

''By putting *all* of myself into those roles and making them as real for me as they were for the audience.''

She was quiet a moment before asking, ''Will you come with me to rehearsal this Saturday and show me how?''

He'd been trying to share some truths with the kid that would make her feel better about her part. He hadn't expected to be roped into giving acting lessons. ''I don't know, Mel. Things are pretty—''

''Busy,'' she completed before he could. ''It's okay. I understand.''

If she had said the words with pique or self-pity, he would have happily let the matter drop. But the damn kid really did sound like she understood and accepted.

''All right, I'll be there,'' Jack said. ''But you have to give me your word of honor that you won't grow up to be a professional actress. Your mother would kill me.''

Mel's giggle was rich with delight, a sound so much nicer to hear than her earlier disappointment.

"JUROR NUMBER SEVENTEEN CUT OUT a story about Connie's upcoming trial that ran this week," Shirley announced as she held up the newspaper sheet with the telling hole. "Since she lives alone that can only mean she's following the case in direct defiance of the judge's admonition to stay away from all media reports."

"Well done, Holmes," Jack said, meaning it.

The four of them sat in a circle on the living room floor at Baby Lane, sorting through the trash that Jack and Mel had picked up that morning from the homes of their prospective jurors. Whether it was part of her mental capacity or part of the persona of her fictional character, Shirley continued to impress him with her uncanny ability to make sense out of the discarded debris.

"What does our psychological profile show on this juror so far?" Diana asked.

Mel picked up the sheet for juror number seventeen. "She's in her early sixties, four times divorced, three adult children—all who have moved to other states—and five grandchildren, none of whom she's allowed to see according to a note of complaint she wrote on her questionnaire. She's a retired auditor from the county assessor's office, would like to be a judge on Court TV, and if she won a million dollars, she'd buy a nice casket and burial plot since she knows none of her ungrateful children will do it when she goes."

Diana shook her head as she stretched out her legs. "A very unhappy, judgmental person. Mark her file as one to be excused."

Jack pulled his eyes away from the enticing sheen of bare skin before him.

When Diana had arrived home late from the office,

she'd changed into shorts and T-shirt before joining them. Her clothing was appropriate for the very warm temperatures that had arrived with the muggy afternoon skies. But it wasn't helping Jack's rising blood pressure.

Which was why he'd deliberately chosen to sit with the firm barriers of Mel and Shirley between them.

"Jack, I think I've found something, too," Mel said as she passed him a treasure from their hunt.

Mel's voice had been high with excitement all day. What surprised Jack wasn't so much that the kid had enjoyed herself, but that he had actually enjoyed having her along. She'd worked hard and hadn't complained once, not even when he'd given her the task of going through the nonpaper trash to make note of food consumption choices of the prospective jurors.

"So what's significant about this receipt from Barnes and Noble?" Jack asked as he glanced at the sheet she had handed him, pretty sure he knew what she was getting at, but wanting to give her the chance to say it.

"The book titles. This juror has purchased four books on how to deal with and survive cancer. I think he's sick."

"Does he live alone?" Jack asked.

Mel took a moment as she referred to the man's questionnaire. "He's forty-seven, divorced, his address is an apartment and his only son lives in Massachusetts."

"Are there any other concerns we've noted about him?" Diana asked.

Mel shook her head.

"His illness doesn't disqualify him in my mind, if he feels well enough and chooses to serve," Diana said.

"Will you ask him about being ill in *voir dire*?" Jack asked.

She shook her head. "If he doesn't volunteer the information, it will remain his business. I'm only interested in matters that might interfere with someone rendering a fair verdict.''

"Speaking of fairness," Shirley said, "I think you need to take a look at these.''

Jack accepted the two stubs she'd handed him, but puzzled over their significance a moment before it finally hit him. "These stubs are from Staker's political fund-raiser last week.''

Shirley's nod was that of a pleased professor for a bright student. Jack smiled at her before turning to Diana. "That political fund-raiser was by invitation only, right?''

"And cost five hundred dollars a plate," Diana confirmed. "Who's the juror, Holmes?''

Shirley picked up the label that had been affixed to the plastic bag. "Number one hundred and two.''

Mel opened the binder that contained the prospective jurors' returned information. "Number one hundred and two claims here that he has never heard of Staker. He's the financial officer at a local bank. Married. Two kids. Ages ten and twelve.''

"Since the kids obviously didn't attend that fund-raiser," Diana said, "the Mr. and Mrs. must have. Not only has this guy lied about knowing Staker, he obviously wants on the jury so he can support Staker by convicting Connie.''

"When Staker sees him in the jury box, he'll have to excuse him," Jack said.

"If he recognizes the guy," Diana said. "I understand that a thousand invitations were mailed out for that fund-raiser and close to four hundred people showed up. If this guy is trying to get on the jury panel quietly, I doubt he's made himself known to Staker.''

"What are you going to need to expose him?'' Jack asked.

"A list of the attendees to that fund-raiser," Diana said. "Can you get it?"

"Give me a day or two," Jack said. The smile she sent him was worth whatever trouble it was going to take.

"You were right when you said we could check to see if jurors filled out their questionnaires honestly. Between the Internet searches and this trash pickup, there's a wealth of information available. Can I get you on retainer to perform these tasks on all my trials?"

"As long as the deal includes your daughter's help," Jack said.

Mel sent him a pleased grin. "Jack nearly got into a fist fight with this one guy who wasn't on our list, but insisted we take his trash anyway. Then this raccoon leaped out of a garbage can and landed right on Jack's shoulder, making him jump a foot. And this huge dog chased Jack up the block. And—"

"Sounds like *you* had a lot of fun," Diana said to her daughter.

"It was certainly productive," Shirley announced.

Jack looked over to see Shirley holding up a piece of paper.

"What is it?" Diana asked.

"Ruth Vinter, prospective juror number sixty-four, listed her profession as clergy, but this pay stub in her trash clearly shows she's a driving instructor at the local high school," Shirley said.

"If she makes her living teaching teenagers how to drive, she probably needs to pray a lot," Diana said with a smile. "What character did she pick to play on TV or in the movies?"

"Oprah because she has such a good heart."

"Great answer," Diana said. "Flag Ruth's file and I'll clarify the employment point with her if she winds up in the jury box."

They continued sorting for a few more minutes before Mel let out an audible yawn. Diana checked her watch. "Past your bedtime, Cute Stuff."

Jack wasn't surprised when Mel didn't protest. She'd been up since dawn and was pretty sensible for a kid. After stacking the last of the papers on her lap into a neat pile, she stood.

"I, too, must retire," Shirley said as she got to her feet. "Tomorrow will prove another busy day perusing these clues. Come, Hound."

Diana called a good-night to Shirley as her aunt started toward the stairs, the cat dogging her feet.

Mel gave her mom a hug and a kiss on the cheek. When she walked by Jack, she stooped and gave him a quick hug. Jack was so startled he nearly fell back on the floor. As he watched her disappear up the stairs after Shirley, he shook his head in bona fide bewilderment.

"Well, now, that's a first," Diana said, sounding as astonished as he felt.

Jack looked over to see her smiling at him. "Does *every* female you meet succumb to your charm?" she asked lightly.

The meaning inherent in her words immediately tightened every muscle in Jack's body.

"Have you, Diana?" he asked, not lightly at all.

Her eyes dropped to the papers on her lap. "Time to call it a night."

That had been a polite way of closing the subject and asking him to leave. A sensible man would have taken the hint. But Jack didn't feel particularly sensible at the moment.

What he felt he could no longer ignore.

"Diana?"

When she looked up, the expression on her face was all he needed to see. The next instant he was beside her on the floor, right beside her, drinking in her scent—already dangerously close to the edge.

"Jack, we want very different things from life."

Her words were full of sense, but her skin was flushed and her voice breathless.

"Diana, right now what I want more than anything is to kiss you. And I'm going to if you don't tell me to get lost or beat me off with something. There's a heavy binder on the floor in front of you and a fireplace poker to your right. Words or weapons—choose quickly. You have three seconds."

She didn't waste a one of them. With an inarticulate murmur, she pulled him to her.

IT WAS RAINING SOFTLY, the kind of summer rain that made no sound. As Diana gazed out her open bedroom window, she could see the silky curtain of beaded drops caught in the muted moonlight. She inhaled the heady scent and sighed.

Jack's arm held her firmly against the hard curve of his body. "You smell so good," he said as he kissed the back of her neck. "Better than the rain, than summer, than a man's deepest dreams."

Her spine tingled. Heaven couldn't feel any better than this.

How they'd gotten to her bed was a blur. But everything they'd done here would forever be embedded in her memory. Jack was the kind of lover most women only got to dream about—so totally focused on giving pleasure that her tiniest movement or sound was responded to as though it were his own.

No guy should be this good. How could a woman ever be satisfied with anyone else?

"What's wrong?" he asked as he nuzzled her ear.

"Why do you think something's wrong?"

''Your sigh had a sadness to it.''

He could sure read her all right.

She'd become what she'd promised herself she would never be—one of Jack's women. Asking him where their relationship was going was unnecessary. She already knew. From the first, he'd told her he was a confirmed bachelor.

They were going nowhere.

''What now, Jack?''

Heaven help her, she'd asked anyway.

''I can't go back to just being your friend,'' he said. ''Even if I wanted to. And I definitely don't want to.''

An evasion of the real question she'd asked. Maybe that was kinder than honesty. Maybe she should shut up and take what he had to give. Even she heard the sadness in her sigh that time. So much for all her bold self-talk.

''Diana?''

''It's almost two, Jack. I'm not comfortable with Mel finding out that we've…you've spent the night.''

''I'll be out of here soon,'' he promised in a heated whisper against her ear. ''But first…''

Even if she had wanted to resist, there wasn't a cell in her body that would have let her. Not when the hard perfection of his body was so close and his eager, expert hands were already claiming her as his.

IT WAS AFTER FIVE in the morning when Jack pulled the van he'd used for trash pickup the previous day into the large garage behind the White Knight Investigation offices. He parked the vehicle, turned off the engine and sat for a moment in the quiet darkness.

He'd been greedy and selfish keeping Diana awake all night. But he couldn't help himself. If she didn't have a daughter in the house, he'd still be in bed with her, and in a few hours, doing everything in his power to convince her to call in sick to work.

But she did have a daughter in the house—a daughter he'd made a promise to. He'd broken that promise, as well as the one he'd made to himself—a promise not to get involved with a woman who had a child.

We want very different things from life.

Diana was right. Making love to her had been a mistake. But it was a mistake he intended to go right on making.

Jack huffed in frustration as he got out of the van. He started stripping off the sign that identified it as part of a neighborhood recycling program.

The van was a multipurpose vehicle. Depending on the sign they put on the sides, it could pass for a delivery truck, utility vehicle, or assume any number of other handy camouflages a private investigator might need on a case. After he removed the sign, Jack would give it a good wash inside and out to get rid of any lingering odor.

"The lady must be special," a familiar voice said suddenly. "You almost stayed for breakfast."

Jack started, and turned to smile into the warm gray eyes that greeted him. He walked over to his mother, gave her a hug. Alice Knight had an unbeatable knack for sniffing out a secret. Of course, his returning the van at this time of the morning was a dead giveaway he'd been too busy the night before to attend to it.

"What has you up so early?" he asked.

"Richard's been on an all-night surveillance. I'm going to take over the watch for a few hours to give him a break. Tell me about Diana Mason."

Oh, no. Jack wasn't going to let a guilty conscience trip him up again. His answer was delivered in neutral tones. "Very intelligent. Ethical. She's doing her best to do right by her client."

Alice smiled. "Like her that much, do you?"

"What do you mean?" Jack asked.

"This is the first time you've failed to tell me how beautiful a woman is that you're interested in."

"What makes you think I'm interested in Diana?"

"Your oh-so-careful attempt to sound so uninterested," Alice said on her way to the old pickup in the corner. "Please call Jared and straighten out whatever it is that has you two not talking."

Jack didn't bother to ask his mother how she knew he and Jared weren't talking. Keeping a secret from anyone in his family was clearly an exercise in futility.

"Why couldn't I have been born to acrobats or musicians or safe crackers?" he asked the roof.

His mother's laughter sang out in the darkened garage.

DIANA HAD NO SOONER WALKED IN the door of Kozen and Kozen the next morning when Gail pulled her into her office and closed the door.

"He's getting it on with our clerk," Gail said, her tone both angry and sad.

Recognizing the hurt beneath her friend's words, Diana figured out what Gail was referring to. "Staker and Kelli are having an affair?"

Gail nodded as she paced the office, her movements jerky, her hands fists at her sides. "I dropped by to talk to him about the baby thing yesterday after work. When he didn't answer the door, I used the key under the doormat and went inside to leave him a note. I was writing it when he and Kelli came in the back door and walked right past the study on the way to the bedroom. She was pulling his shirt off, her blouse already gone. They were so... involved they didn't even see me."

Diana let out a sad sigh for her friend.

"I gave up my job for him. I was ready to have a baby with him. And all the time he was..."

Tears spilled out of Gail's eyes. Diana walked over to her friend and put her arms around her. "Staker's not worth one of your tears, Gail. He never was. Your first impression of him was right. He's a bastard."

"I thought he'd changed."

"There are two theories about how a woman can change a man," Diana said. "Neither works."

"I'm such a fool."

Diana understood the feeling. At the moment, only too well. "From the age of puberty until they plant us six feet under, the females of our sorry species are subject to all the slings and arrows of outrageous romantic fortune. And not even the strongest, smartest and sanest among us are spared."

"Kelli's been taken in as well," Gail said. "I found a birthday card George sent her stashed in the bottom drawer of her desk. Lying bastard gave her the same line about loving her, and never wanting any woman but her."

"He's used Kelli, too."

"And she's used us. Kelli's our office leak."

"That's why she was always in our offices, ostensibly to replenish supplies."

Gail nodded. "I even had to ask her to leave once when I was discussing confidential matters over the phone. But it wasn't until after I saw her with George that I got suspicious and came back here to break into Kelli's computer files."

"When did you become a computer hacker?"

"A guy I prosecuted a couple of years ago gave me a few pointers," Gail said nonchalantly. "Kelli sent George what she overheard or read on our cases through an online e-mail account in which she identified herself simply as 'a friend.'"

"Are you saying she sent the information anonymously?"

Gail nodded. "Since she was careful not to use our office e-mail address, he probably doesn't know she's the one sending him the stuff."

"Gail, he's got to know."

"He might think it's me," Gail said in a small voice.

"But you didn't compromise your ethics—not even for love."

"My one solace in this whole sorry mess. I gave Ronald and Vincent all the evidence when they got in this morning. They confronted Kelli, and she admitted to the affair, but swore George didn't know who was sending him the information. They dismissed her quietly. Won't press charges for fear of bad publicity. The locks to the doors will be rekeyed by the end of today."

"Do the Kozens know you were intimate with Staker?"

"No, I spun them a yarn about becoming suspicious after seeing Kelli in George's car last evening. Ronald thanked me for proving there really was an office leak and allowing him to plug it. They swore me to secrecy, but I had to tell you."

Gail's voice broke on the last word. Diana wrapped an arm around her friend's waist. "What we need is some coffee and a couple of chocolate bars I have stashed here in my shoulder bag. We are going to gorge ourselves and plot revenge on that two-faced, two-timing, slimy son of a slug."

Gail wiped her eyes. "What kind of revenge?"

"For starters, bright and early tomorrow morning you're going to march into his office, tell him you're pregnant, you've decided to have the baby, and then enjoy watching him fall out of his chair."

Gail's lips lifted a fraction as she mulled over the image. "We did forget to use protection once last month. He might fall for it."

"Make sure you leave before he can ask any questions

and don't answer any of his calls,'' Diana cautioned. "Let him sweat blood for a few weeks. When you finally allow him to corner you, casually tell him not to worry. It's someone else's.''

"He'll flip,'' Gail said, her face suddenly alight with anticipation. "The two-timing bastard has a jealous streak a mile wide. What next?''

Good. Gail was getting into the spirit of things. She'd taken a first step on the long road to mending a broken heart. Good thing Diana was re-familiarizing herself with the journey. A sinking feeling told her she'd be taking those steps soon herself.

She led the way to the door. "There are so many options it boggles the mind. Let's go get that coffee to go with our chocolate. My best plotting always comes after the proper brain stimulation. What do you want to do about the baby now?''

"You think I'd force an innocent child into a relationship with a piece of slime that has the gall to call itself a man? No way I'm having a baby.''

For her friend's sake, Diana was relieved. Motherhood was not something to be entered into in grief or anger or any emotion—save love.

CHAPTER FIFTEEN

"THIS IS JUDGE WEATON. If you want to talk to me before the trial, it will have to be now."

Diana had called Judge Weaton twice at her office after she'd promised an interview on the news. Each time Diana had left both her office and home numbers. But she never expected a call at her home at midnight.

"Did you hear me, Ms. Mason?"

"Yes, Your Honor. But it's late and—"

"I will be at Clare's all-night Coffee Shop across from the courthouse in forty-five minutes. Your next opportunity to ask me questions will be in court."

Dial tone blared in Diana's ear. This was how Barbara Weaton was going to satisfy her promise. Diana should have guessed after the way Lyle and Audrey had acted. There was no way she could get a court reporter this late. She bit back her irritation as she tore off her nightgown and jumped out of bed.

Racing to the closet for some clothes, she punched in Jack's home number. When his deep voice answered after the first ring, relief streamed through her. He listened to her hurried explanation and plan, and without a moment's hesitation said he'd arrange it.

As she tossed the cordless phone onto a chair and reached for her slacks, Diana tried to count her blessings.

*He's a first-rate private investigator and a hell of a lover.
What more could you ask?*

She could think of a few things.

JUDGE BARBARA WEATON WAS already seated in a front booth when Diana arrived. She beckoned Diana to take the seat opposite where a cup of coffee waited.

When Diana attended law school, Barbara Weaton was already a rising star in jurisprudence, a major contributor to law journals, a woman to be admired. Appearing in her court had not diminished Diana's respect. But as she sat across from the judge now, Diana could feel her scalp tightening. Something wasn't right.

Barbara stirred sugar into her coffee, took a sip, made a face. "This is dreadful."

Diana moved her cup away, thankful for the excuse. She couldn't drink coffee this late at night if she wanted to sleep. Pulling a pad and pen out of her purse, she said, "Shall we begin?"

"I didn't see Connie Pearce kill my son as you very well know. I'm not answering any personal questions about myself or my family. Let's stop playing this stupid game and deal with each other as two intelligent women of the law should."

Diana flipped her pad shut and shoved both it and the pen back in her purse. "Why did you bring me here, Judge Weaton?"

"Plead your client guilty, and I'll get Staker to reduce the charge to second-degree. William Gimbrere will give her the minimum sentence. My guarantee."

Diana studied the woman before her, trying to read what thoughts were going on behind those keen eyes.

"Why would you do that?"

"Last year I had lost my child and husband. I wanted revenge." She paused, looked down at the cup in her hand. "Now, Ms. Mason, all I want is to put that dreadful day behind me and my family so we can get on with our lives."

Diana knew Judge Weaton was waiting for an answer. Her body was telling her to be careful about what answer she gave.

"As a mother, my heart goes out to you for your loss," Diana began. "As Connie Pearce's attorney, I assure you that I will discuss with her any offer the prosecution makes."

"I heard she was talking now."

The muscles tightened all the way down Diana's back. Who had told Barbara Weaton that? Had Judge Gimbrere passed on the information after hearing it from Ronald Kozen?

"Did she say she was…sorry?"

"Judge Weaton, you know I cannot discuss my client's privileged conversations with you."

"A judge isn't sitting across from you now, Ms. Mason. You're looking at a grieving mother who has had enough pain."

And, Diana reminded herself, a woman politically in bed with the prosecutor on the case.

"I'm prepared to forgive her," Judge Weaton said. "But when she makes her allocution to the court, she has to be sorry. If you truly understand my loss as a mother, then you will understand this as well."

What Diana understood was that this conversation was totally inappropriate. Barbara Weaton had no business using her position or her personal relationship with Staker and Judge Gimbrere to fish for information or attempt to influence the outcome of this case.

That she was doing both made Diana more than uneasy. It made her suspicious.

"DID YOU HEAR EVERYTHING?" Diana asked as she got into Jack's car in the café's parking lot after watching Barbara Weaton drive away.

"And got it all on videotape," Jack assured as she

handed him back the miniature camera and mike he'd given her to wear. "What do you make of her offer to have the charge reduced?"

"Either she wants to put the death of her son behind her as she claims, or she doesn't want Connie to go to trial because she's afraid of what will be revealed about her son. Could be Staker has told her Bruce was involved in Amy's hit-and-run."

Jack nodded. "I sensed she was hoping you'd tell her something when she asked you what Connie said."

"Barbara Weaton's up for an appellate court appointment. She risked a lot telling me she could influence Connie's case. Of course, she might be counting on the fact that if I said anything, it would be my word against hers."

"You could get her in trouble if you sent this tape to the right people," Jack guessed.

"I don't want to get her in trouble," Diana said. "The woman's been through hell. I only want her to back off and let me do my job."

"Did you suspect she'd pull something like this? Is that why you wanted your conversation on tape?"

"I only knew that a call this late at night was an attempt to fulfill her promise of meeting with me while at the same time circumventing my getting a formal deposition. Having a record of what she said seemed like a good idea."

Diana grasped the car's door handle. "Thanks so much for coming on such short notice, Jack. Tonight's been both above and beyond the call of duty."

"Tonight's only begun, Diana." He pulled her into his arms. Her instant of hesitation was barely perceptible before she returned his kiss with a fervor he had come to know and love.

When she pulled back a moment later, her voice was barely a whisper. "It's late. I have to get home."

He snapped her seat belt into place and started the engine. "My home."

"Jack—"

"Diana, I had all of thirty minutes sleep last night. Yet it was the best thirty minutes I've had since meeting you. If you send me home alone to toss and turn, I'll be nothing but a wreck tomorrow. You wouldn't be so cruel."

Her sigh was a half laugh. "Is that what I am to you? A thirty-minute sleeping pill?"

Jack shoved the gearshift into reverse and backed out of the parking space. "And my employer, don't forget. Without enough sleep, I might screw up my continuing investigations on Connie's behalf. Do you really want that on your conscience?"

Out of the corner of his eye, he saw the smile on her lips. "This is extortion. And kidnapping."

"Call it anything you like, counselor," Jack said as he gunned the engine and laid rubber out of the parking lot. "Just don't start screaming until you're in my bed and I'm giving you something really great to scream about."

"THAT'S THE DEAL, Mason. If you're smart, you'll tell your client to take it."

Diana had come to Staker's office as requested because he said they had important information to discuss about the Pearce case. Two days had passed since her meeting with Judge Weaton. Now, as Judge Weaton had predicted, Staker was offering a reduction of the charge to murder two if Connie pled guilty.

"Have you learned anything new about the Pearce case that has resulted in this offer?" Diana asked.

Staker scowled at her. "You've gotten everything the law requires I give you, Mason."

Diana doubted that. The sheriff had had plenty of time

to tell Staker about Jared's investigation into Amy's hit-and-run.

"You haven't added anything new to the evidence against my client in ten months," Diana said. "Something has to have changed your mind."

Staker came forward in his chair. "I've got your client dead to rights. If you want her to go to trial and get life, that's fine with me. You have twenty-four hours to decide."

Hungry anticipation shone on Staker's face. And that's when Diana knew. He didn't want to offer Connie this deal. What's more, he was hoping she'd turn it down.

"STAKER DOESN'T KNOW about Bruce being involved in Amy's death," Diana began. "That can only mean—"

"Jared didn't tell the sheriff what he found," Jack finished for her.

She'd driven from Staker's office directly to Jack's to tell him the news. The revelation brought Jack a sharp stab of remorse for what he had said to his brother the last time they talked. No wonder his twin had been a no-show at Sunday dinners since and had not answered his calls.

"Damn it," Jack said as he slammed his hand on his desktop.

"You're more upset at him now for jeopardizing his career to help you than you were when you thought he was going to follow the rules."

"He's an idiot," Jack said with heat.

"A very nice idiot. I'd like to meet him sometime."

Her look was tender with understanding. Jack's irritation at himself and his twin faded as he folded her into his arms and kissed the smile on her lips.

"I was about to call you and whisper all the latest case secrets into your sexy ears. But your dropping by is so much better. Give me a moment to lock the door."

She held his arm, restraining him. "Jack, please. There's so much to discuss. Trying to concentrate when you're in the same room is enough of a challenge."

He was inordinately happy to hear it.

A second later she had slipped out of his arms and put the length of the desk between them. The discovery that she had more discipline than he did wasn't an agreeable one.

"I'm certain Judge Weaton convinced Staker to make that offer today," Diana said after a moment. "If she knows about Bruce's involvement in Amy's death, Staker didn't tell her. Someone else did. Or she's known all along."

Jack considered the implications as he rested against the edge of the desk. "You think that's the real reason she doesn't want the case to go to trial?"

"Except, logically, if she were trying to hide her son's crime and her involvement in covering up that crime, why has she waited so long to get the case settled out of court?"

"Maybe Judge Weaton tried to convince Staker to settle earlier but he balked until she supported him politically."

"She went public with her support five months ago," Diana said. "Earl Payman would have gladly pushed Connie into pleading to second-degree if Staker had offered the deal then. No, this change of heart has come up recently."

"Nothing was being done in Connie's defense until you got the case. She might have assumed her son's involvement in Amy's death would never come out. Now she could be worried it might. By the way, I got that list of people at Staker's political dinner. You have the proof you need to excuse that prospective juror who attended. And I also tracked down the Duesenberg."

Her smile was full of relief. "Jack, that's great. How?"

"By putting an offer on Ebay to pay twice its worth to anyone willing to sell one. A private car collector in Tacoma e-mailed me this morning. I've talked with him by phone. He told me he bought the car from an Evelyn Farrell nearly five years ago."

"Farrell?" Diana voice repeated, rising an octave. "Farrell's Originals is the jewelry business that Audrey Weaton co-owns with her mother."

Jack nodded. "Evelyn Farrell is Audrey's mother. The Duesenberg was registered to her at the time of Amy's death, which is why I know the car has to be the right one. Along with the fact that Audrey *Farrell* was issued a moving violation on the day of Amy's death."

Jack took the record off his desk and handed it to Diana.

As she read the contents, she shook her head, her tone reflecting a disappointment clearly directed at herself. "Audrey still uses her maiden name on her driver's license because she went into business under that name. Why didn't I think of that?"

"Because you're the brilliant, beautiful attorney with every nuance of the law at her fingertips, and I'm the hardboiled, albeit tender, dig-out-the-clues private eye."

She flashed him a grin.

"The deputy writing up the report labeled the offense as driving while intalksicated," Jack said. "That's a new one on me."

"Having accidents while using a cell phone, whether hand-held or hands-free, is becoming more common," Diana said. "Guess it was simply a matter of time before a new term emerged. Except we both know that Audrey lied. She wasn't the one driving that day. Did the new owner of the Duesenberg mention if it arrived with a few dents?"

"Quite a few. Unfortunately, he had them repaired. But he has pictures of the before and after, which might help.

Shall we go see Audrey Weaton and find out what she has to say?''

Diana was already· halfway to the door. ''Do you have that hidden camera and microphone handy?''

''I have every recording and listening device you can imagine—and a lot you probably can't. Even one that fits in a belly button if·that gives you any ideas.''

She chuckled. ''I think the one that passes as a broach will be all I need today, thanks.''

THEY TRACKED AUDREY Weaton to a store at the mall where she was meeting with the proprietor who carried several pieces of her jewelry. While Jack stayed in the car to monitor the conversation, Diana intercepted Audrey when she emerged from the store, carrying a jeweler's sample case.

''Audrey, do you have a minute to talk?''

The woman was startled to see Diana, but didn't appear alarmed. ''Well, yes, I guess. What about?''

''A few loose ends. Come on, I'll buy you a soft drink.''

Diana purchased the drinks at an open concession stand, and she and Audrey took a table in the corner.

''What do you need to know?'' Audrey asked as she sipped her drink.

''I'm aware of Bruce's alcoholism. I also know that five years ago when he got in an accident, you covered for him. What you did was against the law.''

Audrey bit her lip. ''I never thought about it being illegal. Honest. I was only trying to…''

''To what?'' Diana prodded when Audrey hesitated. ''Tell me so I understand.''

The woman's shoulders sagged as she sat back in her chair. ''Lyle was off at a softball game that Sunday. I heard the roar of the engine and looked out the window in time to see the car jump the curb and hit one of our trees. I ran outside and found Bruce behind the wheel, a deep gash in his forehead.''

Either Audrey was a very good actress, or she was telling the truth. Holding judgment on which for the moment, Diana asked, ''Was Bruce drunk?''

''Very. I was so mad at him—and my husband. He was driving my mother's car—a classic 1932 Duesenberg SJ— part of our company's business image of original quality. She'd loaned the car to me the day before so I could meet one of our clients at the airport. Lyle forgot to get gas for his car so he took the Duesenberg to the softball game without telling me.''

''How did Bruce come to be driving the car?'' Diana asked.

''He told me he'd dropped his car keys somewhere at the park. When he couldn't find them, he lifted the keys to the Duesenberg out of Lyle's jacket. Stupid thing to do. He didn't know how to drive the car—especially not drunk.''

''You took Bruce to the E.R., didn't you?''

She nodded. ''Before my mother killed him for bashing in the front of her car, I figured I'd better get him patched up. I told the E.R. doctor he'd driven off the road. Never occurred to me that the doctor would contact the sheriff. When a deputy arrived, I panicked and called Lyle on his cell. He told me to tell the deputy I was driving.''

''So you told him you were on your cell phone when you lost control of your car and hit the curb.''

''I was holding my cell phone when I pulled the deputy aside. I'd driven my Cadillac, not the Duesenberg, to the E.R. It was the only explanation I could think of on the spur of the moment.''

''I'm confused. Why did your husband ask you to take the blame for something Bruce did.''

''Lyle and his dad were always covering for Bruce's

drunkenness so the good name of the real estate business could be preserved. And to protect Barbara.''

"Protect her standing as a judge?''

"It was more than that. When Bruce got a DUI in his twenties, she convinced herself—with his help—that it was all due to youthful exuberance. Lyle and Philip let her go on believing that, thinking it kinder than the truth.''

"Are you saying Judge Weaton didn't know her son was a drunk?''

"She didn't want to know. Bruce could be real charming when he chose to be. When he was around his mother, he turned that charm up full blast. He was her favorite and knew it. We all knew it.''

"Must have bothered Lyle being second best.''

Audrey shook her head. "Lyle fed on the feeling of superiority he got being the good boy who kept his mother ignorant of her favorite's drunken sprees and womanizing. Every time he bragged about how he'd gotten Bruce out of another mess, I could hear the satisfaction in his voice.''

"That doesn't explain why you took the blame for Bruce.''

Audrey's eyes dropped to the soft drink in her hands. "I did it for my husband's sake.''

Diana might have believed her if she'd maintained eye contact. "Where did you take Bruce after the E.R. doctor released him?'' she asked.

"Back to the house to sleep it off.''

"Your house?''

She nodded.

"And your bed?''

Audrey's eyes came up at that. "You can't think—''

"As you said, Bruce could be very charming,'' Diana interrupted. "I rather doubt it was coincidence he was heading for your home that day, ten miles out of his way. You were expecting him, weren't you?''

She lifted out of her chair. "If you want to have me arrested for saying I was driving, go ahead. But I don't have to talk to you about—"

Diana halted both the woman's words and retreat with a firm hand on her arm. "Yes you do, Audrey. If not here, in court. Would you prefer I ask these questions in front of a judge and jury?"

Audrey's voice was close to a sob. "You're going to anyway."

"As long as your relationship to Bruce has no bearing on Connie's defense, you have my promise I will say nothing about it in court. But I need the absolute truth from you now. Did you really see Bruce drive your mother's car into a tree in your front yard?"

Audrey dropped back into her chair. "You think I made that up? Lyle saw the damage to the car later when he got home. So did my mother. They'll tell you. Ask them. I'm not lying."

No, Diana didn't think she was. Which meant that Bruce not only hit and killed Amy that day. He really did strike a tree in Audrey's front yard.

"What happened to the Duesenberg?" Diana asked.

"Bruce drove it home that night when he finally sobered up. He promised he'd get everything fixed. Only when he called around, no one could match the original paint. Far as Mom was concerned, the car was worthless without everything being original. She sold it to a collector in Tacoma. Bruce paid her the difference between what she got and what she would have gotten had the car not been damaged."

"Did your husband find out about your affair with Bruce?"

"No."

"How long did the affair last?"

Audrey took a sip of her drink and swallowed before

answering. "Not long. I didn't realize it at the time, but he must have been really shaken up by hitting that tree. He joined AA the next week and told me he couldn't see me anymore."

"Did that upset you?"

She shrugged. "Bruce was all window dressing. He pursued me for weeks, kept telling me how much he wanted me, couldn't live without me. I knew he was lying. The week after he crashed the Duesenberg, I found out he'd been sleeping with at least three other women besides me. I was a conquest to him, nothing more."

"If you suspected he wasn't being truthful from the first, why did you take up with him?"

"For all Lyle's superiority, he's no better than Bruce when it comes to playing around—simply more discreet. Having an affair with Bruce was my way of getting back at Lyle."

"Even if he never knew?"

"*I* knew."

Audrey's words carried the small triumph of a wounded heart.

It was on the tip of Diana's tongue to ask her why she stayed with a man who cheated on her. She didn't ask because knowing wasn't necessary for Connie's defense. And she'd already trespassed into this woman's personal life enough for one day.

"I'M MORE CONFUSED than ever about this," Diana admitted as she joined Jack in the parking lot after her interview. They stood beside their cars, parked side-by-side at the far end of the lot. "If Audrey didn't know Bruce killed Amy on his way to her house that day—and I don't believe she did—then who knew?"

"Way I see it, one of two things happened," Jack said. "Either Bruce told someone, or when the report of Amy's hit-and-run made the news, someone figured it out from the description of the car, the fact that Bruce was in the area, and maybe some damage to the Duesenberg that wasn't consistent with having hit a tree.''

"All of which means it had to have been someone who knew Bruce.''

"And that someone blackmailed Bruce into joining AA. Diana, the only people close enough to Bruce to figure out what he'd done and with a motive for forcing him into making a life change was his family.''

"You don't think Tina could be a candidate?''

"She might have blackmailed him into giving her a job, but she never would have required him to get sober as part of the deal. According to Bud Albright and Audrey Weaton, Bruce's father and brother were the ones Bruce went to when he got in trouble. They also knew him best. My money's on one of them.''

"Barbara Weaton is also a possibility. When she met with me the other night, I could sense the fear in her.''

"When do you have to give Staker your answer about that?'' Jack asked.

"I'll call him at his office after I see Connie. She'll go with my advice and turn it down, of course.''

"Seeing how Barbara Weaton responds to that might be your clue as to how much she knows.''

"Still, discovering the person responsible for Bruce's joining AA won't be required for Connie's defense. We have the forensic evidence tying Bruce to Amy's death and Craig Sutherland's testimony firmly putting Bruce behind the wheel of the car. I'll call Audrey Weaton to the stand to testify that she was the woman in the E.R. who lied about driving. That will close any loopholes Staker might try to use. The accident reconstruction specialist's testimony will prove that Connie did try to avoid hitting Bruce. Evidence-wise, we have a strong case for acquittal.''

"Sounds like all you have to do now is put the right jury in the box."

"Thanks to you," Diana said with a smile. "Are you going to tell Jared about Audrey being the woman with Bruce and where he can find the Duesenberg?"

"I'll make an anonymous call to him. Until he starts talking to me again, it's the only way we're communicating these days. Although if I know Jared, he's already aware of where the Duesenberg is and that Audrey was the woman in the E.R. that day."

"And yet he said nothing to the sheriff. Is he going to get into trouble, Jack?"

"If there's a way to explain why he didn't tell the sheriff what he's discovered and how it relates to the prosecution's case against Connie, he'll find it."

"Is there anything we can do to help him?"

"Try not to pin him down to the specific dates and times he uncovered the evidence when you get him on the stand."

Diana nodded. "I'll be requesting the subpoena for the E.R. doctor and the medical records on Bruce from Judge Gimbrere right before *voir dire* begins on Monday. When you make that call to Jared, why don't you tell him to go ahead and fill in the sheriff."

"You'll be giving Staker the whole weekend to respond," Jack warned. "I thought you wanted to spring the subpoenas on him as a way to distract his attention from the jury selection process?"

"I did. But I'd gladly forgo that strategy now if it means Jared's job won't be at risk. Besides, this will give me a chance to see how fast Staker discloses the information about Bruce's involvement in Amy's hit-and-run."

"Shall I plant a hidden camera and microphone in his office so you can see his response when he's told?"

Diana smiled. "Tempting, even with the jail sentence we'd both have to serve for illegal eavesdropping."

Jack moved closer. "Speaking of tempting, tell me you don't have anything pressing to attend to tonight."

"Ah, but I do. Shirley will be giving me the last of her insightful reports on the treasures she's found in the pro-spective jurors' trash so I can finish my *voir dire* selections this weekend. I also promised Mel I'd listen to her do her lines for her debut tomorrow night. She's actually gotten excited about the play since you've been coaching her."

"Then I'll be by with dinner for four at six. All healthy, I promise."

"You want to spend your Friday night on casework and Mel's play rehearsal?"

"Foolish woman. I want to spend the night making love to you after Shirley and Mel go to bed."

JACK KNEW the exact moment when Diana had fallen asleep. He could feel her slow, rhythmic breathing now as she lay in his arms. Tonight had been even better than their times before, despite the fact he'd been certain that would be impossible.

It seemed nothing with her was impossible.

Or enough. Fighting the stirring of his body, he forced himself to let her sleep. He owed her that at least after all the pleasure she'd given him over the past few hours.

He'd never experienced anything like this before. Being with her felt as natural as arriving at the destination he'd been heading to all along. That should scare him. It did.

Their first night together, she'd asked him where the relationship was going. Had she been any other woman, he would have told her straight out that he wanted to be with her for as long as it pleased them both.

But he couldn't say that to her, because he was afraid

of losing her. So, he'd evaded answering her question. And she'd let him.

That wasn't like him—or her.

Unless she wanted the freedom to walk away from him?

Next week *voir dire* started. Following that would be the trial. His contract with her kept him on the case until the trial's conclusion.

And then? What would he be to her then? Nothing but an inconvenient lover who could cause friction between her and her child?

She moved against him, sighing in her sleep. To hell with letting her rest. Every minute with her was a gift too good to be squandered. His hands played over her skin, willing her to wake.

A moan of pleasure rose in her throat. He wanted—needed—to know she was responding to him and not from the sweetness of some dream in which she was still encased. Feathering his fingertips over her breasts, he smiled as he felt her come alive beneath his touch.

She rolled over to face him, molding her softness to him with an eagerness that hammered the blood in his ears.

"Don't you ever get…tired?" she murmured, a pleased if somewhat amused wonder weaving through her tone.

"Actors need lots of rehearsals to get it right," he said, pulling her as close as skin.

"I thought you were a private investigator now?"

"That's hard-boiled private investigator, ma'am, with the accent on hard."

Her laugh vibrated through him. His mind was already hazing over with the feel and scent of her. But before he completely lost control, there was something he wanted—no needed—to say.

"Diana, the other night you asked where this was going.

I didn't know then. I don't know now. I only know I want to be with you when we get there.''

Then he molded his mouth to hers and there was no more breath for words. Or time for thoughts. There was only her.

CHAPTER SIXTEEN

DIANA WATCHED in awed pride as Mel played her small part. She'd not only immersed herself in the role. She was pulling it off like a pro. When the fatal moment arrived for Matter to be murdered, a wonderful surprise stole over Mel's face as she sank slowly and convincingly to the stage floor.

Only knowing that such an act would horrify her daughter kept Diana from jumping up and clapping like the very proud mother she was. For years she'd been enthralled by Mel's mental prowess, a true gift of nature. Tonight she was even more impressed to see Mel accomplish something that had taken a lot of hard work.

A fellow performer rested on his bony knee beside Mel's quiet form, putting an exploratory finger against the pulse in her neck. "Dead," he announced in a voice that squeaked.

Diana recognized him as Thackery, an eleven-year-old who was already so well versed in the string theory of physics that he was challenging assumptions made by known experts in the field.

Beside him stood Rosemary, the fourteen-year-old host of the TV Game Show. She could play a piece of music on any instrument like a virtuoso after having heard it only once.

"One of our contestants in the studio tonight is a murderer," she said, looking pointedly at the other performers left standing on the stage. "Before this game is over I will name the culprit and bring him—or her—to justice."

As the curtain closed on Act One, a murmur of appreciation wove through the community center's auditorium, filled this Saturday with the families of the gifted children performing the Game Show Murder.

Jack sat on Diana's right, the feel of him producing both a gladness and an ache inside her. He'd helped Mel accomplish what she had tonight. Diana loved him for it—and for so many other things she'd lost count. But she could never tell him.

From the first he'd let her know he was a confirmed bachelor and that children were not part of his life plan. And yet she'd still chosen to have an affair with him. Last night he'd told her he didn't know where their relationship was going. She did. At the end of the trial, she'd say goodbye. She had to. If she didn't do it then, one day he would. And that would be so much harder for her heart to handle.

Diana sat back and watched Act Two unfold. Mel was backstage, Shirley helping her remove the heavy Matter costume, while on stage the clever sleuth ferreted out the murderer by asking the remaining contestants questions and tripping them up by their answers. When the culprit was unmasked and admitted to the foul deed, the play was over and all the performers piled onto the stage to take their bows before a cheering audience that had come to its feet.

Diana was looking for Mel to emerge for her bow when the cell phone in her shoulder bag rang. Thankful the call hadn't come during the performance, she dug out the phone, put a finger in one ear to drown out the clapping and answered.

"Diana Mason?" the strange, breathy voice asked.

"Yes," Diana said, straining to hear. "Who's calling?"

"Plead your client guilty right now. If I don't hear you've done so on the news tomorrow, you will never see your daughter again. Keep this secret to your grave or I will put you both in one.''

JACK FELT Diana stiffen beside him, saw the shock that drained her face. He clasped her shoulders, gently turned her toward him. ''Tell me.''

She repeated what the caller had said in a voice devoid of life.

Capturing her hands in his, he held on tightly, willing the warmth of his touch and voice to reach her. ''Diana?''

A shudder ran through her as her glazed eyes cleared and focused on him. ''I'm all right. Let's go.''

They hurried backstage while the clapping continued. Darting through the layers of curtains, they found Shirley crawling on the floor near the exit. She held her middle, her breath coming out in gasps.

Jack recognized a hit to the diaphragm when he saw one. As Diana dropped to the floor beside Shirley, he pulled out his cell phone and called for an ambulance.

''Grabbed...'' Shirley said, struggling to get the word out.

''Did you see who it was?'' Diana asked.

''Mask,'' Shirley gasped. ''Tall. Dress.''

''Judge Weaton,'' Diana said.

Shirley grabbed her arm, shook her head as she fought for breath.

''Smell...man,'' Shirley gasped.

Jack dropped to his knee and studied Shirley's face, noting the steady look in her eyes.

''Lyle Weaton,'' Jack said. He shot to his feet. ''The ambulance is on its way, Diana. Stay with Shirley.''

''Jack—''

''I'll get Mel back,'' he promised.

Before Diana could say another word, he was gone.

''JARED, I NEED TO KNOW where Lyle is,'' Jack said into his cell after having quickly related the situation. ''The

Global Positioning System in his Cadillac should pinpoint his location.''

''Hold on,'' Jared said.

No argument, wasted words or hesitation. Jack never appreciated his brother more than at this moment.

He was in the auditorium's parking lot, sitting in the Porsche with the engine running. As he waited for his twin to return to the line, he pulled an emergency tool kit out of the glove compartment, wishing he hadn't left his gun at the office. Richard had often warned him that a private investigator should never be without his weapon. But the last place Jack had figured he'd need one was a kid's play.

His nerves stretched raw as the seconds crawled by and his blood pounded for action.

The abduction had been carefully planned. The only people even aware of the performance tonight were supposed to be the organizers of the event and their families. But the auditorium had been open during the rehearsal Jack had attended—and probably all the others. All Lyle would have had to do was walk in and take a seat in the shadows in order to learn about the date of the performance and when Mel would be backstage.

Only thing he hadn't counted on was Shirley being with her.

After what seemed like an eternity, Jared came back on the line.

''His Cadillac DeVille's been located at Park Street and Twenty-Third downtown.''

As Jack listened to his brother's directions, he accessed the Porsche's Communication Management feature and fed in the coordinates. The electronic road map showed the quickest way to get there.

''Got it, Jared. Thanks.''

"Jack, I need time to try to get a search warrant for his car. You understand?"

"Perfectly," Jack replied as he flipped his cell closed and shot out of the parking lot.

What Jack understood was that his brother's chances of getting a search warrant were slim. And even if he got one, it would only be for Lyle's car. If Mel wasn't in the vehicle, his brother would be forced to walk away.

Jack wasn't bound by any such constraints. Very little of his journey registered in his conscious thoughts as he sped through the night. His reflexes were on automatic.

Mel's bright eyes, her smile, her face so brimming with life filled his mind. When the image of Diana's stark white face replaced it, Jack pushed the gas pedal to the floor.

Following the electronic road map lit on the dash, he zoomed down the streets of the business district.

When he turned the far corner of Park Street, he saw the neon lights blinking outside a bar, behind it a full parking lot. Cutting the Porsche's lights and engine, he turned into the lot, slipping into the shadows. The second the car had rolled to a complete stop, he was out of the driver's seat.

Silently and swiftly, Jack wove through the parked cars. He found Lyle's DeVille at the far end, its hood still warm. Pulling a flashlight out of his tool kit, he checked the interior then grabbed another tool and forced open the trunk. Empty.

Jack checked inside the bar, including both rest rooms. Lyle wasn't there.

That's when Jack realized Lyle had parked at the bar as a ruse. He knew the man couldn't be far. Back on the street, Jack began to search the surrounding stores. Everything was locked and shut up for the night. At the end of the block, he turned right and proceeded on foot to the next street, all the while conscious of the precious passing time.

Finally, three doors down on the right, he found what he was looking for. The sign on the darkened diner read, For Sale by the Weaton Real Estate Company.

Jack peered into the window and saw a faint strip of light coming from behind an interior door. His heart started to pound. Lyle was in there, and he had Mel with him.

The lock on the front door was connected to an alarm. Jack checked the windows and also found them alarmed. He moved to the side of the building and located a solid metal exit door. Getting through it would take nothing less than a battering ram.

Setting off an alarm might be a good way to get Lyle out of there. But before he tried anything, Jack knew he needed to make sure all the exits were covered. He was reaching for his cell phone to call to his brother when a blue Cadillac came into view.

Jack ducked into the shadows. The Seville came to a screeching halt. Barbara Weaton jumped out of the driver's seat and charged at the front door of the diner, banging loudly on its door.

"Lyle, it's me," she yelled. "Open this door immediately."

Jack could hear the noise of an interior door, the footsteps that shuffled to the front. Lyle must have deactivated the alarm because when he opened the door for his mother, no blast ensued.

"What are you doing with that gun?" Barbara screeched.

"It's protection," Lyle said. "What in the hell are you doing here? Go home. I told you. I'm handling things."

"With a gun?"

"Why don't you yell a little louder. I don't think they heard you in the next county."

"Lyle, I don't care how bad things are. I won't let you kidnap a child."

"You're too late. It's done. Now get in here before you attract attention."

Jack heard Barbara's gasp, the shuffling of feet, the close of the door.

Leaving his hiding place, Jack circled to the front of the diner, peered through the window to see the door closing at the back. He turned the knob and pushed the door open, exhaling a breath of relief when the alarm didn't sound.

Noiselessly, he made his way through the darkness to the sliver of light beneath the storeroom door. He could hear the voices clearly through the closed door.

"Lyle, why have you done this?"

"To clean up Bruce's last mess so you don't lose out on that appellate court nomination. Same way I've cleaned up all his other messes in order to protect you."

"This is insane!"

"No, insanity is your continuing to cherish his memory like he was some choirboy. He was a no-good drunk who killed a kid and left us all to pay for it. If the news gets out, my business is doomed and so is your career. I had to do this, Mother. You know I did. Mason wouldn't talk the damn woman into taking a plea."

"Lyle, I tried to tell you on the phone but you wouldn't listen. Even if Mason agrees to plead Connie Pearce guilty now, Staker's going to turn it down."

"What are you talking about?"

"Connie Pearce's motive was the only weak point in Staker's case—the only reason I was able to even talk him into offering second degree in the first place. Now that he has the evidence proving Bruce killed Connie's child, he's going to let nothing stand in his way of taking it to court."

"Get on the damn phone and talk to him. Here. Use my

cell. Tell him he has to plead her out. Tell him you'll withdraw your backing of his candidacy if he doesn't.''

''I already withdrew my backing,'' Barbara said in a voice weary with defeat. ''He insisted I do it. He didn't want to be tainted by any connection to your brother through me. I also withdrew my candidacy for the appellate court. It's over, Lyle. The announcements will be on tomorrow morning's news.''

A moment passed in silence followed by a slew of Lyle's curses.

Jack had a feeling that the object he'd heard hitting the wall had been Lyle's cell phone.

''I'll kill him,'' Lyle screamed. ''I'll kill them all.'' Then there was a click—the unmistakable sound of the hammer snapping into firing position on an automatic.

An angry, desperate man holding a gun, with the life of a child in his hands.

Knowing he hadn't a second to lose, Jack kicked open the door and charged inside.

DIANA RAN DOWN the corridor toward the E.R. She recognized the man in the dark blue suit who stood by the receptionist's counter, although she had never seen him before.

''Jared Knight, I'm Diana Mason,'' she said holding out her hand.

He shook her hand and stared at her with eyes the exact color as Jack's.

''Your daughter is fine,'' he said. ''What I told you over the phone has been confirmed. She was chloroformed, but otherwise unhurt. When she came to a few minutes ago, she had no memory of being abducted. Happened too fast. They'll keep her overnight for observation. You'll be able to take her home tomorrow.''

Diana allowed herself a blessed respite of deep gratitude before asking, "What about Jack?"

"The E.R. doctor is with him now."

Diana's heart squeezed tightly in her chest. "How bad is it? Please tell me."

"When Jack tackled Lyle, the guy's gun went off, but the bullet only grazed Jack's arm. He'll be okay."

The relief surging through Diana left her weak. She gripped the counter and felt Jared's hand rest briefly on her shoulder.

"Don't be alarmed if you see blood on your daughter's clothes. It's Jack's. He got it on her when he picked her up. Lyle had dumped her on the floor."

Diana had watched nature programs where mothers who were half the size of predators would fight so fiercely in defense of their young that the predators would run off. She understood what those mothers had been feeling now.

"I could kill the bastard with my bare hands," she said in a voice even she didn't recognize.

"Jack dislocated Lyle's shoulder in their fight over the gun. Help any?"

Diana smiled. "And he kept telling me he was the wimp in the family."

"When Jack believes in what he's fighting for, he's as tough as any of us," Jared said very quietly.

Diana took a closer look at the man before her. Other than a deep scar in Jared's cheek, the brothers were identical feature-wise. But looking into Jared's eyes, Diana knew she'd never mistake the men. She had the strangest sensation that at some point in Jared's life, he'd fought an internal demon—and lost.

"How's your aunt?" he asked.

"Wonderfully resilient. Doctor says she'll be sore and

sporting a whopping bruise for a while, but otherwise will fully recover. May I see Mel now?''

He nodded. ''Follow me. I'll get you in.''

JACK FOUND THEM in Mel's room as soon as the doctor had finished bandaging his arm. Diana was sitting on the edge of the bed, Shirley standing beside it. Mel was propped up on the pillows. When she saw him, she smiled.

''I can't believe that twice in one night I missed out on all the action,'' she said in a voice brimming with disappointment. ''I don't remember a thing!''

Her hair was matted and there was a small cut on her forehead, but her color was warm. Compared to the pale face and lifeless body he'd held in the twenty minutes it took for the paramedics to arrive, she looked wonderful.

''Thank you for rescuing me, Jack.''

He came to a halt in front of her bed, touched by the simple sincerity in her words. ''You're thanking the wrong person. We wouldn't have known who took you if Holmes hadn't seen through the disguise Lyle wore.''

''And Holmes took a painful blow trying to stop Lyle,'' Diana added, sending her aunt a look of gratitude and love.

Being the object of three sets of staring eyes seemed to make Shirley self-conscious. She cleared her throat and puffed some nonexistent smoke from the pipe in her mouth as she looked down at her feet.

Mel stared at her great-aunt with an expression on her face that Jack had never seen before. ''Thank you,'' she said. Simple words, but their meaning was not.

Shirley eased onto the edge of the bed. ''You would have done the same for me, my dear Watson.''

''I'm not that brave,'' Mel admitted.

''Bravery is simply the brain listening to the heart,'' Diana said. ''Don't ever sell either of yours short, Cute Stuff.''

''She's right, Watson,'' Shirley said. ''Women generally are about these things. We men think we're out there doing the brave deeds that will insure a better tomorrow. But it's the women who are holding the future in their hands, because they are holding the hands of the children.''

As Mel smiled at Shirley, she gently captured her great-aunt's hand in hers.

Jack glanced over at Diana's face to see the tears glistening in her eyes. He slipped his fingers through hers.

"You'll excuse us a moment?" he said in the general direction of the bed as he pulled Diana out into the hall.

As soon as the door was closed behind them, she turned to him, her smile a dizzying gleam. "Thank you for bringing Mel safely back. You're my hero, Jack."

And at that moment, he never felt more like one. Folding her into his arms, he kissed her with all the need inside him. When he finally released her, he found them surrounded by an appreciative audience of patients and hospital personnel.

Jack took Diana's hand and bowed to their audience. Diana chuckled at that as much as the onlookers. When the others had dispersed a moment later she brushed a kiss over the bandage on his arm. "Does it hurt?"

"Just a flesh wound. Hot damn, I always wanted to say that line."

Her laughter was the best painkiller of all. He told her then of finding Lyle and listening to the conversation he had with his mother.

"Did they say anything after you got the gun away from him?" she asked.

Jack nodded. "Lyle figured out Bruce had killed Amy after hearing about the hit-and-run on the news and seeing the blood on the car fender. When he told his father, they confronted Bruce together and got him to admit he'd deliberately crashed into the tree to try to hide his crime."

"And Lyle and his father threatened to turn Bruce in if

he didn't join AA and stay sober,'' Diana said, understanding. "What about Judge Weaton?"

"Lyle claims they never told her because he and his dad knew that as a judge, she'd have to turn Bruce in. When Lyle found out that Bruce was going to marry Connie to give her a child to replace the one she'd lost—"

"*That's* why he wanted to marry her," Diana interrupted. "Dear God. Like one child could simply replace another."

Jack nodded. "Sick bastard's idea of Step Eight. Bruce deliberately let the air out of her tire that first day so he could drive by and play good Samaritan. His subsequent meeting with her was also planned."

"When did Lyle and his father find out what Bruce was doing with Connie?"

"Not until that day of the barbecue. Both Lyle and his father were shocked to learn who Bruce had been dating and what he intended. They were trying to talk some sense into him when Connie bolted from the garage. Lyle thought she'd overheard their conversation. He's believed all along that she hit Bruce with her car because of what he did to Amy."

"When did he tell his mother that Bruce had killed Amy?"

"Not until after you deposed him. That's when he started to worry about what you might uncover. He told her about Bruce so she'd lean on Staker to plead Connie out. Barbara told me she met with you because after hearing what Bruce had done to Amy, she really did want to forgive Connie for killing him and put it all behind her."

"So she was telling the truth," Diana said. "I feel terrible for her. It's bad enough that Bruce turned out to be a criminal. Now Lyle has shown himself to be one, too."

"Before Jared walked in, Lyle told me right out he'd deny everything he said."

Diana exhaled in disappointment. ''Shame. Lyle could have given the jury all they needed to know about Bruce's motivations for pursuing Connie.''

''Then this should come in handy,'' Jack said as he pulled a tape out of his pocket and placed it within her palm. ''Unbeknownst to him, I recorded Lyle's confession.''

Diana's fingers closed over the tape almost reverently. ''Well, that cinches it, Jack Knight. You are definitely my employee of the month.''

Jack laughed, so lost in her lovely smile that he didn't care if he ever found his way back.

''ON THE COUNT of murder in the first degree,'' Jury Foreman Ralph Montgomery announced in a strong voice that carried to the corners of the courtroom, ''we find the defendant, Connie Pearce, *not* guilty.''

Diana hugged Connie as the spectators in the courtroom came alive with excited murmuring and applause. Judge Gimbrere pounded his gavel to restore order, but all Diana heard were the words being whispered into her ear.

''Thank you, Ms. Mason. You've saved my life.''

Diana pulled back to see the tears of gratitude slipping onto Connie's cheeks. She gave her client another hug. ''You're so welcome, Connie.''

Catching a movement out of the corner of her eye, Diana turned her head to see Jack sitting with Mel, Shirley, her mom and Ray—all of them smiling at her and clapping loudly, heedless of the pounding gavel and the call for order.

At that moment she wondered why anyone in her right mind would choose to be anything but a defense attorney.

DIANA WAS ON HER WAY to join Mel and Shirley in the witness room where Jack was protecting them from reporters when Ronald Kozen appeared, bringing her to an abrupt halt in the hallway.

"You've made a powerful enemy today, Mason," he said in his gruff tone. "Staker's never going to forgive you for making him look like a complete idiot on such a high-profile case. You realize all this bad publicity is going to cost him his judgeship?"

Diana faced the senior partner straight, knowing this was one of those occasions when speaking her mind was an absolutely necessity. "I sincerely hope so."

Ronald studied her quietly, that perpetual half smile reflecting back at her like a smirk. "Gail kept telling me I'd underestimated you. Should have listened to her. Damn good job, Mason. You beat Staker a few more times like this and your name will be coming up for junior partner one of these days."

Diana was so shocked that several seconds passed before she noticed that his hand was extended toward her. "Thank you," she said as she shook it. "But what about Gail's junior partnership?"

He smiled, a real smile. "She has it, Mason. Told her this morning. We were only waiting to be sure that foolish affair with Staker was behind her."

"Excuse me?"

"You're not the only one who has the sense to hire White Knight Investigations when something needs to be checked out."

With that Ronald released her hand and disappeared down the hall. Diana was so surprised and relieved, she burst out laughing.

"GREAT GOING, MOM," Mel said when Diana entered the interview room.

"A verdict full of justice," Shirley declared.

Jack watched as she hugged her daughter and aunt in turn.

"Grandma and Ray have gone ahead to get the celebration feast started," Mel said. "Can we go now?"

"Sounds good to me," Diana said.

The fleeting look she sent Jack was inviting. Unless he was merely seeing his own feelings mirrored in her eyes? She'd been even more diligent over the past couple of weeks trying to keep the nights they spent in each others' arms from her daughter. He'd once joked that she was ashamed of being seen with him.

Didn't seem like much of a joke now.

All his business reasons for being with her had ceased. She could end the personal one with a word. That she had the discipline to do it he had no doubt. That she might at any moment sent a chill through his heart.

"Hungry, Jack?" Mel asked.

Only one thing scared him more than what he was about to do. And that was not doing it.

Before Diana could take more than a step, Jack positioned himself in front of the door, barring her way. She halted, looking up at him quizzically.

Jack held Diana's eyes as he addressed her daughter. "Mel, I can't be just your mother's friend. I'm in love with her."

"I know."

"You know," he repeated, surprised by both Mel's immediate response and the blandness of her tone.

"She loves you, too," Mel said.

"How do you know?" Jack asked, his pulse quickening as his eyes darted to the girl's face and found her smiling at him.

"Because she looks at you the same way you look at her. Holmes and I have been wondering when you were going to tell us."

Jack stared into the beautiful face before him. "Diana, do you love me?"

She chuckled as she wrapped her arms around his waist. "And still he has to ask. Some detective."

He pulled her close to his fast-beating heart and brushed his cheek against her hair, every nerve ending in his body happily humming with the message in her words.

"Maybe I can hire Holmes to give me some pointers," he said in a voice not quite steady.

"Always happy to be of assistance," Shirley assured. "Although I will have to admit, Watson and I are going to miss the fun of watching Jack trudge through the backyard at four in the morning trying to find his car in the trees."

"And tripping over the weeds," Mel said with a giggle.

Jack shook his head in amusement. What had ever given him the idea that he was a good actor?

"You're all right with this, Mel?" he asked, not taking his eyes off the gentle radiance on Diana's face.

Mel's responsive sigh was full of dramatics. "I suppose if Mom *has* to lose her mind over a man, she could do a lot worse than a great drama coach."

Jack smiled. "Diana, I may not be a fan of kids, but I've sure fallen for this little supercomputer of yours. And having Sherlock Holmes in the family is a dream come true for any private investigator. Looks like the only way I'm going to be able to gain custody of them is for you to marry me."

"Marry?" she repeated, and he was all too aware of the astonishment in her voice. "I thought you weren't that brave?"

He traced the exquisite curve of her cheek with his fingertip. Until this moment he hadn't known she'd given herself to him so unconditionally. For the woman she was that had taken a lot of love. A feeling full of gratitude and rightness poured through him.

"Bravery is simply the brain listening to the heart," he quoted.

Her lips drew back in a smile. "I seem to have heard that somewhere before."

"An actor always steals the best lines."

"Ah, but you're a private investigator now."

"Which is why if you marry me, I can promise you'll never have to pay full rate for private investigation services again."

"I'd think twice before turning down such a generous offer," Shirley said soberly. "I've seen Jack's bill."

"Say yes, Mom, or we're never going to eat," Mel chimed in. "He's blocking the door."

"Diana, I love you so much we're going to beat the hell out of the divorce statistics. Be brave. Please. Tell me the answer is yes."

Diana's sigh was a happy sound as she wound her arms around his neck. "Of course, it's yes. Doesn't the hero always get the girl in the end?"

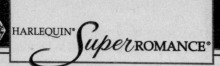

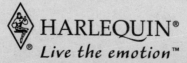

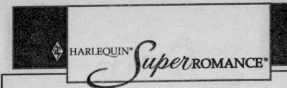

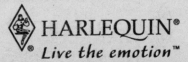

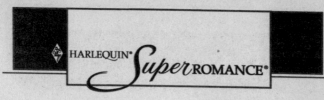

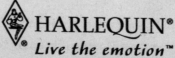